Low
Light

Colin Youngman

The Works of Colin Youngman:

Low Light (Ryan Jarrod Book 6)

Operation Sage (Ryan Jarrod Book 5)

High Level (Ryan Jarrod Book 4)

The Lighthouse Keeper (Ryan Jarrod Book 3)

The Girl On The Quay (Ryan Jarrod Book 2)

The Angel Falls (Ryan Jarrod Book 1)

**

Standalone Novels:

The Doom Brae Witch

Alley Rat

DEAD Heat

**

Anthology:

Twists*

*Incorporates the novelettes:DEAD Lines, Brittle Justice, The Refugee and A Fall Before Pride (all available separately), plus a BONUS READ: Vicious Circle.

Colin Youngman

This is a work of fiction.

All characters and events are products of the author's imagination.

Whilst most locations are real, some liberties have been taken with architectural design, precise geographic features, and timelines.

Seaward Inc.

ISBN: *979-8-44358-8-407*

Cover based on an original image courtesy of Sam Leighton

DEDICATION

To
John Ramsay

*My teacher at the age of ten who first spotted some potential in my
writing and offered me his time and encouragement.
He wasn't a bad football coach either, come to think of it.*

'If you prick us, do we not
bleed?
If you tickle us, do we not laugh?
If you poison us, do we not die?
And if you wrong us - shall we
not revenge?'

William Shakespeare

'Something wicked
this way comes.'

William Shakespeare

CHAPTER ONE

Kathy Spencer never could hold a tune, but her doctors told her singing was good for her. It'd increase her lung functionality, they said. So, sing she did. Strictly to herself, though. Never to an audience.

She wasn't convinced her doctors were right about it improving her asthma, but she was sure of one thing: practice didn't make perfect. All the years of tuneless trilling hadn't enhanced the quality of her voice.

Fortunately for her neighbours, the white noise of the cordless Dyson drowned out the racket Kathy made as she warbled and strutted around the lounge of her Gateshead home, set above the town in High Fell.

She mistook Fred Mandel's synthesiser bridge for a Brian May guitar solo as she lifted the cleaner from the carpet and played air guitar before breaking back into song.

'But life still goes on
I can't get used to living without, living without,
Living without you by my side
I don't want to live alone.
God knows, got to make it on my own.'

Kathy heard the doorbell on its third ring.

'Okay. I'm sorry. I'll stop singing.'

The bell rang again.

'I've stopped. Listen – all's quiet. See?'

This time, she heard knuckles rap against the door. With a sigh, Kathy swung it open. 'Was I really that bad?'

Another woman stood on the other side. A stranger. 'Can I help you?' Kathy asked.

'Hello, Kathy.' The woman barged past her, knocking Kathy aside.

'Hey, you can't…'

'I just have,' the woman replied.

Kathy studied the stranger. Dressed entirely in navy blue with matching eyeshadow and nail varnish, the woman's face bore a serene smile. Kathy was sure she'd never set eyes on the woman before.

'Who are you? What do you want?'

'I think you know the answers to both those questions. In fact, deep down, I know you do.' The woman flicked the lock on the door.

'What're you doing?'

The serene smile morphed into a snarl. 'You. That's what I'm doing.'

The woman snatched the Dyson from Kathy's hands and swung it at her head.

Kathy went down, blood warming the side of her face. 'HELP ME. SOMEONE, PLEASE!'

No-one heard Kathy's scream. The intruder had started up the Dyson. It drowned out all other sound. She held it against Kathy's head. Hair tore from her scalp. Began clogging the mechanism. Before it overheated, the woman switched it off. She grabbed Kathy by the arms and part dragged, part hauled her into the kitchen dining area.

Kathy was a slight woman. Barely five foot two and slender with it. It was a simple task for the heavier-built intruder to get her sitting upright on one of the high-backed padded dining chairs.

Kathy screamed again. No sound came. She had no memory of the woman sealing her lips with gaffer tape, but that's what she'd done.

With the tape around her mouth, Kathy struggled for breath. She felt the familiar tightness in her chest, a rising panic, and a tingle between her shoulder blades. An attack was on its way.

Within moments, she felt herself losing consciousness.

As soon as Kathy slipped into her inner darkness, the woman strapped her wrists to the chair. She spun her victim towards the table and lined up three objects on its surface.

The intruder pursed her lips. Ripped the tape from Kathy's mouth, allowing her to breath once more. 'Now, we wait,' she said to her unconscious prey.

When Kathy Spencer regained consciousness, the items on the table would be the first things she saw.

**

She fluttered open her eyelids, but the darkness of night imposed itself on her vision. She felt sick, her head woozy.

Then she remembered.

The woman at the door.

Kathy tried to move, but she was tethered to the chair. She jerked her body to release her from the restraints. All she achieved was to topple the chair onto its side, still strapped to it.

She thrashed her legs like a gazelle brought down by a cheetah, yet Kathy couldn't raise her chair from the floor.

I've got to break free, she thought to herself, all irony lost as panic welled up once more. She coughed. Gasped in air. Heard a high-pitched whistle as the oxygen squeezed through constricted trachea.

Easy, girl, she told herself. She slowed her breathing. Kept it regular despite the growing pressure in her chest. Kathy inhaled and exhaled several times, slow and easy. She closed her eyes. Tried calming the fear inside her.

As the asthma receded, so her awareness increased. She heard a scratching noise and saw a weak flicker of light. The match flame danced closer to her, before it passed above her head and licked the wick of a candle.

In the darkness of the house, the candle flared as brightly as a beacon.

'Hello again,' the woman said.

'Please, just take what you want from me and leave.'

Kathy felt her chair right itself as the woman hauled it and its occupant upright.

'If only it were so simple,' the woman sneered.

'It is. Please, just take it. Take anything you want. Take everything. Just, leave me alone.'

The woman's face seemed to pulse in front of Kathy's eyes as the candle cast flickering shadows over it. 'What I want isn't here. I made sure of that.'

'I don't understand.'

'I want what you took from me.'

Kathy froze. She felt blood drain from her body. It coagulated in a leaden pool at her feet. 'Jane?'

'Eureka!' the woman cried, moving back into shadow. 'Yes, it's Jane. Who else would it be?'

'I had nothing to do with your break-up. You and Dave had been apart for months. He told me. Showed me proof.'

The woman called Jane ignored her. 'He was my world, and you took him from me.' The words were slow, deliberate, and menacing.

'You hurt him. You stabbed him with a broken bottle. In the neck, for Christ's sake. That's why he left you. It had nothing to do with me.'

'He would have come back. He always did. Until YOU got your claws into him.'

'Jane, none of it had anything to do with me. People break up all the time. Shit happens, you know?'

Jane rotated her neck until it made a cracking noise. 'Not this kind of shit, it doesn't.'

'Please, if I thought there was any chance he wanted back with you, I wouldn't have got involved. I'm not like that.'

'Bullshit!' Jane brought her fist down on the kitchen table, making Kathy jump.

Jane's hand, invisible in the shadows, picked up the candle so it seemed to hover in the air. She held it close to the objects on the table.

'What are they?' Kathy whispered.

'This?' Jane's hands picked up something. Rotated it in the air. 'It's not much,' she said. She set the object back down. 'You think you're so superior to me, don't you?'

'I don't even know you, so no: I don't think I'm better than you.'

'So much prettier,' Jane continued, ignoring the girl in the chair, 'More intelligent. More independent.'

She walked around behind Kathy. 'I can't do anything about most of those things…' Jane grabbed Kathy's long black hair and yanked it back. Kathy cried out in pain. 'But I can do something about your looks,' she hissed into Kathy's ear, tossing her head forward roughly.

'Jane, you can't. It had nothing to do with me. HELP, HELP!'

Jane picked up the roll of tape from the table and looped four lengths of it over Kathy's mouth before tearing the tape with her teeth. She set it back down.

Next, Jane pulled on a pair of heavy gloves. She raised a bottle from the table. Unscrewed it. Made as if to take a sip from it.

'No, no, no,' she said wagging a figure at Kathy and laughing. 'This isn't for me. It's for you. All of it.'

Kathy prayed for an asthma attack. Wanted the agonising effort of struggling for breath. Willed herself to pass out.

She'd never wanted anything more in her life as she watched Jane raise the bottle above Kathy's head. She wanted it because she knew the bottle didn't contain water.

Kathy looked up with saucer eyes as Jane upended the container.

The first searing cascade of sulphuric acid ate away Kathy's scalp, burnt through her eyelids, and flowed downwards to ravage her lips and tongue beneath the gag.

The last thing Kathy Spencer heard was the sound of Jane singing to herself on her way out.

'I can't get used to living without, living without,
Living without you by my side.'

11

CHAPTER TWO

Eighteen Months Later
March 2022

'How the hell's it taking them so long?'

Ryan Jarrod jumped at the sound of DI Lyall Parker's voice, and coffee spilled from the cup in his hand.

'I mean, it's obvious she's guilty as sin,' Parker continued, 'But these gowks cannae see the wood for the trees.'

Ryan's hand steadied as his nerves settled. 'Doubt it'll be much longer. Judge said he'd accept majority verdict.'

Lyall snorted a scornful laugh. 'Should never have come to that.'

'We're not the jury, Lyall. And we could be a tad biased, know what I mean?'

'Is that what you really think, lad?'

'Nah. She's guilty as sin alright but, like I say, we're looking through blinkers.'

Ryan and Lyall were sat in a small private room just off Crown Court Three in the Law Courts building on Newcastle's quayside. Like most rooms inside the modern edifice, the walls were clad in light oak panels, the furniture manufactured from the same material.

The door to the room opened. Ryan's heart raced as he swung his head towards the man entering the room. Lyall also turned and looked expectantly at Matty McNair of the Crown Prosecution Service.

McNair shook his head.

'So, you've come to tell us you've nothing to tell us,' Lyall complained.

McNair dropped an armful of files onto the desk. The noise made Ryan jump again.

'A bit nervy, are we?' a bewigged McNair chided. He reeked of cardamom and cedar wood as if he'd bathed in Pour Homme.

Lyall and Ryan exchanged glances. 'He's okay,' Lyall said, even though he knew Jarrod was far from okay. How could he be with a drug gangmaster's threats hanging over his head for months?

'Anyway,' McNair continued, 'It's not the sexiest case any of us have dealt with, and these things take time. We're all used to the machinations of the law.'

'Machinations, you call it? I call it taking the piss. We've better things tae do with our time than sit on our arses.'

McNair held up his hands. 'Sorry I spoke, I'm sure. No-one's forcing you to stay for the verdict. It's not part of your job description.'

Ryan sighed. 'Lyall, get yourself back to Forth Street. Like you say, you've got better things to do with your time. Not like me.'

'Don't do yourself down, laddie.'

'I'm not. It's just the way things are, isn't it? I know the Super thinks she's doing me a favour, keeping me out the limelight and as far away from Benny Yu as she can, but I might as well be seconded to DCI Kinnear's crew if I'm only going to work shitty cases like this.'

'Ryan...'

'Don't even pretend the Super's not side-lining me, Lyall. I know she is. I'm not pulling my weight; I'm costing the force a fortune with the extra security deployed on me – and I know all the lads think they're carrying my workload.'

'That's not what we think, Ryan. None of us, from Superintendent Maynard down. Once we get Yu and his cronies under wraps, you'll be back on the good stuff.'

'Really? And when do you think that'll be – before or after he's wiped out my family?'

McNair picked up his files. Shuffled them. 'I'll leave you two to your little spat. I'll be back for you when the verdict's in.'

'The verdict's in.'

It wasn't an echo. The words came from an usher standing in the doorway.

'We'd better get back into court.' McNair bustled out the room, a halo of man scent around him.

'Aboot bloody time,' Lyall Parker grumbled.

**

'All rise,' the Court Orderly instructed.

'Court is back in session for the case of The Crown versus Roberta Cavell, presided by The Honourable Mr Justice Hogarth.'

Eton Hogarth entered the courtroom through a side door leading from his chambers. He boasted thick eyebrow overgrowth beneath which his eyes, pale with age, hid behind half-moon spectacles.

Hogarth took his position before the court, dipped his head, flicked back his robes with unnecessary drama, and lowered himself onto his chair.

The court officials followed his lead, giving brief yet reverential bows to the Royal Coat of Arms behind the judge, before they took their seats. A rumble grew as the press corps and the members of the public did likewise.

In the dock to the judges right, Roberta Cavell, too, sat down.

She'd followed her team's instructions to the letter. '*You're young and pretty. The men on the jury will notice that. So, too, though, will the women. Go minimal on the make-up, and dress smart like butter wouldn't melt. Nothing low-cut, short, or sexy.*'

Roberta - or Bobbi as everyone outside the courtroom knew her - had grimaced but reluctantly obeyed. She'd opted for a high-waisted pencil skirt of knee length and a pale pink cardigan which could have come from the rails of Primark.

Wearing no jewellery and sensible, flat shoes, Bobbi Cavell felt uncomfortable - but she did look the picture of innocence. In reality, she was a spoilt brat.

The only child of the Chief Executive of a local Building Society, she believed employment of any kind beneath her. Or, she had done until her parents forced her hand by cutting off her generous allowance.

That's when she'd taken it upon herself to find alternative ways to fund her lavish lifestyle; 'alternative means' of the kind resulting in her appearance at numerous magistrate courts over the last twelve months, but never a Crown Court.

Not until now.

Bobbi looked around her, taking in the detail of the modern grandeur of the court as a way of calming her nerves. The overpowering scent of polish emanated from every inch of the wooden walls, the multitude of desks and benches, even the handrail around the dock in which she sat.

The carpet was predominantly sea-green in colour dappled with a blue diamond pattern. The gallery chairs looked as uncomfortable and fixed as church pews.

At the very front of the court, at an angle to her and raised high above the rest of the courtroom, Justice Eton Hogarth sat beneath a large motif of the Royal Arms and its *'Dieu Et Mon Droit'* motto.

On a lower platform, a man and a woman sat with fingers poised on keyboards. The female stenographer was a prissy-looking woman dressed all in blue. Her male colleague wore Clark Kent glasses and dishevelled hair which flopped in front of his face. Bobbi expected him to pick up a baton at any moment and start conducting an orchestra.

Facing Justice Eton Hogarth and the recorders, the prosecution team sat at one end of a longer desk, Bobbi's counsel at the other. Her barrister turned towards her and offered a reassuring smile. Bobbi nervously gnawed on her bottom lip and turned her attention to the left of the courtroom.

The twelve jurors – eight men and four women – avoided eye-contact with her. Not a good sign, until she realised they weren't looking at anyone else in the courtroom, either. Some looked as nervous as Bobbi, others appeared bored, one so much so he seemed asleep.

While the assorted barristers and legal teams prepared themselves for the verdict and Judge Hogarth took a final scan of his notes, Bobbi's eyes settled on two men sitting in the gallery.

The younger of the two, the one with fair hair and scarred hands, glanced around the courtroom with the nervousness of a shelter dog. The other, the silver-haired Scotsman whose genteel charm masked a steely underbelly, stared right back at her.

Bobbi gave DI Parker an exaggerated 'Here's Jonny' type smile, only to receive a curled lip in reply. The younger, attractive one's eyes continued to search the gallery with the intensity of a North Korean border guard until Eton Hogarth cleared his throat noisily; a signal for the Court Clerk to stand.

Bobbi's defence barrister stood and motioned for her to do the same. She smoothed down her skirt and noticed her hands were trembling. *'This is it,'* she mouthed silently to herself. *'This is what the last twelve boils down to.'*

A solid weight shifted in her stomach. Sweat beaded her upper lip. She shook uncontrollably. Scratched at an imaginary itch on her cheek. Twisted a strand of hair.

While the clerk readied himself to enter the spotlight, Judge Hogarth addressed the jury.

'Before you adjourned to consider your verdict, I consented to accept a majority verdict agreed by at least ten of you.' Hogarth removed his glasses and rubbed his eyes before continuing. 'Your verdict must depend on your belief that the prosecution has proved beyond reasonable doubt that Roberta Cavell knowingly committed the crime with which she is charged.'

He took a sip of water from his glass and looked over the rim of his spectacles in the direction of the clerk.

The clerk puffed himself up. 'Will the foreperson of the jury please stand?'

A red-faced woman in her forties stood self-consciously, hands clasped in front of her.

'Have you reached a verdict upon which at least ten of you agree?'

Bobbi Cavell took in a lungful of air and held it. In the gallery, Lyall Parker followed suit

The woman cleared her throat. 'We have.'

'Do you find the defendant guilty or not guilty?'

CHAPTER THREE

Murmurs turned to words, words to shouts, shouts to cheers, cheers to abuse.

'Never in holy creation. How the hell did they come up with that one?' Lyall Parker fumed.

Ryan shook his head. 'Months of work up the spout. The system's bollocks, it really is.'

'Corrupt, more like. The case was crystal clear. All she had going for her were her looks and fluttering eyelashes. Bet they were false, as well. Jesus Christ. I give up.'

In the dock, Bobbi blew kisses towards her team, used her hands to mime a heart shape at a friend in the gallery. Waved to another. Laughed and pointed towards a third.

Matty McNair turned towards the detectives and shrugged his shoulders. The gesture said, '*That's the way the cookie crumbles.*'

'I've seen enough,' Parker said. 'I'm oot o' here.' He squeezed passed Ryan even before Jarrod could stand.

'Aye. I'm with you. Let's get back to the station. We'd better let DCI Danskin and the Super know they've hoyed more money down the drain on this one.'

Bobbi saw the detectives leave. She stuck out her tongue and raised a middle finger in their direction.

'Ignore it,' Ryan said to Lyall.

'Aye. She'll get her comeuppance one day, sure enough. I just hope I'm the one tae see it.'

As Bobbi watched Jarrod and Parker exit, her eyes caught sight saw of Eunice Paddock. A short woman with wiry grey hair, Mrs Paddock sat alongside her husband who took her hand in his while she dabbed her eyes with a handkerchief held in her other hand.

A dark-haired man draped an arm around Mrs Paddock's shoulder. He looked up and stared into Bobbi's eyes. She willed herself to break his gaze, but she couldn't look away. Her knuckles whitened around the dock rail until, with a shake of his head, the young man turned away to kiss his mother on the top of her head.

Eunice Paddock let out a piercing cry. Tears streamed down her flushed cheeks. Mr Paddock tried to console his wife, but his face betrayed the family's shock.

Bobbi looked away and tried to swallow the lump wedged in her throat.

Justice Hogarth waited for the commotion to die down before turning towards the dock.

'Miss Cavell, the jury have found you Not Guilty. This concludes all proceedings against you. Bail no longer applies, and you are free to leave this court without condition.'

The Court Orderly stood to formally close the session.

'This is all wrong!' A voice broke over the general hubbub. 'The witch up there took everything my mother had. Her life savings. Her dignity. Her pride. And you're setting her free to do it all again. How can't you see her for what she is? How can you let it happen to someone else?'

'That is quite enough, sir,' the Court Orderly intervened.

'No. It's not nearly enough. This is the nothing but the start.' The icy stare of Eunice Paddock's son froze Bobbi to the dock floor.

'Ssshh, Tyler,' Eunice urged. 'I don't want a scene.' She pulled on her son's hand dragging him down into his chair. His eyes never moved from Bobbi's ashen face. Bobbi was transfixed; free to go, yet afraid to do so.

'Congratulations, Bobbi.' It was her defence lawyer, Martina Thomas. Martina bore hair the colour of jet piled high on her head. Her green eyes smiled with the delight of a job well done.

'It's really over?' Bobbi asked in a voice devoid of emotion.

19

'It is.'

'Oh my God.' Bobbi breathed for what seemed the first time that day. She watched folk stream out the courtroom. She'd lost sight of the Paddock family and breathed once more. 'What happens now? I just go? Just like that?'

'Almost. You've some paperwork to sign at the foyer desk then, yeah – you're free to leave.'

'Thank you.' She wiped her nose on the back of her hand. 'I don't know what more I can say.'

Martina smiled. 'You don't need say a thing, Bobbi. It's all in a day's work. You can do one thing for me, though.'

'Of course. Anything.'

'You can pay my invoice today. End of the month, and all that. We've all got bills to pay. It won't be a problem, will it?'

Bobbi grinned. 'No. I've got plenty of money, don't worry about that.'

Martina gave her a curious look. 'Okay,' she said holding up her hand. 'I don't think it's wise to say anything else. I really don't want to hear any more.'

The defence lawyer pulled her iPhone from beneath her robes. Scrolled through a stream of messages. Without raising her head from the screen she asked, 'Is someone here to take you home?'

'Yes, my flatmate should be here.'

'Okay. Goodbye, Bobbi.' She dipped her head towards the door. 'Time for you to get those papers signed. An usher will show you the way.'

'I just want to hear it from you once more: I'm free to go.'

'Yes, you're free to go.' Martina looked up from her messages. 'Take care, Bobbi. And keep that mouth of yours shut. I do not want to see you here again. Understand?'

Bobbi saluted. 'Received and understood.'

Martina was in no mood for small talk with a stuck-up immature rich kid. Especially one who was quite clearly guilty as charged. She turned on her heels and left Bobbi in the hands of the usher.

Sometimes, Martina Thomas really hated her job.

**

Lyall Parker stood a discreet distance away as Ryan Jarrod made one of his regular calls. Three times a day, Ryan called his dad. Every time, his heart stopped beating until he heard Norman Jarrod's voice.

'All okay?' Ryan asked.

'Aye, son. Hangover from hell, like, but everything's okay in the sense you mean.'

The *'sense he meant'* was the fact that neither his father nor brother, or his grandmother, had been kidnapped, butchered, or worse by Benny Yu, despite the Chinese gangmaster's threat to Ryan and his family.

'James?'

He heard his father exhale.

'Dad – how's James?'

'He's nee different. Not out of bed yet. Or, if he is, he's applying his bloody Goth make-up again.

Ryan sighed. 'It's Emo, not Goth.'

'Aal the same to me, son.'

'I know, dad. I wish he'd talk to somebody.'

'Talking won't do any good, man. He's a changed lad since…' Norman didn't need finish the sentence. Ryan knew.

'Has he taken anything?'

'If you mean drugs, no. Divvent think so, anyway. He was on the piss last night but there again so was I so I can't complain.'

'And gran?'

'I've just spoken to the home. She's fine. And, before you ask, they haven't recruited any new staff. Yu can't get to her that way, Ryan.'

The occupants of Court Three began to disgorge themselves into the foyer.

'Yu can get anybody, anytime he likes.'

'Son, man, your lot have more security looking after us than Prince William.'

Ryan saw Lyall tap his wristwatch impatiently.

'I've got to go, Dad. As long as you're okay, that's all I wanted to know.'

'We're fine, man.'

'Love you, Dad.'

'Hadaway, you big soft shite,' Norman Jarrod said as he ended the call.

Ryan called out to Lyall. 'Ready when you are.'

'Aye, just a minute, lad.' It was Parker's turn to linger. He stared coldly across the lobby as an usher led Bobbi Cavell towards a desk.

'Next,' an officious woman said from behind the counter.

'Oh. Err, I'm not sure what I have to do. My name's Roberta Cavell. I just left Court Three and my brief told me there's some forms to complete.'

The woman typed Bobbi's name into her computer. Her head jutted forward until her face was inches from the monitor. She squinted, hit print, and waited for a swathe of paper to scroll from the printer.

The woman scribbled a number of 'x's on the paperwork. 'Sign and date here, here, and here. Sign, date, and write your full name in block capitals on the last sheet. Try not to write outside the box.'

Bobbi did write outside the box. She did so because she heard Tyler Paddock scream at her from across the foyer.

'Don't even think this is over, you bitch!'

Bobbi turned towards the voice and saw the man stomp towards her. She glanced around, searching for security. Two guards rushed to her side. The young detective, the one who'd identified himself to her as DS Jarrod, stood between her and a furious Tyler Paddock while a third guard grabbed Paddock's arm.

'I'll make you pay. Do you hear? You're not getting away with this.'

Ryan left Bobbi with the security guards and walked towards the red-faced son of Eunice Paddock.

'Sir, I understand this is a difficult time, but you must calm down.'

'Who the fuck are you?'

Ryan flashed his warrant card.

Tyler's face dropped. 'Yeah, yeah. Okay. I'm going.'

He shrugged off the guard's hold.

Mr and Mrs Paddock waited for their son to join them at the exit. He walked towards them with head bowed. His last words before leaving were delivered over his shoulder and directed towards Bobbi.

'Just remember what I said. This isn't finished. Not by a long chalk.'

CHAPTER FOUR

Ryan and Lyall Parker exchanged curious glances.

'Did you no' hear what I said, sir?' Lyall questioned. 'They found Cavell not guilty.'

'Aye, I heard you. So what? You win some, you lose some,' DCI Stephen Danskin shrugged.

'But the man-hours the pair of us spent on it. The effort Ravi's computer forensic team put into trawling through bank transactions: all for nothing. And I tell you what, she's as guilty as sin, so she is.'

Danskin rocked back in his chair in his third-floor office. 'I've no doubt she is.'

'So how come you're so blasé about it?' Ryan asked.

'It's the way the cookie crumbles.'

Ryan snorted down a laugh. 'That's what the CPS said.'

'Look, Jarrod, I know this wasn't the type of case you're usually assigned to, and I appreciate it's been a long and complicated process. Fraud, embezzlement – they're always complex. Far too complex for Joe Public to decide on, which is why we can never be sure which way a jury will jump. They're more likely to pass their verdict on the closeness of the defendant's eyebrows, or whether he or she has a nice smile, than they are on the evidence.'

'But it was cut-and-dried, sir.'

Danskin sighed. 'No. It wasn't. You can never trust what a jury is going to do. Some of the intricacies of these cases are way above most people's level of understanding. I mean, if the public voted a buffoon into Downing Street, if they agreed to Brexit; then you can't trust 'em to do owt right.'

'Aye, I suppose,' Ryan conceded. 'It just boils me piss, sometimes. All the effort and expense that goes into pursuing a case.'

Danskin rubbed his jaw. 'Speaking of costs: Lyall can you leave us for a minute? The Super and me would like a word with Jarrod.'

Ryan instantly stiffened. 'Has something happened? Are me folks okay?'

'Relax, Jarrod. It's nowt like that.'

Ryan sunk back in his seat. 'Don't do that to me, sir.'

'Sorry, son. Lyall, leave us to it, yeah?'

'Nae problem.'

As soon as Parker closed the office door, Danskin picked up the phone. 'We're free, ma'am,' was all he said before he replaced the receiver.

Ryan and DCI Danskin sat in a silence so uncomfortable Ryan likened it to a kid watching a sex scene in the company of his parents. He noticed Danskin avoided eye contact as if they were sitting opposite each other on the Metro.

'What's going on, sir?'

Danskin was relieved he had no time to answer. The door opened and Sam Maynard walked in, a gentle smile on her face.

'Detective Sergeant Jarrod. Ryan. How are we?'

Ryan's brow furrowed. 'I'm fine, ma'am. At least, I was. I'm not sure how I'll be in five minutes time. What's this about?'

Sam Maynard lay a hand on Ryan's shoulder as she moved around him to perch on Stephen Danskin's desk. 'We're approaching a new financial year. As ever, we'll have budget cuts. God knows, it's hard enough managing as it is, but more reductions…' she shook her head.

Ryan shifted uncomfortably. 'So?' he asked.

Superintendent Maynard tapped a manicured fingernail against the underside of Danskin's desk while she considered what she was about to say.

'Ryan, I can't afford to have one of my best MIT detective's arse-farting around on work better suited to DCI Kinnear's crew.'

'I'm back on the team, then?' he said, eyes brightening. 'The juicy, high-profile stuff? Proper coppering?'

Sam Maynard laughed. 'Yes, proper coppering, as Stephen would call it.'

'Great. Can't wait. What you got for me?'

'Nothing yet, Jarrod,' Danskin said.

'Well, what are we waiting for? Let's find us summat.'

Danskin caught himself mesmerised by Sam Maynard's eyes as they shared a glance. He dragged himself away by saying, 'There's a bit more to it than that.'

'Huh?'

Superintendent Maynard once more put her hand on Ryan's shoulder. He looked at it curiously.

'How have things been lately?' she asked.

Ryan resisted the temptation to roll his eyes. 'In what way, ma'am?'

Again, he noticed Maynard and Danskin exchange a look. Stephen Danskin seemed to incline his head ever so slightly before the Super exhaled and continued.

'Okay. Let's cut to the chase. It'll be six months next week since Benny Yu made those threats against you and your family. Since then, we've seen neither sight nor sound of him. The YuTube drugs line has gone off-radar. None of his known accomplices have surfaced, and even the Met have lowered him down the Op Tower priority list.'

'What are you trying to tell me, ma'am?'

Air escaped her mouth with a hiss. 'We think Benny Yu has left the country and, with no more threats against you, it's time to scale back your security cover.'

Ryan waited while the rumble of a passing train died down. He used the time to gather his thoughts. 'What exactly does *scale back* entail?'

'It means we can no longer afford to deploy an officer on twenty-four-hour surveillance. As you know, we've had an unmarked car patrol between your house, your father's house, and your grandmother's care home. We've had an officer constantly monitor the CCTV feed from the cameras around your property. That's going to stop.'

Ryan rubbed his brow. 'So, that's it. We're on our own now, is that what you're saying?'

'Steady down, lad,' Danskin said. 'We can't do this forever, you know, and it's been half a year since there were any credible threats against you.'

'That's okay, then, is it? Remember what Yu told me: *'I'll be watching you for as long as it takes,'* is what he said; words to the effect of.'

Sam Maynard intervened. 'You're not being cut adrift, Ryan. The cameras will be left outside your house. You'll still be able to watch the feed yourself. See anything suspicious – anything at all - just hit the panic button and someone from the Whickham station will be there in minutes. We'll still store your Peugeot in the station pound and continue to provide you with an unmarked car to travel to and from Forth Street, which means no-one will know what you're driving from one day to the next. We'll also continue providing you with a route home which varies from day to day. All of which means it's highly improbable anyone can follow you, and even less likely for you to be intercepted on route.'

Ryan arched his eyebrows and sighed.

'That's what I mean by scale back,' Maynard continued. 'We're not leaving you hanging out to dry. We've still got your back. We just need to count the pennies, that's all. How does that sound?'

Ryan stared out the window, along the Tyne and up towards the hill on which Whickham village sat.

'For me, I get it. I really do. It's my family I'm not sure about. Doesn't sound like they've got any cover at all.'

'I've got to be honest with you. They haven't.'

'Shit,' he mouthed.

Maynard bent forward and touched his knee. 'I'm sorry, Ryan. It's all I can do.'

He considered it for a moment. 'Doesn't sound like I've much choice.'

'You don't, I'm afraid.'

Ryan appreciated her honesty, if nothing else.

'Stephen – have you anything to add?'

Danskin shifted in his seat. Cleared his throat. 'Aye. About Hannah …'

Ryan shot into defensive mode. 'What about her?'

'I'd prefer it if you still kept away from her.'

Ryan snickered. 'It's fine for you to shaft my family but don't involve your stepdaughter in any of it. That's rich.'

Danskin couldn't meet his eye.

Ryan let out a whimper. 'Sorry, sir. That wasn't fair of me. Don't worry. I'll keep away from her. You know I wouldn't do owt to endanger her. We've kept apart for six months now. A little longer won't make any difference.'

Danskin offered a grim smile. 'Thanks, son. I appreciate it. Really, I do.'

Ryan stood. 'But I'm back on proper duties now, yeah?'

'You bet your life you are,' Danskin said. 'Welcome back. We need you.'

Ryan knew the words were genuine. 'Thank you, sir. I need you lot, an' aal. More than ever.'

Danskin put an arm around Ryan's shoulder. 'Good. Let's see if we can't find a case for you to get your teeth into.'

'Champion,' Ryan said, rubbing his hands together. 'Just make sure whatever you give me has nowt to do with Roberta-sodding-Cavell.'

**

Roberta-sodding-Cavell opened the door to her apartment with an elbow and raised a bottle of champagne aloft in each hand. Behind her, a girl clung to her waist conga-style and pushed the door shut with her foot.

'*I'm free to do what I want - any old time,*' Bobbi sang. Both girls giggled.

'I can't believe it. I mean, I *really* can't believe it,' Leanne Soulsby said, collapsing into a mocha-coloured leather sofa. She kicked off her shoes and folded her legs beneath her.

Bobbi sat next to her. 'You better believe it, girl – and I'm gonna party like it's 2022.' She tossed back her head and laughed. 'C'mon. Let's get these bottles opened.'

'Warm champagne? Heck, no. A few minutes in the freezer will do the trick.' Leanne took the bottles from Bobbi and wandered over the zebra-patterned carpet in the Knott's Flats apartment the girls shared. Her bare feet touched cold black and white checked tiles as she reached the kitchen area, where she slipped the bottles into the freezer's middle drawer.

'Give them a few minutes and we'll get the party started,' Leanne said.

On her way back, she lit a couple of scented candles sat on a white shelf beneath a framed print of a Maasai warrior silhouetted against a golden sun. It was daylight outside, but the candle's flames tossed a soft, flickering glow over the picture as if the sun rose from beneath the Great Rift Valley.

Leanne stood back and admired the portrait for a moment. More Boho than shabby chic, it was at odds with their home's décor, yet Leanne loved the boldness of the artwork, the serenity in the warrior's face, and the lean musculature of his rangy frame.

'Penny for them,' Bobbi said.

'I dunno what I'm thinking, really. I suppose I'm looking at our friend here,' she nodded towards the portrait, 'And thinking about freedom. To us, he looks free as a bird but, in his world, is he? Does he have the same worries as the rest of us?'

'Ooh, get you, Simone de Beauvoir. Frankly, my dear, I don't give a damn what he thinks. All that matters to me is the fact my nightmare's over and I can get on with life.'

Bobbi tipped back her head until it melded into the sofa's soft leather. She felt a calmness swaddle her; something she hadn't felt for a long while. The sensation was so alien to her, she immediately felt uncomfortable.

She breathed deeply, taking in the candles' fragrance. Lemon drizzle scent, sickly sweet, filled her nostrils; stuck in her throat. Bobbi felt the anxiety, which only a moment ago had begun to escape her, build in her gullet along with the realisation today's outcome could have been so very different.

Bobbi felt herself gag.

She sprinted past Leanne, flung open the balcony doors, and rushed to the concrete barrier.

Her eyes were glassy. Her hands went to her mouth as she choked. Bobbi screwed her eyes tight. Bent over the barrier. A thick rush of fluid filled her mouth, spilled out, some splashed the balcony beneath, the rest fell as a congealed mass onto the clifftop five stories below.

She opened her eyes, tipped her head skywards, and breathed in a lungful of fresh air. Slowly, the tears cleared from her eyes.

Off to her left, the Collingwood Monument shone white on the clifftop. Straight ahead, the mouth of the Tyne gaped wide, a flotilla of trawlers winding into the river's maw. A flock of quarrelling seagulls followed their every move, their cries piercing the still air – and Bobbi's consciousness.

She spat once to rid herself of the bitter bile taste. Stared across the river from where the spider-legged, robotic-looking Herd Groyne lighthouse glared back at her from the south bank.

That was the moment she truly realised she was back home. Not in a cold prison cell, but in the comfort of her own home.

'Is that champagne ready yet?' she shouted back into the flat. 'I'm gagging for it.'

CHAPTER FIVE

The woman was of indeterminate age, a result of her horrific injuries. She hadn't been wearing a seatbelt at the time of the accident, and she was catapulted through the windscreen. She landed thirty yards down the country lane.

Now, years later, her facial scars remained raw. The surgeons had tried to save her left leg, but it had proved futile. Worse, she emerged from an induced coma with permanent brain trauma.

The hospital argued against her discharge, but they were given no choice. The woman left, and the bed she was confined to did not lie in a hospital ward. Instead, her permanent carer tended to her every need from the woman's home. And her needs were many.

Gently, her carer replaced the catheter in her urethra and attached its transparent bag to a metal stand. A milky liquid dribbled from her mouth from the feeding tube. The woman's carer wiped it away with a tissue and lightly smoothed down her hair.

The woman moaned.

'I'm sorry. I'm being as gentle as I can,' the carer soothed. 'I know it's not nice. It'll soon be over.'

Tears glistened in the woman's eyes before they were wiped away. Her attendant caressed the scar on the woman's face with the back of a hand. 'There, there. I'm finished now. Wasn't too bad, was it?'

The woman moaned again.

'And,' the carer added, 'I have some exciting news for you. I think I have found one. I'm afraid it means leaving you alone for a while, but I promise I'll be back as soon as I can.'

Another tear trickled down the woman's face.

'I know, and I'm sorry you must be alone but, by the time I'm home, the world shall be a better place. It'll be better because she won't be a part of it.'

The carer bent forward and kissed the woman's forehead.

**

Stephen Danskin whispered into Ryan's ear as he led him through the bullpen from his office. 'Listen, there's a couple of things the others know but you don't. Try not to act surprised.'

'Oh aye? What sort of things?'

'I'll explain later.'

Todd Robson met them halfway. 'How you doing, mate?'

'Todd, man, I've been sitting opposite you for the last four months. Nowt's changed in the few hours I've been away today.'

Robson squinted into the sun which streamed through the third-floor window. 'Everything's changed, man. You're away from all the boring shitty cases and back on the team.'

Ryan smiled. 'You've heard, then?' He nodded towards Danskin. That's what the DCI had meant. 'Aye, it's true – so you better have a queue of cases I can supervise you on.'

'I have. Boring shitty cases, mainly.'

The trio laughed.

'Thing is, Jarrod,' Danskin said, 'You're asking the wrong person.'

Ryan looked around. 'DI Parker's not here so there's no-one else to ask.'

'Aye, there is.'

DC Lucy Dexter looked up from behind a monitor like an inquisitive meerkat. She gave Ryan a wave.

Lucy Dexter was the youngest and most inexperienced member of Danskin's team. The rest of the squad – Todd Robson in particular – thought she had a thing for Ryan.

'You'll be working with Dexter for a while.'

'Oh, will I, indeed?'

Danskin looked Ryan in the eye. 'Yes. You will.'

'Why not Todd? Or Treblecock?'

The DCI paused. 'Dexter could do with your experience.'

Todd chortled. Lucy stifled a giggle.

'How long for?'

'A while,' Danskin responded.

Ryan glanced at Todd and Lucy. ''Scuse us a minute.' He led Danskin away by the arm.

'What's going on, sir?'

Danskin scratched the back of his neck. 'I was going to tell you. Super doesn't want you out on your own. Not yet. Still a bit early, you know?'

Ryan nodded. 'Benny Yu, you mean. Surely if the Super's worried, Todd's the man I should be with, not Lucy? I've more muscle in my fingernail than she has in all her body. She's tiny, man. All you're doing is putting her in danger by assigning her to me.'

'Howay, man. She's not in danger. Yu's long gone. It's just…precautionary, you know?'

'My arse, it is.'

'Look. It doesn't matter what you think, the Super's not letting you out on your own. Either you pair up with Dexter…'

'Pair up? This isn't LA. We don't *pair up* over here.'

'Don't get cocky with me,' Danskin said through his teeth, 'We do now. You either pair up with Dexter, or you're back on desk cases like the Cavell one - only you'll be part of DCI Kinnear's team, not mine.'

Ryan began to protest. Realised he had no choice. 'One month. Okay? I'll give it a month then that's it.'

'Good.' Danskin glanced at Lucy Dexter who was studying them with a grin on her face. 'Besides, she might keep you away from Hannah for a while,' he whispered. Danskin saw Ryan's face. Held up his hands. 'Joke, Ryan. It was a joke.'

Ryan caught Lucy watching him. She gave him a coquettish wink.

'I'm not sure it is a joke,' he said under his breath.

**

Bobbi popped the cork on the second bottle of Moet. Bubbles frothed over the rim, cascaded down the bottle's neck like pyroclastic flow from a volcano.

'Whoa!' Bobbi brought the bottle towards her to avoid spillage on the carpet. She cupped her hand against the side of the champagne bottle. Sparkling liquid pooled in her palm.

Once the flow stopped, she licked the champagne from her hand and sucked her fingers dry.

Leanne narrowed her eyes and pursed her lips. 'You're a dirty mare,' she laughed.

'You don't know the half of it, girl,' Bobbi teased back. She filled two flutes, entwined her wrist around Leanne's, and said 'Cheers,' as she clinked the glasses together.

'To us,' Leanne slurred.

'And to good old British justice.'

The girls clinked glasses once more. Bobbi smacked her lips together. 'This is the life,' she said, staring at the ceiling. 'The only thing which could make it better is if I was drinking this on a yacht somewhere off the St Lucia coast.'

'Nah. Not for me. Monaco. That'd be my choice.'

'Just as well you're not coming with me then, isn't it?'

Leanne took another sip of champagne. 'Dream on. I can't remember last time I was away, what with travel restrictions and all that malarkey.'

'Which is why I'm gonna do it.'

'The yacht and St Lucia?'

'Yeah. Or Barbados. Why not?'

'Money, for starters.'

Bobbi waved a hand dismissively. 'That's what money's for.' She refilled her glass.

'It is if you've got it,' Leanne added wistfully.

For once, Bobbi had no reply. Instead, she gave an enigmatic smile and drained her glass. She topped up Leanne's flute before trying to fill her own.

'Ah man. Empty,' Bobbi turned the bottle upside down as if to prove her point. The few remaining drops glistened like tears as they fell into her lap. She pushed herself up from the sofa, swayed slightly, and sat back down. 'Whoa. It's good stuff.'

'Where were you going?'

Bobbi stared at her with glassy eyes and flushed cheeks. 'Fridge. Prosecco's in there. It mightn't be shampoo but it's still bubbles, and I need more bubbles.'

'I'll get it.'

Leanne unfolded her legs from beneath her, steadied herself, and headed to the kitchen whilst Bobbi chanted rhythmically, 'I need bubbles. I need bubbles,' over-and-over again.

Once her glass was charged, Bobbi said, 'You can come with me. To St Lucia. Or Barbados. Or wherever it was you said you wanted to go.' She put a hand to her mouth as a loud belch escaped her.

Leanne rolled her eyes. 'What with? Like I said, I've no money.'

'Oh yeah; I forgot. You're less a wannabe, more a never-will-be, aren't you?'

Leanne looked at her coldly. 'At least I try. It wasn't my fault they never aired my X Factor audition. And I was on standby for Love Island, remember.'

'As if you'd let me forget. Remind me again – were you called?'

Leanne stared into her glass. 'That's not the point.'

'It's escatly the point.' Bobbi stumbled over the word. 'Escatly,' she tried again. 'You know what I mean,' she settled for.

'What about the modelling I did for that fashion catalogue?'

Bobbi tipped back her head and roared with laughter. 'You know where that led, don't you?'

'Yes, actually; I do. An offer for a professionally produced portfolio.'

Bobbi's fizz dribbled from her glass as she pointed it towards Leanne. 'From your post on Purple Port, and an offer from a photographer whose studio,' she made air quotes around the word, 'Was a terraced house in Ashington, where all he wanted was to get in your knickers.'

Leanne arched her tattooed eyebrows.

'What's worse, you were daft enough to let him,' Bobbi added.

'I'm going to bed,' Leanne announced.

'No, no, no, no,' Bobbi clung to her friend's arm. 'I didn't mean it. Stay here with me.'

Leanne folded her arms across her chest, but she retook her seat. 'At least I've got a job,' she said.

'On the Charlotte Tilbury concession store in Fenwick's. Big deal.'

'I take it you won't be wanting any more products from me, in that case.'

'I retackt…no, that's not right, is it? I retrack…I take back my statement. Anyway, your glass is empty.'

She poured Leanne another drink. The recipient closed her eyes and felt Bobbi's head rest in her lap as she stretched her length along the sofa.

'Just think, Leanne. We could be sitting watching the sun sink behind the twin pitons. What do you say? Sun, sea, cocktails - and cock. Lots and lots of cock,' Bobbi sighed wistfully.

'I work, remember. It was hard enough getting today off to support you, and I've booked a duvet day for tomorrow to recover.'

'Pull a sicky.'

'I can't.'

Bobbi stretched up a hand and ruffled her BFF's hair.

'Pretty please.'

'I can't afford it, Bobbi.'

'I'll pay.'

'YOU can't afford it.'

'Can't I?'

The girls remained silent as they looked out the balcony windows at a pink sun setting behind the Fisherman's Memorial on Fiddler's Green. Not quite the same as the twin pitons, Leanne thought.

'Can you really afford it?'

'Yes.' Bobbi raised her head from Leanne's lap. 'Does that mean you'll come?' her eyes sparkled against the alcohol glow of red cheeks.

'*How* can you afford it?'

Bobbi lowered her head into Leanne's lap. Said nothing. After a long silence, Leanne spoke again.

'Bobbi – how did you do it?'

'Do what?'

'You know what I mean.'

'Oh, Eunice Paddock, and all that. I didn't. The nice old man with the glasses and funny wig said so.' She raised a glass to Eton Hogarth, almost spilling the contents onto her head.

'Is that a fact? Well, we live in this fab apartment. You don't work. Your parents stopped subbing you ages ago. You must get your money to pay for this,' she gestured around their home, 'Somehow. Not to mention St Lucia.'

Bobbi swung herself upright and half turned so she could look Leanne in the eye.

'Promise not to tell?'

Leanne made a cross gesture over her heart.

'Promise not to tell on Jamie Dornan's abs?'

'I swear on Jamie Dornan's abs, and all other parts of his anatomy.'

Bobbi licked her lips. 'Okay. We're all out of fizz but there's a bottle of Chablis in the cooler. Go get it, and then - when you're sitting comfortably - I shall begin.'

CHAPTER SIX

Ryan Jarrod flicked down the sun visor as he crawled over the Redheugh Bridge. He had the headache from hell. Staring into a furnace-red sun as it lowered itself from the sky didn't help.

Today's assigned vehicle was a Volvo. It was far too big for his liking, especially in late rush-hour, nose to tail traffic, on the *'Blue Route'* he'd been instructed to take. The concentration needed to manoeuvre it through the traffic increased the tension inside his head even more.

Not only that but, while he waited for the gates of the Forth Street station's car park to open, Ryan also had texted DS Hannah Graves telling her he was back on the team.

Sod's Law meant he caught her on a break from her duties at the Port of Tyne, and she called him at once. Over the handsfree, he heard her tell him she was pleased for him. When he mentioned about the security cutbacks, Hannah had said, 'Take care.' Not, *'For God's sake, be careful - I love you so much I don't know what I'd do if anything happened to you'*, just *'Take care.'*

Ryan tormented himself with thoughts of how she really felt about him, after six months apart. Besides, he'd already promised Stephen Danskin he wouldn't endanger her. The knowledge of the Danskin conversation, and what it meant, only made his head throb even more.

By the time he'd steered the Volvo onto Askew Road and began the crawl towards the A1, he consoled himself with the understanding he'd soon be balls deep in complex major investigations and would have no time for DS Hannah Graves anyway.

He did, though, have time to think about his family.

He took the A1 south for less than half a mile to the Lobley Hill interchange where he joined a queue of stationary traffic. Ryan drummed his fingers on the steering wheel, turned up the radio, but still fears for his father, brother, and grandmother's safety filled his brain.

So much so, he barely realised the traffic had started moving again, and him with it.

So much so, he didn't notice the transit van - half on the footpath, half on the road - with its hazard lights flashing until he almost ran into the back of it.

So much so that, when the rear doors opened in front of him and a figure stepped from its back holding a weapon, he knew it was one of Benny Yu's men come for him.

Instead of braking, Ryan increased the Volvo's speed and aimed it directly at the person in front of him. At the last moment, he got a clear picture of his assailant.

She wore a navy-blue blazer and grey tartan skirt. In her hands, she gripped a hockey stick. She was no more than twelve years old and bore the Grace College high school uniform.

Ryan stamped on the brake pedal. The Volvo slewed slightly, straightened again, and came to a halt inches from the transit's rear bumper.

The girl had leapt back into the safety of the van. Ashen-faced, she cried and trembled like a jellyfish.

A furious looking man in a postal worker's red jacket sprinted around from the front of the van and consoled the girl.

Ryan stepped from his car and apologised. The father turned to confront him; fists clenched.

'What the hell do you think you're doing?'

Ryan blushed shame-facedly. 'I'm sorry, I…'

'Sorry? You nearly killed wor kid and all you can say is sorry?'

'I thought…'

The man jumped from the van and grabbed Ryan by the scruff of the neck. Instantly, Ryan snatched the man's wrists and wrenched them from his throat. He twisted the man's arms, forcing the girl's father to turn with the movement, away from Ryan and towards the maw of the van's open doors.

The girl screamed, 'Daddy, daddy!!'

'Get off me, you madman! I'll call the police.'

As calmly as he could, Ryan said, 'I am the police, sir.' He released his hold and brought his warrant card from a pocket.

Cars behind them tooted their frustration. Some drivers stepped from their vehicles and craned their necks to watch. A bus driver travelling downhill brought his double-decker to a halt. He slid open his window and shouted, 'I'll call the cops, mind' as his passengers pressed their noses against grimy windows in order to get a better view.

'DS Ryan Jarrod, City and County CID,' Ryan said to the driver of both van and bus. He waggled his ID towards the stationary number 97. Satisfied, the bus driver released the air brakes and in a plume of blue smoke continued with his journey.

'If you'd let me explain,' Ryan said to the van driver, 'I was about to say we've had a report that a van matching this description has been involved in a hit and run. I can see now that this isn't the vehicle in question.'

It was a bare-faced lie and Ryan hated himself for telling it, but all he wanted was to get away from there so he could check on his dad and brother.

'Aye, well. That doesn't change the fact you scared my Annabelle half to death.'

'I know, and I'm sorry. I'll file a full report on this, sir, and let my superiors know of my error. There's a police complaint process if you wish to lodge one.'

Annabelle's father shook himself down. 'Nah. No point. No harm done in the end; I suppose. Just be more careful in future, yeah?'

'I will. Thank you for your co-operation. I'll let you be on your way. Take care, sir. And you keep going to your hockey practice, Annabelle. You'll be a star, one day.'

The girl nodded swiftly, tears drying on her cheeks.

Ryan climbed back into the Volvo and waited for the van to pull away before he put his head against the steering wheel and shed more tears than Annabelle ever had.

**

Bobbi Cavell screwed her face at the first sip of the Chablis; the contrast of its bitter minerality too much to the sparkle which went before.

'I'll get used to it soon,' she said.

'Never mind the bloody wine. Tell me how you did it.'

'Oh, that,' she waved her hand. 'I'm coming to it.' She took a second sip. 'Aah – much better already, see? Anyway, do you remember Bernard?'

Leanne thought for a moment before shaking her head.

'You do. Posh bloke. Always wore a suit. Lives in Gosforth.'

'Oh, yes. The old bloke you went out with for a while. I do remember.'

'He wasn't that old really. Well, okay, I guess he was nearly forty so that is old,' she giggled. 'Old and very, very rich.'

'What's he got to do with Eunice Paddock?'

'Nothing apart from the fact he lived around the corner from her.'

'Okay. Go on…'

'Anyway, he lived on Westfield Drive, and I always met up with him on Graham Park Road.'

'Why not just go to his house?'

'Err, hello? Because of wis wife, stupid-head.'

Leanne shook her head. 'You're a minx, Bobbi Cavell; you really are.'

'So, this day, I was standing outside this posh house; so posh its owners didn't want anyone so common as a postman walking down the drive. It had one of those letterbox-on-a-stand things. The ones that look like a bird house, like they have in America.' She took a draw from her glass. 'Anyway, the postie came along, saw me standing outside and, because I was done up to the nines, he assumed I lived there. He said something like, '*Might as well just take this, love, rather than me put it in your letterbox,*' so I did.'

'What happened next?'

'I put the mail in my bag and forgot about it.'

Leanne yawned and looked at her watch. Her eyes struggled to focus through the alcoholic haze. 'I'm nodding off here. Get to the point, for God's sake.'

'You wanted to know, girlfriend,' Bobbi said, faking a Bronx accent. 'When I turfed my bag out a few days later, I saw all the post addressed to a Mrs Eunice Paddock. And, I opened it.'

'What was it?' Leanne asked, suddenly alert.

'Loads of things. A bill from the vets, an invitation to a Christening, some insurance letters from Saga, and a couple of bank statements. I nearly fell off my chair when I saw all the zeros on the end of her savings account.'

She paused, savouring the moment, a beam of a smile on her face. 'I had the TV on in the background, and that little bald bloke was presenting one of those beware of the scammers-type programmes. It got me thinking '*I could do that*'

'Shut up!' Leanne exclaimed. She took a sip of wine, missed her mouth, and swore.

Bobbi was in her stride now. 'I found the phone number for the Paddock's. Fortunately, it's not a common name. I invented a persona for myself, practiced a posh accent and deepened my voice, and rang her.'

'What did you say to her?' Leanne shifted position so she could look directly at her friend.

'Good morning, Mrs Paddock,' she said in a voice so alien even Leanne didn't recognise it. 'I'm Katherine White, and I'm calling from your bank to introduce an exciting new product available only to our most trusted clients.'

'That's *sooo* good,' Leanne fawned.

'I told her the product was a low-risk investment account with guaranteed yield, fully FSCS protected, but the guaranteed rate only applied to those signing up today.'

'How do you know all this stuff?'

'Because Dominic Littlewood had just told me, silly.' Both girls laughed so loud they startled a couple of pigeons settling on their balcony for the night.

Between hiccups, Leanne told Bobbi to continue.

'I said I had to run through a few security questions. Pet's name, first school, favourite actor; that sort of thing.'

'Hang on. How did you know the answers?'

'Well, the pets name was on the vet bill. The others, I just told her she'd given the correct replies and she had passed security.'

Leanne's eyes widened and her jaw dropped. 'O.M.G!'

'Next, I asked her to confirm her online banking username, password, account number and such like.'

'What? And she gave them to you? Just like that?'

'No questions asked. I went to the library, used one of their computers so it couldn't be traced to me, and transferred the money.'

'Simple as that?'

'Yep. Simple as. Obvs, I withheld our number when I dialled Paddock from here so it couldn't be traced back to us, and anyone could have used the library computer. I thought the cop computer boffins would be able to stitch me up, but they didn't. Probably too much pressure investigating murderers and such like they skimped on investigating me. So, you see, any evidence against me was circumstantial. At least, that's what my defence barrister, whatever her name was, told the jury.'

Leanne sat on the edge of the seat, gobsmacked.

'You see, my dear, that's how I can afford to pay for your holiday. Come with me. Please, pretty, please – say you will, won't you?'

Leanne set down her half-full glass. 'I can't. I already told you. I can't get off work.'

'Aw man.'

Leanne stretched, yawned, and hiccupped all at once. 'And now, I'm totally pissed and ready for my bed.'

'It's only half six, babes.'

'Don't care. I'm done in. I'm taking to my pit and the do-not- disturb sign is going on all night and all tomorrow. You know what I'm like with a hangover. Don't you dare interrupt my duvet day.'

She hugged Bobbi. 'Goodnight, you clever, evil, dirty witch, you.'

Bobbi returned her embrace. 'You sure you won't come?'

Leanne was already rising to her feet. Unsteadily, she made her way towards the smaller of the two bedrooms. 'Sorry, sweet. I can't.'

Bobbi let out air. Drained her glass and sighed again. She flipped open her laptop and, without even a glance at destination or cost, booked the first flight and accommodation her fingers stumbled upon.

She slurred the words of a Madonna song.

'Holiday. Celebrate.'

Bobbi reached for the wine bottle.

Empty.

'Oh shit. Still, plenty time to get more,' she mumbled to herself.

She pulled on a jacket, fumbled for her purse, then her phone.

'I'm all booked,' she texted Leanne, followed by a string of emojis.

Low Light

Bobbi banged her thigh on the sofa as she made for the door. She lay a hand against the wall as she tried to grasp the door handle. It took three attempts.

'If we took a holiday
Took some time to celebrate
Just one day out of life
It would be, it would be so nice.'

She pushed at the door rather than pull. When she got it right, it opened so swiftly she fell face-first into the corridor.

Bobbi Cavell's quest for more alcohol had not started well.

It would end much, much worse.

**

Ryan sat in the black Volvo outside his father's house in quiet Newfield Walk planning how he would tell his father and brother that they were on their own. No security, no back-up, no nothing.

Ryan was confident Norman Jarrod would be okay. It was his brother, James, he worried about.

With still no plan in mind five minutes later, he got out the car, knocked on the Jarrod's front door, and walked straight in.

The sickly aroma of two-day old cooking oil greeted him. At least it took his mind off the headache.

Faithful old Spud limped arthritically towards him. Ryan bent double and picked up the ageing family pet and carried him into the living room where James Jarrod lay snoring on the sofa in front of Look North.

Ryan dropped the pug onto his father's lap.

'What the...'

'What have I told you about locking the door, Dad? I could have been anyone walking in here.'

They both knew who Ryan meant by *'anyone.'*

'Sorry, son. I divvent think owt's gonna happen after all this time, but I know what you mean.' Norman rubbed sleep from his eyes.

'Is James upstairs? I've got something to tell the pair of
you.'

'Oh aye? What's that, then?'

'You both need to hear it.'

'Your brother's not in.'

'Bugger. How long will he be?'

Norman Jarrod shrugged his shoulders. 'Not 'til
tomorrow. He's staying with Muzzle tonight.'

'You what?'

'He's at Muzzle's.'

Ryan pulled a face. 'Who's Muzzle when he's at home?'

'He hasn't told you? Somebody he met on that online
gaming site he's never off these days.'

Ryan stiffened. 'What's this Muzzle's real name?'

'Nee idea. They all use nicknames, apparently.'

'And let me guess – James calls himself Jam Jar, yeah? The
name everyone but us calls him. Doesn't take a genius to
work out it's him.'

'Aye, well...'

'Dad, man. He can't go off meeting people he doesn't
know. Especially anonymous ones. It could be one of Benny
Yu's lot. It could be Yu himself. Jesus Christ, man!'

'Cool your jets, son. It's nothing like that. I've met Muzzle.
There's no problem there.'

'How can you be so sure? He could be anybody.'

'He's not. He's a she, for starters. They've met up a few
times now.'

Ryan wasn't convinced. 'What do you know about her?
What's she like?'

'Ryan, man. What's with all the questions? Relax. You're
not at work now.'

DS Jarrod closed his eyes. 'Tell me what you know about
her.'

Norman pulled himself upright. 'Well, she's one of those
Goth Emo types an' aal, whatever it is you call them. She's

got more metal in her face than there is in Shepherd's scrapyard, but she seems canny enough.'

'Where does she live?'

'Lemington way, somewhere. Look, what's this all about? I'm worried enough about James since you-know-what happened. He's not thinking right. I thought having a mate, a lass, might help. Is that such a bad thing to want for my son?'

Ryan cast his eyes downwards as Norman continued.

'The last thing I want is you going the same way. Now, what do you want to tell me?'

'Couple of things. Firstly, I'm back on MIT duties.'

'Thank the lord. You might feel happier now.'

'Not really. The second thing is, we've lost our security. Our protection. At least, you, James, and Gran have. Mine's been scaled back.'

Norman pinched his nose. Grimaced. Finally, he nodded. 'Good.'

'Good? How is any of what I've just said good?'

'I can have Shania Twain come visit me anytime I like, for starters.'

'Dad, can you not be serious for a minute?'

'You want serious? Okay; I'll give you serious. I'm pleased security's gone.' He held up a hand to quash Ryan's protest. 'I'm sick of having your folk drive round the block. Checking in with me every now-and-again. What with lockdown and facemasks, kidnappings and death threats, not to mention Saudi takeovers and Putin throwing a wobbly, I just want me quiet life back. Normal, like it was before. Boring, but normal.'

Ryan dragged his eyes away from his father's. 'Has it really been that bad?'

'Aye, if I'm being honest. It has.'

Ryan sighed. 'Okay. I'll leave you to it. Let me know when James is back. I need to break the news to him, too. I'm not sure how he'll take it.'

'I wouldn't bother if I was you.'

'He has to know, Dad.'

Norman Jarrod smiled. 'He already does. The local copper came around and told us. James is cool about it.'

Ryan's mouth dropped open. 'You both knew? You let me waffle on like an idiot for ten minutes and you already knew?'

'Aye. I have to get a bit of fun somehow,' Norman laughed.

Ryan picked up a cushion and tossed it at his father. 'You bugger,' he smiled. 'Right, I'd better head back home and make sure everything's okay over there. I'll let you know when I'm in safely.'

'Hadaway, man. You're not a fourteen-year-old lass. I know you'll be fine.'

Ryan chuckled as he made for the door.

'Ryan,' his dad said. 'Look after yourself. This mightn't be over yet, so don't be ower complacent, yeah?'

'Thanks,' he said, knowing full well he'd never be complacent again – not until Benny Yu was safely behind bars.

CHAPTER SEVEN

The first thing she noticed was the smell. Fermented cheese, or stagnant yeast left over from a brewing process. One of the two. Either way, it was so bitter she could almost taste it.

Her head lay to one side, resting against her bare shoulder. She opened her eyes and knew what the smell was. She saw the remnants of her last meal, soured by bile and diluted in champagne, splattered across her flesh.

'Oh God. Never again,' she mouthed before her eyes closed once more.

Then came a different smell: the eye-watering alkalinity of strong bleach.

'Shit. I'm sorry,' she mumbled realising her housemate had cleaned up the mess.

She shivered. She was naked, and icy cold. She felt for the duvet. Instead, her fingers touched cold metal. Confused, she tried to sit up but, as soon as she moved, her headache forced her back down.

Her eyes opened again. She was immersed in inky darkness. She realised it was not yet morning. Another shiver rippled through her.

Her subconscious mind registered a familiar sound – a rhythmic pulse or beat, yet she couldn't put a name to it. As she strained to make it out, she became aware of another noise; an occasional creak of metal, like a shed door rattled by an invasive wind.

They lived in a fifth-floor apartment. They didn't have a shed. The girl willed her eyes to focus, but there was nothing to see except the infinity of night.

She heard a click, a hum of static, and saw a light flicker briefly before it sprang fully to life. God had divided the light from the darkness, and she bathed in harsh fluorescence.

Her eyes took a moment to adjust, and she wished they hadn't. She gazed up at a stainless-steel canopy suspended above her. Her own reflection, distorted and grotesque, stared down at her.

The girl saw she was indeed naked. Worse, she was chained to a metal lattice-work table. A wide leather band strapped across her forehead pulled her long hair back and to one side so her extensions cascaded over the side of the table.

She felt bile rise once more. Her heart raced inside her, and a squeak escaped her throat.

'You're awake.'

She jumped at the sound of the voice; jumped so hard the metal chains cut into her wrists.

The voice, muffled and indistinct behind her, came again. 'I was beginning to lose patience.'

'Please…'

'Shut up!'

'What – what do you – want?' she pleaded through short, sharp breaths.

'Didn't you hear me? I said SHUT UP!'

A face suddenly appeared above her own; a face hidden behind the mesh of a beekeeper's headgear, or a swordsman's face guard. Hot tears clouded her vision.

When they cleared, she saw her captor was clad in a thick white protective suit, almost that of an astronaut. 'Do you know who I am?' the voice asked, androgynous and monosyllabic.

'No.'

'Do you know why you're here, then?'

'Please. Let me go,' she sobbed.

Her kidnapper moved to one side, and she felt eyes roam her naked body.

'Your tan is false,' the voice said. Fingers entwined themselves in her hair. 'Nice hair. You've no need for those extensions. Your eyelashes – they aren't real, either.' The figure dragged gloved fingers down her arm and over her curled fingers. 'And no-one has nails like those. No-one.'

The voice remained silent for a moment. The girl wept while nervous convulsions washed down her in waves.

'What about these?' She felt a finger prod a breast. 'False as well, are they?' the speaker asked.

She shook her head frantically. Squeezed her eyes so tight she thought they might explode. When she opened them, the figure still lurked above her.

'You're a fraud, aren't you? All of you. There's nothing real about you. Everything is false. Don't you find that a little ironic? I do.'

Her lips moved, but no sound came.

'Fine. We'll do it my way, if you're not going to speak to me.'

The suited figure turned its back on the girl.

She kicked at her restraints, wrestled with the chains on her wrists.

'Oh dear. You'll hurt yourself doing that. We wouldn't want you to cut yourself, would we?'

She gave a frantic shake of her head.

'Good. Because that's my job.'

The girl felt a flood of urine escape her, heard it flow through the griddled table beneath her, and splatter on the concrete floor.

'Do you know where you are?' the captor asked.

No response.

'DO YOU?'

'N..no.' A mouse-like squeak of an answer.

'We're in a unit in the fish market.'

The rhythmic sound made sense to her now, the gentle swell of the tide trapped within the sheltered gut separating the North Sea from the River Tyne.

'The fishing boats are out to sea. It'll be a while until they return. We've plenty of time. All the time in the world.'

The girl shuddered again. 'What are you going to do with me?'

'Good question,' the captor mused.

The doors to the unit rattled and creaked like the chains of Jacob Marley's ghost. The girl's eyes darted towards the entrance, praying someone had come to her rescue.

But it was just the wind.

When she looked back, the figure was alongside her again. Its gloved hand held an implement aloft. When she saw it, she screamed so loudly no sound came.

'When the fishermen eventually return with their catch, they'll put this to good use. Do you know what it is?'

'A knife.' The words came out quieter than a whisper.

'Not just any knife. It's a filleting knife. The sharpest blade around. It's used for gutting fish. At least, that's what the fishermen use it for.'

'No, no. You've got the wrong person. It's not me you want.' She had no idea who the intended victim was, but it wasn't her. It couldn't be.

For a moment, she saw her captor consider the possibility. 'I don't think so.'

Was there a trace of doubt in the voice? She tried again. 'You have. I haven't done anything.'

More hesitation.

'Please, let me go.'

She heard her captor sniff loudly behind the mask, almost like a bear scenting quarry.

'Have you been drinking?' the voice asked.

'I don't drink often. I'm a good girl.'

An unearthly laugh came from behind the helmet.

'I am. Honestly. We were just celebrating. A one-off.'

She saw the mask slowly bob.

'Thank you for confirming I DO have the right person.'

'Please. Please – let me go. I'll pay you. Whatever you want, I'll pay you.'

The laugh again. 'You'll pay, alright. Trust me, you'll pay.' The figure toyed with the blade. 'Though perhaps not in the way you imagined.'

'Why me? Why are you doing this to me? I've done nothing to hurt you.'

The air in the shed thickened. She heard her captor's breath come in hisses.

'They talk about justice,' the voice said almost to itself. 'It's a joke, all of it. Defence lawyers lying through their teeth, prosecution lawyers on fixed fees not giving a toss whether they win or lose, and judges – out of touch, biased, prejudiced. Corrupt, even. Almost as corrupt as juries.'

The voice was ranting now, lost in a world of its own.

'Idiots, the lot of them. Idiots in a system that's immoral and rotten to the core.'

The girl saw the mask turn to face her. 'I think we're better off taking the law into our own hands. Do you agree?' the voice behind it said.

'I...I don't know. Honestly.' She hardly heard her own words, so loudly did her heart beat in her chest, so stridently her pulse sang at her temples.

'*You – don't - know*,' the voice repeated sarcastically. 'In that case, I'll ask you one last question; a question even a fraud like you can answer.'

'Anything. I'll tell you anything if you'll just please let me go.'

There was a moment's silence whilst the figure behind the mask considered the words.

When it came, the question sliced through her like the blade in the gloved hand.

'Why did you choose Eunice Paddock?'

The girl had no time to answer.

Nor had she time to scream.

**

A door slammed shut.

The bedside clock read three-fifteen, and someone was in his house.

Ryan sat bolt upright in bed, instantly alert. He stretched a hand over the side of the bed and felt beneath it. Slowly, silently, he pulled out the three-wood golf club and weighed it in his hands.

He strained to hear. Thought he heard whispered voices, realised they were a figment of his imagination, then doubted himself once more.

He pulled back the duvet and swung his feet onto the floor, careful to ensure neither mattress nor bedsprings creaked.

Another door closed: a car door on the street below.

He sprinted to the window and peeked through the curtains.

Outside, The Drive was dimly lit. His eyes roamed the crescent-shaped road, but he saw no-one. Yet, there had been someone. He'd heard them.

An engine fired up. Immediately beneath him, headlights flared.

And Tommy Wright, Ryan's next-door neighbour, ran to the roadside blowing kisses in the direction of his departing lover.

'For fuck's sake,' Ryan swore, taking a breath for the first time in minutes.

He took a moment to compose himself, decided he needed coffee or something stronger, so headed downstairs.

Ryan spent the next three hours burning toast and fast-forwarding, rewinding, and watching hours of CCTV footage from front and back of his small semi-detached house.

Apart from the ghostly image of a wayward fox casually making its way from the fields behind Washingwell County Primary School and along The Drive, he saw nothing until

Tommy Wright's bit-on-the-side drove off into the moonlight.

Ryan made a mental note to listen for bumps in the night next time Tommy's air-hostess missus was on long-haul.

At six-thirty, Ryan received his daily automated text message. It informed him today's journey would follow the yellow route. This required him to leave Whickham in the wrong direction, head towards Blaydon, and cross the Tyne via the Scotswood Bridge. From there, he knew traffic along Scotswood Road into Newcastle would be gridlocked from seven-fifteen onwards.

'Bugger.'

Still unshaven, Ryan made for his unmarked Volvo, the telescopic pole with mirror attachment in his hand, and checked beneath the car for suspicious objects.

All clear.

'Why does life have to be so complicated?' he complained to himself.

Little did he know, life for Ryan Jarrod was about to get more complicated than he ever imagined possible.

CHAPTER EIGHT

Ryan slipped through the lift doors before they were fully open.

He'd made the twelve-step journey from the lift to the bullpen countless times over the years yet, somehow, today felt different.

Butterflies darted inside his stomach almost as if this was first day on the job. To some extent, it WAS his first day - his first day back on the team.

He hesitated outside the bullpen, took a deep breath like he once did before mounting the parallel bars as a kid, fixed a smile on his face, and breezed through the doors.

'Morning. Morning all,' he said as he strode towards the desks occupied by Danskin's squad.

'Christ, somebody's in a good mood,' Todd Robson moaned behind a noisy slurp of coffee.

'Always, Todd. Always.'

Ryan glanced around the bullpen as if he'd never seen it before. A scattering of crime boards lurked against the outer wall of the cavernous office. A few of DCI Rick Kinnear's team huddled around one of them.

The floor-to-ceiling windows opposite afforded panoramic views across the Tyne and its seven bridges, while the omnipresent rumble of trains outside the solid northern wall provided Ryan with a constant reminder of his near-death experience at the hands of Benny Yu.

He shuddered violently as his eyes continued their exploration of the bullpen. At the far corner of the room, the door to Danskin's office remained closed although lights brightened the window's lowered blinds.

Next to Danskin's room, Sam Maynard's office sat in darkness. Ryan checked his watch. Too early for the Super, he thought.

In fact, looking around, he realised it was too early for most. Apart from Todd, only Lucy Dexter was at her desk, though Gavin O'Hara's chair had his jacket thrown around it.

'What you got for us today?' Ryan asked, finally getting down to business.

'Like I said yesterday, boring shitty cases,' Robson replied. 'Lucy?'

DC Dexter looked up and smiled. 'Pretty much the same.'

'Nowt for us to get me teeth into? Howay, man: I'm bursting at the seams to get back on something tasty.'

'Sorry,' Lucy said. She seemed to contemplate something for a moment. 'Can I just say, I'm looking forward to working with you, Ryan. It'll be a real pleasure and an honour.'

Todd spat out a mouthful of coffee as he choked on his drink, drowning the papers on his desk. He dabbed at them with a crumpled tissue.

'So, Lucy,' Todd said, 'You got a fella on the go at the moment?' he tried to hide the mischievous smile on his face.

Ryan shot him a look of horror. Robson gave him a wink in return.

Lucy, her short blonde hair gelled to attention, reddened slightly. 'I don't talk about my personal life.'

'I'm just being friendly, like. Just it would be good to know a bit more about you. You keep yourself to yourself. I don't trust people like that.' Todd thought about what he'd said. 'In the outside world, that is. You're aal reet, though.'

Lucy sat back, still a little embarrassed. 'Okay, then. What would you like to know about me?'

'Have you a bloke?' Todd repeated.

'No comment.'

Todd tried again. 'Do you live with someone? Your folks or a flatmate, I mean?' Before Dexter could answer, he added, 'Or your bloke?'

Lucy cast her eyes downwards. 'No comment,' she repeated.

'Girlfriend, then?'

'Todd man! Give it a rest. You're embarrassing the poor girl,' Ryan interjected.

Todd gave a crooked smile. 'I'm embarrassing you, more like. Come on, Lucy. Give me something to go off. Tell me summat no-one here knows about you.'

Lucy took a sip from a putrid-looking protein shake. 'I'm a twin,' she said.

'There we are. That wasn't too hard was it? Identical?'

She paused. 'Well, I can tell us apart, if that helps. Alison's a fraction taller than me, her hair's a tone darker if you look closely, and she has a tiny chicken-pox scar just here.' She pointed to a spot above her hazel eyes.

Ryan checked his watch again. 'This isn't getting any work done,' he said.

'I already told you there's nowt urgent, man,' Todd said, ignoring Ryan's senior rank whilst revelling in his discomfort.

'Why do you ask, anyway?' Lucy said.

'Hello? Is anyone listening to me?' Ryan said sarcastically.

'I'm curious why you asked if we were identical,' Lucy continued undaunted.

'Ah well, you see. That's where you and me are different. I've no secrets, me.'

'Tell us more,' Lucy chided.

'It's just I used to go out with a twin many moons ago. Far too many moons for comfort, if truth be told.'

'Could you tell them apart?'

Todd looked at her as if she were daft. 'Yes, of course.'

'How come?'

Todd paused. 'Well, Helen was shorter than her twin, for one. But, mainly, it was because her twin had a beard and a dick.'

The three of them exploded into raucous laughter. DCI Kinnear scowled towards them, which only served to set them off again.

'Sorry, sir,' Ryan just about managed to say between giggles, which resulted in Lucy's laugh morphing into a series of Peppa Pig-like snorts.

In his peripheral version, Ryan saw Danskin's door open.

'Ssshh,' he whispered to his colleagues, 'The DCI's in the house.'

'Christ, he looks ill,' Todd said.

Stephen Danskin did indeed look ill. Ashen-faced and pinched of cheek, he beckoned Ryan towards him.

'Shit,' Ryan said under his breath. 'Please God: not Hannah.'

**

DI Lyall Parker was already in the room. He offered Ryan a curt nod as an acknowledgement, while Danskin shut the door behind them.

Ryan tried to gauge the mood of the room. He didn't want to make a fool of himself by bringing Hannah into the conversation, but at the same time he needed to know if this was about her.

Parker remained silent, his mouth a grim line. The diminutive Scotsman's silver hair appeared ruffled, as if he'd combed it with a balloon. The spider-web veins on his nose seemed more florid.

Something was up.

'Take a seat, Jarrod,' Danskin pulled a chair forward for him. Ryan took it. 'I've got a case for you.'

Ryan blinked. 'Is that it? No bad news or anything?'

Danskin and Parker shared a nervous look which set Ryan's foot tapping against the chair leg.

'I need your input on a case.'

'Oh-kay. What case?'

'A seriously fucked-up case, that's what.'

Ryan noticed beads of sweat glistening on Danskin's upper lip. This was a man who'd seen everything. It didn't bode well.

'Despatch took a call from North Shields fish quay around five o'clock this morning. Seems a worker turned up to hose the quay down before the fleet arrived with their catch. He noticed the door to one of the units was unlocked.'

Ryan listened intently as Parker picked up the story.

'Uniform were first on the scene. The officer – Niall Cruickshanks – reported in. He said it was the most horrific thing he'd ever witnessed.'

Ryan swallowed hard. 'What was it?'

'A nude young woman chained to a gutting bench.'

'I've seen worse things than a naked girl first thing of a morning…'

Parker ignored him. 'The worker who found her said there was something *'not right'* wi' her. Apart from being dead, that is.'

'Not right in what sense?'

'Cruickshanks couldn't get any more out of him,' Danskin continued. 'The rest came from Cruickshanks himself.'

Ryan pushed himself from his seat. 'Okay, I'll get down there and talk to Cruickshanks and the workman. See what else I can find out.'

'Just a minute, Jarrod. Sit down. You're going nowhere alone. Take Robson with you.'

'Todd? I thought Lucy was my shadow.'

Danskin and Parker exchanged a worried look.

'Take Robson,' Danskin ordered.

'Hang on, sir. With respect, you can't pick and choose. I'm either with Lucy or I'm not. If I'm not, I'd like to know why.' Lightning struck. 'Hang on, you think Benny Yu's involved. That's why you're sending Todd with me.'

'No, Jarrod; it's not. If I thought it was Yu, I wouldn't have you anywhere near the case.'

'What is it, then?'

Danskin groaned. 'Okay. You win. Go with Dexter – but look after her, won't you?'

'I thought she was there to look after me?'

'It's not something a young lass should see, that's all.'

Ryan looked between his two senior officers.

'There's summat you're not telling me.'

Danskin stood and turned his back on Jarrod. Stared down into the murky depths of the Tyne.

'The girl's been mutilated,' he said.

CHAPTER NINE

Ryan wished he hadn't contradicted Stephen Danskin. It's not that he didn't like Lucy, or think she had the makings of a top-notch detective – after all, it was he who pushed for her to join the team after working with her on the Byker Wall case – but she just wouldn't shut up.

Whether it was nervousness, excitement, or embarrassment, she wittered on from the moment they left Forth Street. By the time they reached the Coast Road, Ryan closed his eyes and pretended to sleep.

It didn't stop Lucy Dexter.

'I've only investigated one murder before, and even then all I did was a few interviews. None of the nitty-gritty. I can't wait to get stuck in.'

Ryan had spared her the gory details and wondered whether this was the time to tell her. Instead, he faked a snore.

Lucy took the right-hand turn onto Billy Mill Avenue sharper than necessary. She glanced sideways at Ryan, who continued to snore. She braked hard. Still Ryan faked sleep.

'No use pretending, Ryan. I know you're awake. I'm driving like a maniac on purpose here. If you'd been asleep, I'd have woken you up.'

Without opening his eyes, he said, 'You'll make a good detective, d'you know that?'

'Thanks.' She smiled to herself and jerked the steering wheel. They skidded onto the A193 at Chirton.

'Jesus, man. Have a care woman,' Ryan complained, eyes open. 'Anyway, you need to turn off soon.'

'Not according to the GPS, I don't.'

'Sod the GPS. I want to recce the scene first.'

'Why?'

'I like to see the surrounding area, possible approaches, hideouts…owt, really.'

'Hmm,' Lucy said, nodding. 'Makes sense.'

'We need to head towards the river. Here!'

She swung right at the Jeera Tandoori and followed Stephenson Street down towards North Shields fish quay.

The quay was a quirky place; a tight-knit community of fishermen and boatyard workers interspersed with Artisan bakers, musicians and artists.

The buildings themselves were equally eclectic. Tall and closely aligned along narrow lanes, their ruggedly built exteriors hid surprisingly upmarket interiors occupied by tapas bars, wine bars, cafes, restaurants, and pubs.

But every silver lining has its cloud. In this case, everywhere and everyone reeked of fish. Lucy closed the dashboard air vents.

They soon spotted the blue lights of a patrol car, an officer alongside redirecting traffic away from the quay. Beyond, two marked cars were parked at odd angles with a forensic van pulled against the kerb. Officers were already erecting incident tents to serve as a temporary control centre.

Lucy and Ryan slowed so the officer could see their ID. He waved them through and shouted something to another officer further along the road. The second uniform beckoned the car towards him and indicated where Lucy should park.

'Slow down, but keep going,' Ryan ordered.

'What?'

'Just do as I say.'

Lucy harrumphed but did as he said.

They drove by Sambuca's and Ryan declined the second policeman's offer of a parking spot. The officer shrugged but let the car crawl on.

Ryan lowered his head so he could see the fish market exterior wall. It reminded him of the outside of a lower league football team's grandstand; one long, solid, dirty-white wall.

He gave the thumbs-up to the driver of a marked vehicle preventing access to the quay from Hodson Street and waved to another doing the same at the convergence of Brewhouse Bank and Union Road.

'Up here.' He directed Lucy uphill to a car park overlooking the mouth of Tyne. 'Right. You can stop now.'

The moment he opened the car door, the wind ripped it from his hand and blew him back into his seat. 'Bloody hell. It's a bit breezy.'

Lucy climbed out to join him. She gulped in the bracing air. 'You can have some of my hair gel, if you like.'

'Hadaway. I'm not using that stuff.'

'Okay. I don't care if you want to look like Boris. Hair's nearly the same colour to start with.'

'I'm not blond,' he said, drilling a finger into Lucy's ribs.

She smiled at him. Ryan didn't seem to notice. 'Okay,' he said, 'What do we see?'

'A red lighthouse thing over there.'

'Herd Groyne. What about it?'

'Could be a hiding place.'

'Wrong side of the river,' Ryan said, holding down his hair. 'Anything else?'

'Yep. Shields Ferry terminal. He could have crossed the river by ferry.'

'Good observation.'

She beamed, until he added, 'One thing, though.'

'Which is?'

'You said *he*. You've already presumed it's a male we're after. What would DCI Danskin say about that?'

'*Don't see what you expect to see.*'

'Exactly. Let's keep an open mind.'

Ryan watched a police launch patrol the river's maw, preventing vessels entering. Already, four fishing boats rocked like noddy dogs in the frenzied tide whipped up by the wind as they awaited permission to enter the Tyne.

A cargo boat laden with containers sat low in the water behind them. Its skipper sounded its horn; five short, sharp blasts. In nautical terms, the signal meant, *'What the hell are you doing, you nobs?'* Neither Ryan nor Lucy understood the maritime signal. Nor did the officers aboard the police launch, which continued to deny access.

Lucy turned away from the flotilla and stared towards the quay and its fish market. 'What's that?' she pointed at a nearby structure.

'Hmm?' Ryan mumbled, distractedly.

'Down there. That white building.' She steadied herself as the wind threatened to topple her.

'Ah. That's the new Low Light.'

'Which is what, exactly?'

Ryan sighed. 'Lucy, Lucy: where's your sense of belonging?'

'You're beginning to sound like me dad. Besides, I don't belong here. I'm from Haydon Bridge originally.' She stared down at the odd-shaped six story construction. 'Anyway, what is it? Wait; don't tell me - you don't know either, I bet,' she giggled.

'Wrong again. It's a lighthouse. Or was until the Herd Groyne had high-intensity lights installed for ship navigation from Tynemouth and along the river. After that, the Low Light was decommissioned. I think they might have turned it into flats or summat, but its main purpose is to function as a way marker for ships in daylight. Keeps them away from the Black Middens.'

'Huh? You're making less sense than a barking gerbil. What the hell are the Black Whats-its?'

'Middens. Black Middens. It's a reef. A dangerous one, at that.'

'So, this lighthouse thing – possible hiding place, or a lookout for picking his...or *her*, victim?'

'I dunno. Let's take a closer look, shall we?'

Ryan already knew the answer, but he wanted to spend some time ensuring Lucy was at ease before subjecting her to whatever lay inside the fish market.

They leant back as the wind threatened to Jack and Jill them down the embankment, and Ryan continued in tour guide mode. He pointed out several ironwork sculptures, the visitor centre, Clifford's Fort, and the lifeboat station.

When they got to the Low Light, Ryan breezed by.

'I thought we were going to see if the murderer could have used it in the crime,' Lucy said.

'Nah. Nee time for that, man. We've got a murder to solve.'

'You're a funny one, Ryan Jarrod,' Lucy muttered to herself as she watched him squeeze through a part-closed steel gate set in a blue metal fence topped with trident-shaped spikes.

She let the wind carry her forward.

'Hold on; I'm coming,' she shouted.

**

They were on the quay now; the narrow concrete pathway slick with age-old fish scales and God-knows-what else.

'Careful,' Ryan said as he stepped around a higgledy-piggledy stack of wooden pallets. 'It's a skating rink in here.'

For once, Lucy didn't have a reply. She was already holding her breath against the stink of fish.

The quay was a Health and Safety executive's nightmare. Piles of discarded multi-coloured iceboxes littered the path. Cages holding fishnets of blue, orange, black, and grey braided polymer stood propped against every wall and stretch of fence as if put there by a haphazard three-year-old.

Ryan stubbed his toe against a heavy-duty Binnacle ring cemented into the pathway. 'Bloody hell, this place is like Ninja Warrior,' he cursed.

He looked back. Lucy Dexter was stationary.

'Is that where it happened?' she asked, her face pallid.

'I reckon so. Are you sure you're ready for this?'

Lucy nodded unconvincingly.

'Howay, then. What are you waiting for?'

From the outside, the fish market had looked like one continuous structure. Inside the quay, it was clear the building was separated into more than a dozen individual units, all with identical blue metal doors.

The one Ryan and Lucy sought was obvious. It was surrounded by police tape, white-suited forensic investigators, and a uniformed cop emptying his guts over the harbour.

Ryan was already showing his warrant card to a duty constable, who lifted the tape for Ryan and Lucy to duck under.

'Who's in charge of securing the scene?' Ryan asked.

'Cruickshanks,' the officer said, pointing to an older man leaning against a wall which had the word '*Amity*' graffitied across it.

Ryan introduced himself and Lucy to Niall Cruickshanks. Ryan noticed Niall's palms were as damp and slick as the quay as they greeted one another.

'Were you first one here?'

'Aye.' He cleared his throat. 'Yes, I was.'

'What have we got?'

Niall put his arms on his hips and took a couple of shallow breaths. 'Never seen owt like it in twenty years.' He shook his head. 'What went on in there, it's inhumane, man. The poor lass.' Cruickshanks lowered his eyes to the ground.

'How long have forensics been here?'

'Not too long. Still doing the preliminaries until the head-honcho gets here.'

'Is it Aaron Elliot?' Ryan asked, hoping the likeable eccentric's dark humour would see Lucy through the grim tasks ahead.

'Not sure. Kuldeep Thakur's in charge until the main man arrives. Do you know him?'

'Nah, but I'm about to.' Ryan stepped towards the door of the unit. He waggled his fingers behind him, which Lucy took as an invitation to follow.

A large Asian man emerged from a unit. The hand-painted sign above the warehouse revealed it went by the name of CW Fisheries.

The man puffed out his cheeks, peeled off his disposable gloves, and removed his facemask. An impeccably curled handlebar moustache sprung into position.

Ryan went through the introductions once more and requested an update.

'Early days,' Thakur said. He looked Lucy up and down. 'Are you sure you're both ready for this?', with emphasis on *both*.

'Yes,' Ryan said.

Lucy's mouth simpered into a reluctant smile.

'If you're sure. But you must not enter yet. We need to take a few more samples first. Please, I'll let you know when we're ready for you.'

Ryan looked around for something to fill the time with. 'Who found her?'

Thakur bowed to Cruikshanks' greater knowledge.

'He's called Timothy.'

'A second name?'

Cruikshanks shrugged. 'Can't get much out of him. Pretty shook up, he was. Can't say I blame him.'

Lucy Dexter found her voice. 'What was he doing here at that time in the morning?'

'It's his job. Swills down the quay before the vessels arrive, and after they leave. He's on call for whenever the tide's right for the fleet to sail.'

'Okay. I'll have a word with him,' Lucy said. 'Where can I find him?'

'Four units down. It's not used so we commissioned it.'

'Good thinking,' Lucy commended. 'I'll go now while we wait for Kuldeep's people.'

'You'll not get much out of him,' Niall Cruickshanks emphasised once more.

'I have my ways,' she winked at Ryan.

'She does,' he muttered to Cruickshanks. 'I'm afraid she does.'

Ryan caught up with her before they got to the disused unit. 'I'll kick things off, then you can come in with your womanly wiles.'

'It can't be that bad in there,' she jerked her thumb back along the quay. 'I'm sure we can get something useful out of him.'

'Listen, Lucy, you need to know something. I think it *will* be that bad in there. I didn't tell you earlier, but it sounds like the victim's been mutilated.'

Lucy stopped in her tracks. 'I thought as much from Cruickshanks' reaction. And Thakur's. Fact is, I'm a big girl now. I'm ready for this.'

Ryan raised an eyebrow but said nothing. Instead, he walked in to speak with Timothy.

Tim was a thickset man. He sat on a deckchair, bent forward until his head almost lay on his knees. Dark hair with a hint of grey flopped downward. An untouched cup of tea stood on a second deckchair whilst, to the man's left, a female police officer perched on an upturned wooden crate.

She looked up as Ryan and Lucy entered. Timothy didn't.

Ryan showed her his warrant card. The policewoman nodded her understanding and walked towards them.

'Go easy on him, please,' she whispered. 'He's struggling.'

'Aye, I bet. Do we have a name yet, other than Timothy?'

'Rice.'

'No way. Seriously? Tim Rice? Oh, what a circus.'

The woman chuckled grimly.

'Has he said anything else?'

'Not a lot. He just said there's something not right with her. Several times, *'she's not right'*, he'd say.'

Ryan let out air through his nose. 'Okay, I'll have a go.' He took a step forward. 'Timothy, I'm Detective Sergeant Ryan Jarrod. I wonder if you could tell me exactly what you saw?'

The man raised his head for the first time and Ryan knew straight away that Cruickshanks had been right: he'd get nothing out of him.

Tim stared at Ryan with narrow eyes set in a flat, round face beneath a broad forehead. The man's mouth hung open; slack jawed.

'*Ah man,*' Ryan thought, filled with frustration and sympathy. Frustration at knowing this was a dead end, and sympathy for Tim.

Whatever horror lay in wait for Ryan and Lucy four units away, he knew it was something no-one with Down's should see. The poor man would be scarred for life.

'We need to get him home,' Ryan said. 'Have you managed to find out where he lives?' he asked the female officer.

'Just about, yes.'

'Nearby?'

'Very. Just as well, really, given his job, and all.'

'I'll get a car sorted.'

'No need. I'll walk him.'

'That close?' Ryan said.

The officer inclined her head. 'It is.'

'Where?'

'He lives with an Aunt. I'm quite jealous, actually.'

'Why's that?'

'I've always thought it must be great to live amongst all that history.'

She looked back at Tim Rice before continuing.

'He lives in one of the converted apartments in the Low Light.'

CHAPTER TEN

'You can come in now,' Kuldeep Thakur said from the darkened doorway. 'Get kitted up first, and don't touch anything. Just as importantly, watch your step. We don't want you treading in anything.'

Once dressed in their coveralls, Ryan had second thoughts about exposing Lucy Dexter to whatever lay within. 'I'll go in first, Luce. You see if you can spot anything outside. I'll call you in later.'

Thakur nodded approvingly and accompanied Ryan into the gloom of the CW Fisheries warehouse.

Kuldeep Thakur slid the door closed. It gave an agonising scream as it struggled in its metal runners.

Deprived of his vision in the darkness, Ryan noticed the smell first. Bleach. Or detergent, or some other powerful cleaning agent. As Thakur led Ryan deeper into the unit, another smell seeped through his face covering.

Initially, Ryan assumed it was a residue of the fish-gutting process, yet it reminded him of something else. He signalled for Thakur to pause while he struggled to identify it. Then it came to him. The smell was more meat than fish.

It was the stench of an abattoir.

'You stopped at just the right point,' Thakur said. 'Any further, and we may contaminate the scene.'

Ryan asked a question to which he feared he knew the answer. 'What's the smell?'

'Good. You've noticed it. I wanted you to be prepared for what you'll see. Now that you know – you do know, don't you? – we can shed some light on our subject.'

The overhead fluorescents sparked to life.

'Fucking hell!'

The sight was indeed hellish. Hellish, grotesque - yet somehow fascinating.

Ryan stood perfectly still while he processed what he was looking at. He was about five yards from the body, the lighting still not great but more than enough for him to see the extent of the girl's injuries.

The victim lay naked, manacled by wrist and ankle chains to a strange sieve-like table. Blood pooled on the floor beneath, its redness tinged green by the cleaning agent. Bright crimson droplets occasionally fell from the table and rippled the surface of Lake Blood.

Ryan moved around the table with care, keeping several yards between himself and the blood splatters. His eyes never left those of the girl. He'd seen terror in the eyes of the dead before, but nothing like this.

It was made worse by the fact the girl's eyelids had been removed.

'Jesus Christ.'

He dragged his gaze to the victim's hair. Or, rather, her lack of hair. She'd been scalped. Long strands of hair lay matted in a bloody pile to one side of the table, flesh still attached to it like a swimming cap.

The girl was unrecognisable, her facial features non-existent. The killer had peeled her face away as if opening a pack of cooked meat; her once pretty face reduced to a distorted gorefest Ryan had only witnessed in horror movies.

He turned away, gagging.

'Do you need some air, Detective Sergeant?' Thakur asked.

Ryan nodded, cheeks billowing.

The forensic lead creaked open the stubborn metal doors. As he did so, someone squeezed past him.

'Ryan, I've been…' Lucy Dexter stopped mid-sentence and mid-stride. 'Oh fuck. Oh God. Oh Jesus.'

'I think you should leave, Lucy,' Ryan said.

'No. No way. Not now.' She stared at the stricken corpse. 'I've seen it. I'm not going now. I need answers or it'll haunt my dreams.'

Ryan noticed Lucy had dehumanised the victim, calling the girl 'it', rather than 'her.' It was the standard psychological response of someone faced with trauma, their way of coping. It was a good sign.

'Ok, Lucy. Stay well back, though.'

Dexter closed her eyes and took a couple of backward steps.

Ryan resumed the examination of the body with his eyes. He noticed an incision in her left breast, the skin pulled back slightly so it exposed muscle inside.

The victim's fingertips had been removed. They littered the floor around the table, nails still attached. Each long fingernail was painted a different garish colour. It looked as if someone had sprinkled confetti on the warehouse floor.

Of all the horrors inflicted on the young woman, Ryan found the last the most unsettling. The killer had carved two words on the woman's stomach.

The word '*My*' lay above her navel, '*Right*' below.

'Who could do this to another person?' Lucy whispered, her eyes searching the ceiling.

'Someone with a purpose. Somebody who thinks they have a right to do it.' Ryan ran a hand down his face. 'Some sick bastard.'

He struggled to get the words out through the tears.

Quietly, he added, 'Somebody like Benny Yu.'

**

Outside, in the fresh air and the salty breeze, Lucy sat on a capstan while Ryan crouched alongside her.

'Do you think she was raped?' Lucy asked, all emotion drained from her voice.

'You've done it again. You need to be careful about that, kidda.'

'Done what again?'

'Assumed it's a man.'

'So did you. Benny Yu, you said.'

Ryan pinched the bridge of his nose. Watched a pair of gulls explore the quayside for traces of discarded catch.

'That was personal. Me feeling sorry for mesel, that's all. Now, I need to look at things dispassionately.'

'How can anyone be dispassionate about that? In there?'

Ryan didn't have an answer.

'A woman would never do such a thing to another woman,' Lucy continued.

'Hell hath no fury like a woman scorned,' Ryan quoted.

'Okay. But humour me: suppose it was a *he*. What motive would he have? Sex? Lust? Revenge?'

Ryan sighed and engaged his brain. 'Possibly all of those things, possibly none. I don't think rape. The poor lass had many things done to her, but the one place there was no blood, no bruising, was down there.'

Lucy stared towards the unit but remained silent as Ryan continued. 'I'm no criminal psychologist, though, so let's wait until Dr Elliot, or whoever the on-call pathologist is if Elliot's elsewhere, examines her.'

'If it wasn't sex, what was it? I mean, someone who decided to have a game of Operation on a real subject?'

'Patience, Lucy. We're not going to get answers until we know more about the victim.'

He gave a sideways nod towards the fish quay exit gate. 'Come on, let's get uniform organised. We want anyone connected to this place interviewed. The manager, fishermen, fishmongers who get their stock here, local residents, and bar staff and restaurant owners. I want them talking to everyone and everybody.'

Lucy tilted her head until it lay against Ryan's bicep. 'I'm pleased I'm with you. If it'd been Todd, or Gav, or Treblecock, I'd be a wreck. I feel safe with you.'

She clung to his arm with two hands as his phone rang. Ryan struggled to bring the phone out of his pocket with Lucy Dexter clinging to him, limpet-like.

'What the hell?' he muttered as he saw the caller ID. Ryan accepted the call. 'What is it, Hannah?'

Lucy relaxed her grip and crossed her arms in front of her as Ryan stood, knees cracking.

'DI Parker told me you were in charge down there,' Ryan heard Hannah ask. 'What's going on? I've got shipping queued up like the Central Motorway in rush hour, a skipper's shouting at me in Albanian or summat, and the fishing fleet are threatening to sue if their catch goes off. Call off the hounds, Ry, and let me deal with the port traffic. That's my job; not yours.'

'I can't, man. We've got a murder investigation going on, and it's not a pretty one. I'm not letting anyone into the Gut or the fish market.'

'Don't be a nob all your life, Jarrod. Get the frigging police launch out of the way and let my vessels in before the tide changes.'

Ryan stared at his phone open-mouthed. He began to speak. Paused as he ran his hand through his hair. 'Okay. Let's compromise. Nothing gets into the fish quay. The fleet stays at sea…'

'No way…'

'Had on, woman. Hear me out. The victim's in one of the warehouses on the quay. You know as well as I do that we can't have folk trampling all over the scene. The deal is, all other traffic can enter the river providing they keep to the south side. They use the South Shields and Tyne Dock passage.'

'They'd do that anyway 'cos of the Middens.'

'Fine. So, you tell Lyall Parker I give permission for the bigger stuff to go into port, but the fish quay remains out of bounds. The fishing fleet stays at sea.'

Ryan sensed Hannah mull it over.

'Deal,' she said. 'I'll get onto Lyall now and prepare to dock the cargo and passenger ferry. And you let me know the moment the fishing boats can dock, aye?'

Ryan stared back at the cordoned-off fish market. 'I will but I think they're going to have to find somewhere else to dock today. We'll be a while yet.'

'Who's *'we'*? Is Todd with you?'

'No. DC Dexter.'

Ryan felt the frigid air down the receiver as Hannah ended the call with a, 'Right.'

'That's all I need,' he moaned into the dead mouthpiece.

'Ah. At last. About time, too.' Lucy stood in front of him, arms still crossed, head cocked to one side. 'I've organised all the troops. Got them out interviewing as you asked. All while you were talking to your *girlfriend.'* She made air quotes with her hands.

'Grow up, man. It was work. Besides, I'm your senior officer. You don't question my actions.'

Ryan saw Lucy's lip tremble. *'Ah don't cry, man. For God's sake don't cry,'* he thought. 'Well done, though. You got that sorted in no time.'

Lucy almost smiled. 'Thank you, *sir,'* she curtsied.

'Come on. It's been a helluva long morning. We need a break.' He left the harbour through the broken gate they'd used to enter the quay all those hours ago; hours that felt like days. His stomach rumbled. 'Let's get a bite to eat while we wait for more forensic details.'

'You are kidding me, right? Food? After what we've just seen?'

Ryan was already on Union Road. 'You'll get used to it. I know you mightn't believe me, but you will. Sad, I know.'

She scurried up beside him. 'I can't face food.'

Ryan sighed. 'Okay. A pint, then. Or wine, whatever you drink.'

'We're on duty.'

'Who gives the orders around here?' Ryan smiled down at Lucy.

'Yes, sir,' she said, spotting a sign for The Ship's Cat up Tanner's Bank.

'Not there,' Ryan said. 'This way. Come on.'

Lucy hesitated as she watched Ryan march towards the Low Lights Tavern. 'There? It looks a bit of a dive to me.'

'It's not,' Ryan assured her. 'And they do a canny pie, an' aal.'

'Can we not go to that one?' Lucy pleaded, pointing towards the Cat.

Ryan played his trump card. 'Do you like Sam Fender?'

'What's not to like? Of course, I do. He's lush.'

Ryan stopped. Shook his head. '*Lush*? You're a detective, Lucy Dexter, not a schoolgirl. We don't say lush in our job. Unless we're talking about the pies in the Tavern.'

'What's Sam Fender got to do with things?'

Ryan stood outside the door. 'Oh, that. The Low Lights is his local. They've got a beer pump made from his Brit Award.'

'No way!'

'Yes, way.'

'Really? Will he be in?'

'Maybe. Who knows?'

Lucy beat Ryan through the door, all thoughts of the fish market horrors and her preference for The Ship's Cat temporarily banished from her mind.

Which was unfortunate for, if they had followed Lucy's wish, they'd have seen a person of interest watching events along the quay from the safety of The Ship's Cat's exterior balcony.

CHAPTER ELEVEN

The wind had dropped but ominous clouds threatened rain as Ryan and Lucy returned to the fish market.

They could see more Forensic Crime Scene officers trooping in and out of the unit like foraging ants. The flare of the SOCO photographer's camera periodically lit up the darkened sky.

Blood Pattern Analysts filed out of the warehouse having completed the examination of the unit's floor and walls. Their task had proved arduous, given the extent of the blood splatter and the presence of the noxious cleaning agent.

Ryan had sought advice from DCI Danskin, who agreed to further extend the exclusion zone. A gathering crowd of restless natives and the presence of assorted media professionals meant it was a no-brainer to send them further back into town.

Ryan's phone rang. 'Jarrod.'

'Well hello there, Sherlock.'

'Aaron. Thank God it's you.'

'Who else?' Dr Aaron Elliot, lead pathologist to the City and County force, laughed.

'When will you get here?'

'About forty minutes ago, give or take. I've been waiting for you.'

'Where are you?'

Elliot's head appeared from behind the door of the House of Horrors. He gave a cheery wave.

Ryan hurried to meet him, leaving Lucy trailing in his wake.

'Still no Watson, I see,' Elliot observed, referring to Hannah Graves by the name he always used for her.

'Nah. She's still at Port of Tyne.'

'I take it this must be Irene Adler, then,' he smirked. 'Sherlock doesn't have any other friends.'

'DC Dexter, actually,' Lucy said, hand outstretched. She quickly withdrew it when she saw Elliot's gore-soaked gloves.

'Charmed, I'm sure. Get kitted up and I'll take you through what Kuldeep's team has discovered so far.'

Ryan and Lucy donned fresh coveralls and re-entered the unit. The smell was metallic now, the result of blood coagulation. The body remained unmoved, although the incision in the girl's breast gaped slightly where Elliot had inserted his fingers and probed for any objects within.

'Poor girl,' Elliot said.

Ryan wasn't sure if the comment was aimed at a grey-faced Lucy Dexter or an unusual show of empathy for the victim. 'What have you got for us, Aaron?'

Above the facemask, Aaron Elliot's eyes glowed as he tucked a strand of hair back beneath his skullcap.

'Let's start from the top, shall we? Obviously, she's been scalped. The killer made a number of semi-circular incisions – here, here, and here – around the hairline. I'm pretty sure the killer then held her head still and yanked down heavily to remove the scalp. The positioning of the scalp on the floor and the angle of incision suggests our killer is right-handed.'

'Male or female?' Lucy enquired.

'Not sure,' Elliot replied.

'Scalping wouldn't be the cause of death, though,' Ryan mused.

'No, no. Just appallingly painful. It seems as if much of her hair was a wig. Extensions, you'd call them,' the medic said, looking at Lucy, 'But that wouldn't make it any less painful.'

Ryan vibrated his lips. 'The eyelids?' he said, subconsciously rubbing his own.

'Excised with the same implement. They haven't been located yet.'

'Why do that?'

Elliot held up his hands. 'Not my job. I'll provide the details and you find the evidence.'

'Helpful as ever,' Ryan snickered.

'The killer used the same weapon, a blade of the sharpest nature, to cut the skin either side of the jawline. Then, just as you would remove a prosthetic mask, he – or she – pared back the skin, lips and all, to leave that.' He pointed towards the girl's face. 'A remarkable sight.'

Lucy felt bile rise in her throat as she asked, 'What makes somebody do something like that?'

Elliot shrugged. 'Who knows? To hide the identity, I would presume if I were doing your job. But I'm not so I'll leave the hypothesis to your good self, Ms Adler.'

'Dexter,' she corrected.

Elliot and Ryan rolled their eyes.

'Presumably this was done post-mortem, Aaron?'

'I'm afraid not…'

'Oh my God,' Lucy exclaimed, hand to mouth.

'Too much blood, sadly. The girl was alive for at least part of the process and, I suspect, all.'

The air in the unit felt spent; drained of oxygen. Ryan and Lucy both struggled to comprehend what Elliot was saying.

'Okay, where next?' Ryan said, voice breaking.

'Let's go to the fingers, shall we?'

Ryan and Lucy both gazed at the fingers dotted beneath the table.

'The stumps remaining on the deceased are jagged and irregular, which strongly suggests they were removed by some other means. Nothing as neat as a blade. I suspect pliers, or something similar.' Elliot looked at Ryan. 'Before you ask, I don't know why. The nails are false though. Her real nails are gnawed way back. Don't know if that helps.'

'Not really.'

'Okay. Just thought I'd run it up the flagpole,' Elliot said, deliberately playing Bullshit Bingo.

'What about the wound to her breast?'

'We're back to the bladed instrument. It looks like the killer has been rummaging around inside for some reason unknown.'

'For fuck's sake,' Lucy wheezed. 'You still think this was a woman, Ryan?'

'I didn't say that. I said we shouldn't close our mind to the possibility.'

'Doc, what do you think?'

'I think Sherlock is very wise. She'd have to be strong, but it's not outside the realms.'

Lucy stared at the bloody floor. 'Has she been interfered with in other ways?'

'Sexually, you mean? I won't know for sure until I can do a proper internal but there's nothing to suggest so. I've given her a quick internal visual and there's no sign of stretching of the labia majora or tearing of her labia minora. I saw no internal bruising to speak of. Of course, I'll check for semen deposits either within her vulva or around the mons pubis when I get her home.'

'Don't you think that's a violation of the girl, Dr Elliot?'

'Pardon?'

'That's a woman we're talking about.'

'Firstly, it's my job, young lady. Secondly, it *was* a woman. Now, God rest her soul, she's just like any other dead carcass. I'm sorry if my language or methods are abrupt for you, but it's how I get through a day, dear. The *only* way.'

Lucy locked eyes with him. Slowly, the ice in them melted to tears. She nodded briefly. Rubbed her face with her gloves. 'Sorry.'

Ryan ruffled the top of his protective headgear. 'Moving on, what about the carving on her stomach?'

'Abdomen, to be precise. Again, the killer used the sharp object. It was the only way he could ensure the writing was readable.'

'Did he cut an artery?' Lucy asked.

'He – or she – did.'

'So, that's how she died.'

'Yes. But not an abdominal artery. She'd have bled out in her own time from her other injuries, but the killer made sure.' Elliot made a slicing motion with his fingers to his throat. 'Her carotid artery was sliced, hence the blood splatter.'

Ryan shook his head. 'I don't get it. She was subjected to so much pain, yet in the end the killer cut her agony short. Why do that? Why not make her suffer even more?'

'Ah, that's where I've out-Sherlocked you, Sherlock. The killer was running out of time. The tide was on the turn. Our man, or woman, couldn't run the risk of the fishermen arriving before she was dead.'

Ryan considered Elliot's words for a moment. 'So,' he said, 'Our killer knows the tides?'

The pathologist played a dead bat. 'You tell me.'

'I *am* telling you, Aaron. Our killer knows the tides. Come on, Lucy. There's someone we need a word with.'

**

Back in Forth Street, Stephen Danskin trawled over Ryan's initial report. The more he read, the more he despaired. This was no ordinary killing.

Superintendent Maynard sat on the edge of Danskin's desk, so close his nostrils flared at the subtle floral fragrance of her perfume.

She crossed her legs and Danskin swallowed hard. He wondered whether she did it on purpose, then decided he'd rather not know, before he noticed she was speaking.

'I said, '*Will Dr Elliot perform the post-mortem tonight*'?'

Danskin checked his watch. 'Knowing Elliot, he'll want to, but I think it's more likely to be first thing. Coroner needs sign-off the paperwork first.'

Sam Maynard tapped her fingernails on the tabletop. 'This one's troubling you, isn't it?'

'Aye, ma'am. It is.'

She placed her fingers beneath his chin and tilted his head until his eyes met hers. 'Why does this case disturb you so much, Stephen?'

He wanted to look away, but he was entrapped by her eyes; he Mowgli to her Kaa.

'It's the circumstances, ma'am. Not so much the method of killing – I'm used to all sorts of sick bastards – but the words carved on her stomach. What's all that about?'

Maynard removed her hand from Danskin's chin. The DCI's head dropped, and her spell over him was broken. 'Are you sure that's what it is?'

'Ma'am?'

'You're not worried it's too much for DS Jarrod, after all he's been through?'

'No, ma'am.' The hesitation in his voice didn't go unnoticed.

'Okay. How about you're worried about his safety?'

'No more than any of my squad,' he said, eyes still at the floor.

'What about those not in your squad? Those like your stepdaughter.'

Danskin looked up. 'What's Hannah, err… DS Graves, got to do with it? Wait…oh, no – you've got intelligence about this. It's summat to do with Yu and his gang. He's back, isn't he.'

Maynard uncrossed her legs. 'Relax, Stephen. There's still no sign of Yu's crew, but I wanted to test your reaction; to see whether you were fit to take on the case.'

'Me? Of course I'm fit for duty, man,' he blustered. 'I thought we wanted Jarrod back on the case.'

'We do, and he is. For now. I need you to have his back, though, Stephen. Something tells me this is a tough nut to crack. Those words – '*My Right*' – mean something. We need to figure out what.'

'And that's my job?'

Maynard smiled. 'Partly, yes. You and a forensic psychologist.'

'Nee way. Not again.' Danskin shook his shaven head vigorously.

'Again?'

'Aye. That Imogen Markham woman. Connor had me work with her a couple of times. She was shite the first case we worked, and only a little better the second. I don't *'get'* profilers. Might as well call on Derek Acorah.'

'Hardly. He died a couple of years ago.'

'Well, that proves my point. He didn't see it coming, did he?'

Maynard lowered herself from the desk, her skirt riding up a couple of inches. Danskin tried to stop his eyes flitting there but failed miserably.

'Decision's made, Stephen. We need to get inside the killer's head.'

DCI Danskin exhaled noisily. 'When does she get here?'

'Who?'

'Markham, of course.'

Maynard shook her head. 'Not Markham. I'm bringing in someone I've worked with before, when I was in Basildon.'

'When does she get here, then?'

'Not sure. I'm waiting for a call. Oh, it's not a she, either. His name's Fola. Fola Fasanya.'

'Christ. Think I got an e-mail from him telling me I'd won squiddlies on some fake lottery.'

Maynard didn't laugh. 'Fola's okay. In fact, he's better than okay. He's good. The best.'

From the faraway look on Maynard's face, Danskin wondered exactly which department Fola Fasanya was *'best'* in.

He hated the bloke already.

**

A frail, stick-thin woman answered the door. She wore huge, hooped, Pat Butcher earrings.

'Yes?'

'My name's Detective Sergeant Ryan Jarrod, and this is DC Lucy Dexter. We're from City and County CID. I wonder if we could come in for a moment?'

'It'll be about the carry on, is it?' the woman said, returning Ryan's warrant card to him.

'That's one way to describe it. May we?' Ryan made a gesture towards the inside of the residence. The woman stepped aside.

The lounge was tiny, cluttered with antique furniture, and nothing like either of them expected. A display cabinet showed off the woman's Royal Doulton, an old-fashioned TV sat on a triangular wooden table, polished so brightly the ceiling reflected in it. Three comfortable chairs which were no longer comfortable made up the living area.

No, the Low Light apartment didn't live up to expectations.

'Is Timothy here? Timothy Rice.'

The woman pursed her lips. She wrapped one arm across the front of her chest, the other hand toying with an earring the size of a hula-hoop. 'He can't tell you anything. He's barely said a word to me, let alone anyone else. He's not one to talk to strangers.'

Ryan gave the woman a smile. 'I've met him before. He knows me. Could we at least try?'

'Timmy!' the woman roared. Lucy jumped.

A door crept open, and the bulky frame of Tim Rice skulked in, head down.

'Hello, Timothy. Remember me? I'm Ryan Jarrod. We met earlier.'

Tim kept his head down but nodded slightly.

'Good. Here,' Ryan said, standing, 'Have my seat.'

Tim glanced at the old woman and, when she inclined her head, he took the chair.

'Timothy, can I call you Tim?'

Another nod.

'Tim, can you tell me how long you've helped out at the fish market?'

'Two years,' the voice was slightly slurred but clear enough for Ryan and Lucy to understand.

'Do you enjoy it?'

A head down nod.

'You must have to get up early.'

'I get him up,' Tim's aunt said.

'Please, can you let Tim answer?' Lucy said.

The woman bristled.

'Okay, Tim. What time did you get up this morning?'

The man shrugged.

'Five o'clock,' the aunt said, 'That's if I'm allowed to tell you, of course.'

'And you went straight to the quay?'

'Breakfast first.'

Ryan breathed in. 'Right. Then you went to the quay, am I right?'

'Yes.'

'Did you notice anything different?'

A shrug.

'What about the unit belonging to CW Fisheries?'

'Door was open. It should be closed.'

'Had you been inside before?'

He shook his head. 'Not allowed. Only outside I work.'

'So, what made you go inside this time?'

'The door shouldn't be open. I only went to close it.'

Timothy Rice looked up for the first time. 'But then I saw the woman. She didn't look right. Auntie Mo always tells me if something doesn't look right, I should ring 999.'

'Yes, Tim. That's good. You did really well.'

Tim beamed.

'Had you seen the woman before?'

Tim shrugged and gazed at the carpet once more. 'I don't know. I don't see any face.'

'*Shit. Stupid question,*' Ryan thought. He rubbed his brow. 'After two years, I guess you'll know when the tide's due to change.'

Tim remained silent.

'Tim, do you know when the tide's about to change so the fishing boats can dock?'

No answer.

'He doesn't understand,' the woman called '*Auntie Mo*' said. 'But if I can answer for him,' she looked at Lucy Dexter, 'I tell Timmy when it's time to go. He gets his brush, goes to the fish market, unwinds the hose, and swills it down like a good 'un. Then, he comes straight back.'

'I'm sure you do, Tim.' Ryan's words brought another nod and another smile.

Ryan waited before asking his next question.

'Do the words *My Right* mean anything to you?' He watched carefully for a reaction. Lowered his head so he could see Tim's face. '*My Right*. Does it mean anything to you?'

Tim shifted in his seat but said nothing.

'Are you uncomfortable, Tim? Have I said something you know about?'

The man shook his head forcefully.

'Of course he's uncomfortable, Detective Sergeant. Wouldn't you be?'

Ryan looked at the skinny woman, little more than a bag of bones. 'No, actually. I wouldn't. It's a straightforward question.'

'To you, perhaps. But not to Timmy. You've embarrassed him.'

'How?'

'DS Jarrod, my Timmy can't read or write.'

CHAPTER TWELVE

Ryan's alarm woke him at six. His sheet and duvet looked as though a crash of rhinos had thundered through it, while matted pearls of sleep glued one of his eyelid's shut.

He'd grabbed no more than four hours sleep by the time he'd updated his report for DCI Danskin and forced the images of the dead girl from his mind's eye. Even a steaming hot shower hadn't fully roused him.

Ryan checked beneath the Corsa he'd been allocated yesterday before taking the green route into Newcastle and straight on down to North Shields.

'Fancy breakfast?' a voice called from across the car park.

Ryan checked his watch. 'Aye, gan on, then.'

'Marvellous,' Lucy Dexter smiled.

Drizzle hung in the air, so they opted for the nearby Molten Gallery Café rather than trail into town. Ryan tucked into a sausage and bacon stottie while Lucy popped the lid off a plastic container which held something resembling wallpaper paste. Both waited for their coffees to kick in.

They ate in silence, each lost in their own thoughts, before sauntering towards the temporary Command Centre set up in the disused unit. They ducked under the police tape and felt the spray from the Gut slick their faces.

Almost immediately, Ryan's phone vibrated with an incoming message.

'Elliot's got the go ahead to perform the post-mortem. He'll let us know when he gets to it.'

'Can't he do it straightaway?'

'He could, but he won't. He'll stick to his running order.'

Kuldeep Thakur approached them, his immaculate moustache still waxed and pert. He held two packages of protective clothing in his hands.

'Morning, Kuldeep,' Ryan greeted him. 'How have your team been getting on?'

'Like clockwork. Bloody hardworking clockwork, too.' He tossed them a package each. 'Please, get dressed. I'll show what we've got.'

Outside the unit four-doors away, forensic officers scrambled around on their knees, their torches focused on one target.

Kuldeep gave them a wide berth and addressed Ryan and Lucy. 'We have a very clever offender.'

Ryan's heart sank.

Lucy saw his face. 'Not Tim Rice,' she said.

'Didn't think it was. It's the word *clever* I don't like. Clever equals evasive.'

They were inside the unit, now. It seemed almost normal without the remains of a dismembered body in its bowels.

'We can't find anything of note,' Thakur said. 'No fingerprints, shoe impressions, not a single strand of hair other than that belonging to the victim.'

'That's impossible,' Lucy said.

'It's not. I told you our killer was clever.' He reached into a battered steel cupboard affixed to the wall. 'We can find nothing because of this.' He held a canister aloft. 'Chemiphase. It's 14% hypochlorite. An excellent steriliser.'

'Shit,' Ryan murmured.

'We found four of them, each five litres. They are all empty.'

'What's special about it?' Lucy asked.

'It is highly corrosive,' Thakur explained in his sing-song accent. 'It degrades many materials. It can break down the epidermal layers of human tissue. The girl's fingers – we have no prints. The surface of the skin had completely degraded. We cannot identify her, no sir.'

'What about DNA?' Lucy asked. 'Surely the killer must have left some at the scene.'

'We have not a single hair to go off. The Chemiphase would almost surely have dissolved any evidence left behind.'

Ryan tried to find a positive somewhere. 'What about your blood analysis guys?'

'There is a standard flow pattern and considerable splatter and pooling. Nothing we wouldn't expect after such a hideous killing. We do have some blood patterns outside of the bleach, but we don't know the significance of it. The lab analysts will work on it.'

'Okay, Kuldeep. Let me know if a miracle happens, yeah?' He turned to Lucy. 'Let's get back to Forth Street and break the news.'

'I'm sure the DCI will be delighted,' Lucy said with irony.

Ryan doubled-up the sarcasm. 'I'm sure he will, an' aal.'

**

'Tell me you've got something, Jarrod.' The DCI sounded as exhausted as Ryan felt.

'Not much more than what's in my reports, sir.'

'Anything, Jarrod. The media office is getting hammered and they don't know what to say.'

Ryan snorted. 'That's ridiculous. It's their job to know what to say.'

'You know that, and I know that. It appears they don't. So, tell me where we are.'

Ryan gathered his thoughts. 'Aaron Elliot is performing the post-mortem as we speak. We'll know more after that.' He took Danskin's silence as a cue to continue. 'The girl was tortured and had as much pain inflicted as a soul could bear, before a major artery was severed. The Blood Pattern Analysts confirmed the cause of death, but we pretty much already knew that.'

'Jarrod, man. I need something new. Something that's not in your reports.'

'We had a preliminary suspect…,' Danskin sat to attention, 'But he's illiterate so that rules him out. At least, as far as the calligraphy on our victim goes.'

'We don't know who she is?'

'Negative, sir. The cleaning agent appears to have removed all trace evidence. We're waiting for Elliot now to see if there's any internal evidence of sexual assault.'

'Fucking hell. What sort of maniac are we dealing with?'

'One to whom the words *My Right* have a significance, sir.'

Danskin screwed his eyes tight. 'The Super's called a favour in from someone on that front.'

'Oh aye?'

'A sodding profiler.'

'Imogen Markham?'

'No, thank God. Some bloke. Shola Ameobi or something.'

'What?'

Danskin wafted a hand in the air. 'Some foreign name. That's the closest I remember.'

'Hope he's more use than Markham.'

'That's what I said. Super seems to think the world of him, for whatever reason.' Danskin crossed his arms defensively.

'Can I speak to him, sir?'

'Na. He's not here yet. Besides, Maynard wants me to collaborate with him.'

They remained silent before Danskin spoke again.

'We need something, Jarrod. And quickly. The media circus will start making things up, sensationalising it, wreaking havoc and panic. We've got to find summat to give them.'

Ryan offered a grim smile. He suspected there'd be nothing quick about any of this.

**

Out in the bullpen, Ryan briefed Lucy on the exchange in Danskin's office.

Todd Robson couldn't help earwigging. 'You'd better deliver, Golden Boy. If Danskin has to front up to the press with a blank sheet of paper in front of him, there'll be shit on more than just the fan.'

'Thanks for the reminder, Todd,' Ryan chided.

Todd held up a hand. 'I'm only sayin', bonny lad.'

Ryan's phone prevented a reply. 'Jarrod.'

'Sherlock, it's Doctor Death here. Can you talk?'

'Aye; sure, Aaron. Can I put you on speaker? Lucy's here, as well. She can take notes.' He mimed a gesture which Lucy took to mean he wanted her to log into a PC.

'Hello, Irene,' Elliot said, his voice tinny and distorted through the speakers.

Todd pulled a frown. Ryan whispered, 'It's an in-joke,' and Todd signalled it was way over his head.

'Dr Elliot,' Lucy said, rather primly.

'Have you finished the post-mortem, Aaron?'

'I have. Straight off, Irene will be delighted to know there was no kind of sexual assault.'

Lucy closed her eyes and nodded.

'The victim was in good health. Judging by her muscle tone and body fat levels, I'd age her at between twenty-three and twenty-seven max.'

'Any sign of drugs, doc?' Ryan asked.

'Apart from copious amounts of alcohol, you mean? I suspect some agent to knock her out. Nothing too sophisticated. Chloroform, probably. An oldie but goodie. I've sent some samples from her nasal cavities for analysis. We'll know more soon.'

'Anything else?'

'Oh yes, but mostly what we already knew. Her hair was a mix of human-hair extensions and her natural hair. Dyed, but natural, if you know what I mean.'

'Does that tell us anything?' Lucy asked.

'We should be able to determine the make of dye which might help you.'

Ryan pulled a face which said he doubted it.

'Cause of death was indeed a laceration to the carotid artery. Death, when it finally came, would have arrived in seconds. The same weapon was used to scalp her. I have to say, the perpetrator did an impressive job.'

Lucy opened her mouth to protest but Ryan hushed her with a finger to his lips.

'Do you think our killer has medical knowledge?'

Elliot chortled. 'If he did, it came from Dr Google.'

Ryan scratched the back of his neck. He was at a loss. 'Do we have a precise time of death, Aaron?'

'Impossible to say with certainty. Definitely the day she was found, and I'd guess no more than forty-five minutes before she was discovered. Probably less.'

Lucy spoke next. 'Any signs of a struggle?'

Elliot hesitated. 'Yes, but I'm afraid to say it was a struggle against her pain, rather than with her captor. Severe bruising of the wrists and ankles and a torn tendon in her left forearm. Consistent with a struggle to escape her shackles, not her murderer.'

Ryan asked about the incision to the girl's breast.

'Now you're asking me to play detective again, Sherlock. If you want me to, I can.'

'Gan on, then.'

Elliot's breathing came over the speaker like a hiss. 'The girl had false hair. The killer removed it. She had false fingernails. They were ripped off. Her eyelids were removed, I'm surmising because she had false eyelashes. If you're asking me to do your job, I'd say our killer was checking for breast implants.'

'Dear God,' Lucy whispered.

'Fucking perv,' Todd spat.

'The face, Aaron?' Ryan asked. 'Why her face? To hide her identity? Is that all?'

'I have no idea. Look, no guarantees, but I took a sample of her cell DNA as a matter of course. That gives us a chance of discovering her identity, but it won't be a quick fix. It'll take time.'

'Time's something the DCI hasn't got,' Ryan said aloud.

'I'll see if I can chase the lab up. I should warn you it won't be straightforward, and it'll only help if there's a DNA match on medical records, such as if she's had a previous predictive genetic test for an inherited condition. I certainly can't promise you anything.'

Ryan smiled enigmatically. 'I mightn't need your promises, Aaron. Not if her DNA is on *our* files, too.'

Lucy eyes shone. 'You mean *we* can trace her?'

'Yes. Fingerprints or no fingerprints, face or no face; if she's got a record, we'll know who she is from her DNA!'

Lucy Dexter squealed with delight and threw her arms around Ryan's neck.

CHAPTER THIRTEEN

Detective Chief Inspector Danskin seemed to have other things on his mind. Ryan had expected the revelation that the victim's DNA may lead to a formal identification to have energised him. Instead, it barely registered.

Danskin instructed Ryan to spend the rest of the day checking the missing persons database for possible leads and ordered Lucy to comb through the interview reports tumbling in from Uniform.

It made the remaining hours of Ryan's shift a laborious chore. He could do with a pint. DC Nigel Trebilcock had already left for the day, Gavin O'Hara had a 'hot date', Parker and Robson were out on a case, and Ravi Sangar's religious upbringing meant he was tee-total, although he allowed himself an occasional lapse on special occasions. This wasn't one of them.

Which left Lucy Dexter.

Ryan thought about it, he really did, but ultimately decided he was better served heading back to Whickham and coaxing his brother out of his self-inflicted bubble.

'Fancy a pint, James?' he called as he entered the family home.

'He's not in,' Norman Jarrod replied.

'Bollocks. I hoped I'd get him down the village for an hour or so. Try to bring him out of himself, you know.'

'I think he's found his own way of doing that, son. He's staying with Muzzle for a few days.'

Ryan's brow creased. 'I can't keep an eye on him there.'

'He'll be aal reet. I reckon it might help. Give him summat else to focus on, and at least he's interacting with a real person instead of that bloody computer. Besides, I doubt anybody will go looking for him over Lemington way. I think if anything, I'd be the easy target.'

'Well, that makes me feel a whole lot better.'

Norman laughed. 'You know what I mean, though.'

'Aye, I do. Suppose I'll just take old Spud for a walk instead.'

'Don't think he's up to. His back end's a bit gammy today. Not very steady on his feet.'

'I wondered why he hadn't come to say hello. Is he eating?'

'Nowt wrong there. He's eating like a horse. Shitting like one, as well.'

Ryan laughed. 'Oh well. Guess it's back home for me.'

'Unless you fancy a pint with your old man. You can take care of the sitting duck, as it were.'

'You know, why not? It's been a while. Get your coat, Dad.'

**

The evening was clear and mild, the drizzle long since cleared, and stars winked down on Ryan and Norman as they cut through Chase Park on route to the village centre.

They emerged close to the Crown, recently rebranded as The Dirty Habit; a name which was enough to put Norman off. The One-Eyed Stag it was, they agreed.

'I had your lass on the phone earlier,' Norman said as they strolled left along Front Street.

'Who?'

'Hannah, you geet lummox. How many other lasses you got on the go?'

'What did she want?'

'Checking we were all okay. Me, James, and your Gran. You've got a good 'un there, son. Don't give up on her.'

Ryan was surprised he felt a flash of guilt. 'I won't.'

Norman stopped and sniffed the air. 'Ah man – get a load of that.'

The charcoal steeped aroma of tandoori chicken, the smell of freshly ground coconut, coriander, a blend of curry odours, and the scent of fresh, flaky naan brushed with ghee from the Jamdani restaurant hung in the still air, rich and enticing as an apple in Eden.

'Fancy it?' Norman asked.

Ryan's stomach rumbled. 'Can't say I'm not tempted but I haven't time, Dad. A quick pint it has to be.'

Next door to the Asian restaurant, the windows of The One-Eyed Stag micropub were, as usual, fogged with condensation. It was a small establishment, homely and popular, specialising in local craft ales with obscure names and even more obscure flavours.

Ryan studied the hand pumps but settled on a bottled lager. Norman chose a cinder toffee stout, much to his son's disgust.

They chewed the fat, avoiding anything heavy, until Ryan's phone buzzed in his pocket.

'Hannah,' Ryan explained, making for the exit.

Outside, once more amongst the fragrances of backstreet Rangpur, Ryan took the call. 'Wassup?'

'Oh, you know - just checking you're still alive.'

'I am, as you can tell. Thanks for checking on Dad earlier, Hannah. I appreciate it.'

'I like him. I care about him. And James, and your Gran, too. But I despise the pickle you've got them.'

'*I've* got them in? It's hardly my fault, you know. I don't particularly like walking around with a target on me back, either.' He scratched his brow. 'Listen, I'm sorry. I'm stressed to the hilt with the case I'm on, let alone owt else.'

Ryan felt Hannah relax at the end of her phone. 'Apology accepted, Ry. Speaking of your case, any idea when I might be able to let the fleet use the fish quay again? The lads are going off it having to use part of the Saft unit across the river 'cos it's got no facilities for them, and Saft aren't happy that their plant now stinks of fish.'

'Oh pity them. It's not a great hardship in the scheme of things.'

'It's dangerous, apparently. Overheating electrical components also stink of fish. Seeing as Saft produce batteries, their guys are hitting the panic button every half hour.'

Ryan gave the matter thought. 'Look, I suspect we might have got everything we need by tomorrow. I'll call in first thing, check it out, and let you know straightaway. Promise.'

'I'll hold you to that, mind.'

Ryan sensed a hint of a smile in her voice. It made him relax. 'The CW Fisheries unit will still be out of bounds, but they can use the unit we've been occupying as a temp operations hub.'

'I'll let the skippers know, you tell the Fisheries and Saft, yeah?'

'You got a deal, Hannah.'

'Good.' A thought struck her. 'You're not travelling there alone, are you? I mean we don't know who's responsible yet and…'

'Chill, man. There's no way I'm allowed out on my own. I'll have my chaperone with me.'

Ryan sensed the tension again as she asked, 'Who?'

'Luce.'

'I see.'

'What do you mean by that?'

'I mean, it's Luce now, is it? Not DC Dexter, or even Lucy.'

'Hannah, man. Don't be like that.'

'I'll be like whatever I like being like. Be sure to tell me when you've okayed your scene for fleet entry. Goodbye, Ryan.'

'Han…' the call died. 'Fuck's sake!' He kicked the kerb.

Ryan turned towards the Stag knowing the remains of his lager would be as unpalatable as Norman Jarrod's cinder toffee stout.

**

True to his word, Ryan and his chaperone squeezed through the Fish Quay gates soon after dawn the following morning.

The forensics team had completed their crime scene work and were ferrying their kit and samples into a forensics van. Much work remained, but it was work which would take place back in the labs. All traces of the crime had been erased from the warehouse.

Kuldeep Thakur strolled over to Ryan and Lucy and confirmed they were done. 'Once we've completed the tests and signed off the forensic register, I'll ping you an e-mail with the findings. Should I copy your DCI in?'

Ryan confirmed Danskin should see it, too. He looked towards the last two members of Thakur's team sitting on the dockside. 'They look done in.'

'They are. Not one of the most pleasant scenes we've worked on. They'll be fine once they've had their debrief. They'll get counselling if they want it, but I suspect they'll just move onto their next job.'

'Thanks for everything, Kuldeep.'

'Pleasure, DS Jarrod,' Thakur said, accepting Ryan's hand. 'Promise me you'll catch the person who did this.' For the first time, the raw emotion came across in his voice.

'We will do, I'm sure, thanks to your efforts.'

Ryan supervised the Uniform presence while they removed the police tape from the fish market, except for the unit belonging to CW Fisheries. Their unit remained cordoned-off for now. Ryan called the owner and offered him the use of the abandoned warehouse instead.

Next, he pulled up Hannah's number. His finger hovered above the 'Call' button, before hitting the 'Message' symbol instead. *'Fish Market back in service. CW Fisheries know the score. All yours now,'* he wrote. As an afterthought, he added *'x'*.

Just the one.

**

By the time Ryan and Lucy marched into the bullpen, the
rest of DCI Danskin's squad were hard at work, desk work
mainly. Sitting amongst them was Danskin himself.

'All clear down Shields, sir,' Ryan confirmed.

Danskin harrumphed.

'Everything okay, sir?'

Gavin O'Hara gave a warning headshake while Todd
Robson made a 'cut' gesture.

'Aye. Why wouldn't it?' the DCI scowled.

'You've got a face like a brickie's radio, that's why.'

Todd put his head in his hands.

'I've been kicked oot me office, for one,' Danskin moaned.
'Maynard's only gone and leant it out, hasn't she?'

'I don't understand. Who to?'

'Anthony Joshua's fucking stunt double, that's who.'

'Who?'

'That Shola bloke. Or Fola, whatever he's called.'

'Oh, the profiler.'

'Aye, him.'

The door to Danskin's office opened. Sam Maynard
beckoned Ryan to her. 'Ryan, Lucy – there's someone I'd like
you to meet. This way, please. Stephen: you, too.'

'Cheers,' Danskin muttered under his breath. 'Nice to
know I'm welcome in me own bloody office.'

The man inside Danskin's office did indeed resemble
Anthony Joshua. He had a menacing presence, yet the
warmth of his smile belied his size.

'I need to start creating a profile for this killer,' the man
said, straight to business.

'Just a moment, Fola,' Sam Maynard interrupted. 'I think
you should introduce yourself to our investigating officers.'

'Sorry, Sam,' Fola said, the familiarity morphing Danskin's
face from brickie's radio to bent crisp. 'My name's Fola
Fasanya, and Sam has brought me in to draw up a
psychological profile of our man.'

'Or woman,' Ryan said, at last bringing a smile to Danskin's features.

'Very astute of you,' Fasanya nodded. 'So, let's get started shall we, if that's okay with you, Sam?'

'Of course. But, please, address me as Superintendent Maynard, or ma'am.'

'Sure, Sam,' the profiler said with a wink.

'Fuck's sake,' Danskin mouthed.

Fasanya continued. 'We'll take a systematic, four step approach. Firstly, we obtain as much information as possible from both the crime scene and the victim. We're looking for anything which suggests what happened, how it happened, why it happened.'

'Already done,' Danskin offered. 'That's basic proper coppering.'

Fasanya beamed. 'Thanks for your input, DCI Danskin. Moving on, we then run through a checklist to determine whether there are any classic signs or symptoms which may lead us to an offender classification. In turn, this may well reveal a motive.'

Ryan turned to face Lucy. Both raised their eyebrows. The man spoke with authority and conviction. They were impressed.

'Step three is to fit jigsaw pieces to the picture. We work out the chain of events before, during, and after the offence.' He smiled at Stephen Danskin. 'Again, I shall defer to the work of your team who I'm sure will have *'proper coppered'* or whatever the phrase you used was.'

Lucy's snigger was cut short by Ryan's finger prodding her spine.

'Once we've gathered all the information for stages one to three, we can hypothesise about the category of offender. We will identify the killer's sex, age, IQ, possibly even their hobbies and, of course, they're mental health.'

'I think we can safely say their mental health is totally fucked.' Danskin's tone was loaded with sarcasm.

'Not necessarily,' Fasanya concluded without further explanation. 'Now, once we've gone through all stages, we can concentrate on offenders who match the profile. Our search will be more focussed, logical, and will lead us to our killer.'

'Excellent, Fola. That's precisely what we need from you,' Maynard effused. 'Now, do we have any questions for Fola?'

Danskin looked at the floor, Ryan worked the approach through his mind, and Lucy raised her hand to ask a question. It was a question which never came.

It never came because Todd Robson burst into the room.

'We've a DNA match. We know who our victim is, and you're not gonna believe it!'

CHAPTER FOURTEEN

It took Ryan less than thirty minutes to pull together the
rudiments of a crime board. He'd pinned maps, times, and
locations to the board with magnetic tiles and plotted
distances and timescales with colour-coded marker pens.

He'd pulled a photograph from the girl's social media
accounts and placed it top centre. Beneath it, he'd attached
two further photographs of the murder scene and a close-up
of the '*My Right*' mutilation.

Ryan stood to one side of the board, Stephen Danskin –
happy to be back in a world he understood – at the other. In
front of them, Lucy Dexter, Todd Robson, and Gavin O'Hara
faced the board.

Superintendent Maynard watched from the rear, with Fola
Fasanya alongside her.

'Our victim is Roberta Cavell, recently found Not Guilty of
fraud and embezzlement charges. It's a case I'm familiar
with, having worked it with DI Parker,' he explained,
mainly for the benefit of Fasanya. Ryan went on to briefly
outline the case of the Crown versus Roberta Cavell.

'Now, from the previous charges against Ms Cavell, I have
identified a number of potential persons of interest we
should concentrate our initial enquiries on.' Ryan looked in
the direction of Danskin. 'Of course, we all know not to see
what we expect to see, but we must have a starting point.'

Fasanya leaned into Sam Maynard. 'What's this kid's
background?' he whispered.

'He's on fast-stream. Came straight into Stephen's team
from being a Special. Stephen spotted his potential straight
away. Good, isn't he?'

'Very,' Fasanya agreed, returning his concentration to the crime board.

'The first question to answer is, '*Why did no-one report the victim as a MissPer?*' Lucy's done some groundwork and discovered our victim shared an apartment with a Leanne Soulsby.'

He affixed am image of an attractive young woman, immaculately made up, to the board before continuing.

'This image has been retrieved from her Insta account. This second picture,' he pinned that to the board, too, 'Is from Soulsby's Facebook account. It shows her with our victim and is tagged '*BFF*'. We need to find out why her BFF decided not to report said BFF missing.'

Danskin and Fasanya both nodded, for once in agreement.

'Lucy, you go talk to her.' Ryan sipped from a mug of stagnant coffee. 'Now, on a similar theme, we have Roberta Cavell's parents.' He appended two more photographs to the board. 'Why would they not report their daughter missing?'

It was a rhetorical question, but Todd had an answer.

'She's a grown woman, Ryan. A grown woman who hadn't been missing for long. I divvent think we should read ower much into it.'

Ryan thought for a moment. 'Normally, I'd agree. There is something else, though. Ravi's had his computer forensic lads run through her social media accounts. It's early days but we now know that our victim tagged her parents into many posts. They, in turn, commented on their daughter's photos and such like. Until, that is, around eighteen months ago. Then, everything stopped,' he snapped his fingers. 'Just like that. We need to find out why.'

'The father looks familiar,' Gavin O'Hara mused. 'Is he known to us?'

'Na, but you'll have seen him in the papers. He's Jackson Lionel Cavell.'

'The building society guy?'

'The very same.'

Gavin let out a low whistle.

DCI Danskin intervened. 'Needless to say, we now need to be even more astute at keeping this out the papers. The Cavell's haven't been informed yet, so they not only need be notified their lass has been murdered, they also have some questions to answer, as DS Jarrod has already alluded to.'

'Stephen, I suggest you lead on that,' Maynard said. 'It'll reassure them we've a senior officer on it.'

'Will do, ma'am.'

'Carry on, Ryan.'

'There's a couple more people we need a word with.' He licked his fingers and peeled another image from his hands before pinning it to the board. 'This is Timothy Rice. He works at the quay and was the person who found the body. Now, DC Dexter and I have already interviewed Mr Rice and, for reasons I won't go into now, I've good reason to believe he isn't our man but, as I said earlier, let's not see what we expect to see so I believe we need to keep him on the radar.'

'He's big and strong enough, that's for sure,' Gavin noticed. 'And the first to the scene is always a prime suspect.'

'Agreed,' Danskin said. 'What makes you think we can rule him out, Jarrod?'

Ryan pointed to Timmy's image. 'I haven't ruled him out, sir, but this crime took meticulous planning. Materials were used to clear evidence from the scene. With all due respect, I doubt Mr Rice has the capacity.'

'He's better than good,' Fasanya whispered to Maynard. She nodded in agreement.

'Also,' Lucy added, 'Mr Rice is illiterate.'

'What's that got to do with the price of fish?' Todd said, oblivious to the irony.

'Because,' Fasanya intervened, 'He couldn't carve '*My Right*' into the poor girl's stomach.'

'Bugger it. Of course, man.' Todd hung his head in embarrassment.

Stephen Danskin checked his watch. 'Okay, time's pressing. Dexter, you go and see this mate of our victim, I'll head off to talk to the Cavell's. Ryan, you co-ordinate things from here. You've Ravi's crew at your disposal.'

Ryan raised a hand. 'We're not quite done yet, sir.'

'You've more PoI's?'

'I think we need to consider the victim of the crime Cavell was acquitted of: Eunice Paddock.'

Todd looked at the picture Ryan planted on the board. 'Seriously? She must be nearly ninety.'

'Not quite. In fact, nowhere near but I take your point, Todd. So, let's move onto other members of the Paddock family.'

Ryan revealed his final photograph. Held it up for all to see. It was an image of a clean-shaven young man with foppish dark hair and eyes like coal.

'I've saved the best 'til last. This,' he tapped the latest picture he'd put on rogue's gallery, 'Is Tyler Paddock, son of Eunice Paddock.'

Todd scratched the scar on his cheek. 'What's so special about him?'

Danskin smiled knowingly. He knew what Ryan was about to say, and he was right.

Ryan looked at DC Maynard as he spoke. 'Because, Todd, Lyall and me were at the court when the verdict was announced. It all kicked off afterwards. I had to intervene.'

He paused for dramatic effect.

'I had to intervene because Tyler Paddock made threats against Roberta Cavell. To be precise, he said, *'Don't think this is over. I'll make you pay.'*

**

Once the hubbub subsided, Superintendent Maynard called those present to attention.

'Given the limited amount of time since our victim was identified, I think we'll all agree DS Jarrod has done a remarkable job here.'

There was murmured agreement, then Maynard did something unheard of: she began a round of applause.

Others joined in. Rick Kinnear and his team looked across in astonishment, Lucy Dexter beamed more than Ryan who's face flushed in embarrassment. Todd whooped 'You're the man,' and Stephen Danskin lapped up his protégé's praise.

When the applause died down, the Super opened the floor for Danskin to outline the next steps.

'I think Jarrod has already pointed us in the direction, ma'am. DC Dexter talks to the flatmate, I'll lead on the Cavell family because of their profile. We'll keep Rice on the backburner for now. DI Parker's due back with Treblecock any minute. I'll send them to interview Tyler Paddock and his mother.'

'Sir, I'd like to work with Lyall, if no-one's got any objections,' Ryan pleaded.

'None here,' Danskin said, looking around at a swathe of shaking heads. 'That's agreed, then. O'Hara and Robson, you liaise with Uniform and pick up on any leads falling out from their enquiries. I'll assign Treblecock to work with Ravi. Sound okay?'

'Sir,' Lucy said, timidly. 'I thought Ryan and I were working together. Should I not be with him?'

'Please don't tell me she's a bunny boiler,' Ryan thought, relieved when Danskin told Lucy he believed Parker was better placed because of his knowledge of events at the Crown Court.

The DCI wrapped things up. 'Okay, I think we're all done here. If there's no questions, let's hit the streets, as the saying goes.'

A raised hand at the rear of the group delayed the squad's dispersal.

'What about me?' Fola Fasanya asked.

'Oh, I reckon you can get yersel' home, don't you? We're about done with psychobabble now we're back to normal police work now.'

Fasanya scowled. So, too, Maynard. DCI Danskin thought on his feet.

'It's nowt personal, mind. You see, we haven't the budget to provide security for some of my own squad, let alone fund your accommodation and fees, seeing as we're back to standard detective work. Isn't that right, ma'am?'

Maynard shifted uncomfortably. 'It is,' she admitted, her eyes for once dull and lifeless.

Danskin kept his smile hidden.

'Thanks for your input, though, Fola; it's appreciated,' he said. 'Have a safe journey back doon south.'

Stephen Danskin chuckled inwardly at his little victory.

CHAPTER FIFTEEN

Newcastle Crown Court
The Law Courts
Newcastle Quayside

William Vickers stood in the defendant's dock, a puzzled expression across his face. He thought he'd misheard. He could have sworn the man had said, 'Not guilty.'

The duty solicitor – Vickers hadn't the means to employ his own – looked up to the dock and give him a thumbs up sign.

Not guilty, he most definitely was.

William let the realisation sink in. He raised his eyes to the ceiling and breathed out, long and loud. He stood like that, hands still slick with sweat, until he realised the judge had left the courtroom and the gallery occupants were filing out the door, two-by-two.

William wiped his hands on the dock rail, then against the front of his coffee-coloured shirt. He'd dressed smart for the occasion, but the shirt was oversized. He could insert a serving spoon between the collar and his throat, and one side of the shirt tail had become untucked.

He hitched up his trousers, crammed the shirt tail inside his underwear, and tightened his belt a notch.

Slowly, he felt the tension leave the few muscles which covered his scrawny frame. He unclenched his teeth and moved his jaw from side to side until it clicked.

The courtroom was deserted apart from Vickers and the dock guard, who urged him to leave. Vickers looked at the man with disdain before striding from the dock with the arrogant smirk of a school bully.

He needed a whiskey, but he'd been told he had to sign the release papers first. The queue at the foyer desk was long. Long, and slow moving.

'Jesus Christ,' he muttered, looking up at the clock below the Royal Coat of Arms. The pointers seemed to move as slowly as a glacier. Twenty minutes later, he was next in line.

'William Vickers,' he announced to the woman behind the counter. She squinted at her monitor, printed off the papers, and pushed them and a pen through the slot in the perspex screen.

He signed the documentation and shoved them back to the woman. He gave her a leer and a wink, the kind of look he'd given *her* just before it all happened.

William Vickers left the court building smiling for the flashbulbs of the paparazzi who were gathered on the steps of the Quayside Law Courts.

Just around the corner, not a five-minute walk from the courts, Vickers settled into a booth facing the oak bar of The Broad Chare.

The Chare, although recently refurbished, had been deliberately stripped back to display painted brick walls and exposed wood floors; the type of pub which largely disappeared around the time of whistling milkmen and buses with conductors.

The Chare specialised in real and craft ales, but it stocked a good enough supply of whiskey (the 'e' being all-important) to satisfy William Vickers. He raised his glass to an invisible companion and licked his lips as the spirit burnt its way down his throat.

He looked into the glass and chuckled. The chuckle became a hearty laugh; the hearty laugh a hysterical, high-pitched giggle.

It was the name of his chosen whiskey which set him off. Bushmills Black Bush.

William Vickers closed his eyes and remembered.

Low Light

**

Carmen Best's father mentioned he'd been invited to a hoity-toity cocktail reception a couple of weeks previously. 'Eat out to help out' was about to become 'drink out to pass out', David Best had joked.

William Vickers had been planning for this moment ever since, and the anticipation built with every passing moment. Now, the time had arrived.

He waited in the shadows of a sturdy ash tree until he saw the taillights of the Kodiaq disappear in the direction of Forest Hall, the silhouettes of David Best and his wife visible through the rear screen.

Peering over the garden wall, he watched as the stairhead light went on, followed by a bedroom light. A window was part-open, and he heard some rap shit booming from it.

He hurried through the open gates and circumnavigated the garden, keeping his back to the wall so he wouldn't trigger the security lighting.

He closed his eyes, held his breath, and fought against his body's urgency.

He tried the front door.

It opened.

His mouth was dry. He'd seen the photographs. He knew what waited for him, upstairs. In her bedroom.

Vickers closed the house door behind him.

He crept up the stairs, avoiding the fifth step which he knew creaked loudly. He heard her voice, sweet and melodic, a paradox to the guttural hip-hop tones of Ice T. Or Snoop Dogg. Or the Notorious BIG, whichever moronic noise she listened to.

He had his hand on the doorknob. He saw his fingers tremble with the anticipation.

'*Oh, I hope you're ready for this,*' he whispered to himself, a fire inside him.

He opened the bedroom door.

The dark-haired girl jumped. 'God, Uncle Will. What a fright! What are you doing here?'

William smiled. 'Babysitting.'

'I don't think so,' Carmen Best laughed. 'I'm sixteen. I'm okay as I am, ta very much.'

'But, honey, you're daddy told me to take real good care of you while he and momma are out.'

Carmen tilted her head to one side. 'Are you okay, Uncle Will?'

He swallowed hard. Licked his lips. Nodded.

'Just you're sounding, I don't know…weird. Like you're in a movie or something.'

'I thought you liked American slang, judging by the fucking shite you're listening to.'

The girl's eyes widened. She'd never heard her dad's best friend swear before. There was something about his face, too. It looked different. Intense. Sweaty.

There was also something about the knife he held in his hand.

'Uncle Will? Why are you here?' she whispered, eyes wide behind her oversized spectacles.

'To see you, sweetie-pie.'

'Stop with the fake accent. It's creeping me out.' Her eyes shifted to Vickers' hand. 'And, please, put the knife down.'

Carmen edged away from him. He caught sight of her Samsung on the bedside table.

'Don't even fucking think about it, bitch.'

'Uncle W…'

'SHUT UP!'

The girl shut up.

'Now, you're going to do what I say. Understand?'

The girl nodded, eyes never moving from the serrated blade in his hand.

'Take off your clothes.'

'What? No! Never.'

'DO IT!' he yelled.

The girl shook with fright. 'Please, think about this,' Carmen said, pulling her *'Simply the Best'* T-shirt over her head. Her glasses came off along with her top. They landed spreadeagled on the bed. 'You don't want to do this, really. Think of my Dad. You're supposed to be his friend.'

She unbuttoned her jeans. Pulled the zipper down and wiggled out of them.

'And the rest,' he said, his voice a whisper.

'No! I won't. You can't make me.'

He barked a laugh. 'I think I can. I've got this,' he held up the knife, 'And this.'

Carmen Best struggled to see without her glasses.

'What's that?' she managed to say.

'It's my phone. And there's some very interesting photographs on it. Photographs of you, sweetheart. Photographs I don't think your Daddy would appreciate seeing.'

She shook her head. 'No. You can't have. Not of me. I'd never do such a thing.'

William laughed. 'Don't play the innocent with me. You really shouldn't trust people, these days. Not even Jonny Bannister.'

'How do you know Jonny?'

'Does it matter? Oh, go on then. I'll tell you. I don't know him. Not personally. But, you see, once you let someone like Jonny Bannister take photographs of you, especially *these* sorts of photographs, they tend to take on a life of their own.'

The girl couldn't comprehend what he was saying. She stood shivering, tears streaming down her cheeks.

'Now, do as I say. Take off the rest of your clothes. Do it slowly.' His voice broke. 'Then, lie on the bed.'

She reached behind her. Unclasped her bra. Crossed her arms in front of her.

'Let it fall.'

He let out a little gasp as Carmen's bra dropped to the bedroom floor and she unfolded her arms.

'Next.' He pointed the knife towards her panties. 'Or Daddy sees the photos. I'm taking what I want regardless but, if you keep your mouth shut and don't tell him, he won't get to see your little photo gallery.'

'I'm only sixteen,' she sobbed.

'Old enough. Take them off and lie on the bed.'

She did as she was told. Lay down with her hands covering her femininity.

He smiled. Gave her a wink.

The smile fell from his face as he hissed, 'Move. Your. Fucking. Hands.'

She did as she was told.

His invasive glare molested her.

Carmen closed her eyes and mouthed a silent prayer.

**

Back in the warmth of The Broad Chare, William Vickers' face lit up at the year-old memory. He raised his glass to the light, rotated it in his fingers, and savoured the sight of the Black Bush.

CHAPTER SIXTEEN

The bungalow stood in two-acres of land in the hamlet of
Hepscott, just outside the Northumberland market town of
Morpeth. The building was impressive; stone-built, double-
fronted, and expansive.

The nameplate alongside the doorbell informed Stephen
Danskin the Cavell family home was called Jackdaw Field.
When the bell rang, its chime came from deep within the
bowels of the house.

'You rang?' the woman who answered announced in a
poor impression of Lurch. Her normal voice returned as she
stiffened at the sight of Danskin's warrant card. 'Yes?'

'Mrs Cavell, Detective Chief Inspector Stephen Danskin.
I'm sorry to trouble you. Is your husband home, too?'

'Yes, he is. What can we do for you?' Mrs Cavell stood
barring entry.

'It's about your daughter.'

She rolled her eyes. 'Roberta. Surely she hasn't done
anything else, not so soon.'

'If I could just come in?' Danskin said, trying his best to be
the sympathetic, assured professional whilst preparing
himself to perform his most hated task: telling a parent their
child has been butchered – not to mention potentially
questioning them as suspects.

'Who is it, Margaret?' Jackson Cavell appeared at the end
of a long corridor, wearing shirt and tie above checked
lounge pants.

'Police,' Margaret Cavell said.

Jackson echoed his wife with a weary, 'What's she done
this time?' He smiled, teeth gleaming white as snow, and
added, 'Come in, Detective Chief Inspector.'

'Please, call me Stephen,' Danskin said as Margaret Cavell reluctantly stepped aside.

Jackson gestured Danskin into a lavishly furnished lounge adorned with marble busts atop mahogany pillars positioned in alcoves dotted around the room. Danskin imagined it probably resembled the interior of London's Carlton Club although he'd never experienced anything grander than his local Buffs.

On the wall, a portrait hung proudly above a log fire. Danskin reckoned it must have been painted about six years ago. It showed Jackson Cavell stood behind a seated Margaret and teenage Roberta. Mr Cavell rested a hand on each of their shoulders.

Danskin took a single-seater studded Chesterfield whilst Mrs Cavell joined her husband on one of three sofas scattered around the lounge.

'You have a lovely home.'

'Thank you, Stephen,' Jackson smiled. 'Now, what can we help you with?'

'I just have a few questions for you.'

'About the Paddock business? Awful, I know. However, our Roberta has done many things, but she didn't do that.'

'Indeed, she was found not guilty,' Danskin agreed in a non-committal response. 'I was just wondering when you last saw your daughter.'

Jackson Cavell seemed oblivious to the downbeat note in Danskin's voice but, call it mother's instinct, Margaret immediately picked up on it.

'Is anything wrong?' Her voice came out hoarse.

'Mr Cavell?' Danskin persisted.

'Not for a while. We had our differences, you see.'

'We used to be so close,' Cavell's wife added. 'What's this about, Mr Danskin?'

'Stephen,' Danskin smiled before returning his eyes to Jackson. 'Could you tell me what those differences were?'

Jackson sighed. 'Roberta lost her way. We sent her to Mowden Hall School but she trundled her way through it. Her results were average at best, despite her potential. You see, Stephen, that sums up our Roberta to a tee. She could have anything, be anyone she wants to be. Trouble is, she thinks she already has everything.'

'And that's why you fell out?'

'In a way, yes. Being our only child, we spoiled her, I'm afraid.'

Danskin immediately picked up on the past tense. 'Spoiled?'

'We no longer do. You'll understand I want our Roberta to find her own way in life. I'm afraid she's become reliant on me – on us – subsidising her. So, I cut off her allowance to ensure she makes her own way in life.'

'Unfortunately,' Margaret Cavell interrupted, 'In return, Roberta has cut us off, too. She never gets in touch. Never tells us what she's up to. We find out most of it from the papers, I'm afraid. As my husband said, Roberta's lost her way. She's getting herself into trouble all too often. But I'm sure you already know all about our daughter's misdemeanours, Detective Chief Inspector. All I can say is, we are so ashamed of her.'

'Don't be. I'm sure you did what you thought was best. None of Roberta's actions are your fault.'

'I wish I could believe you,' Margaret said, sadly.

The room fell silent. Jackson Cavell broke it. 'I'm sorry. May I get you a drink before you tell us what this is all about it?' Cavell stood, towering over his wife.

'Please, Mr Cavell. Sit down, won't you?'

Cavell frowned. 'Stephen?'

'I'm afraid I have some bad news for you.'

Margaret Cavell swallowed hard, knowing her initial fears were about to be confirmed. What followed was much worse.

'Mr and Mrs Cavell, I'm afraid your daughter has been found in North Shields fish market.'

They'd seen the news. Read the papers. Heard on the radio about the discovery of a body. The Cavells knew what was coming, but it didn't soften the blow.

Danskin wished he needn't say the words, but protocol insisted he did. He was pretty sure they'd already guessed.

'I'm terribly sorry to inform you, your daughter's been killed.'

Margaret Cavell's high-pitched shriek echoed through the bungalow.

At least Danskin learned one thing from his visit. Their reaction was genuine. He was two suspects down in the search for the murderer of Roberta Cavell.

Or so he believed.

**

Two things about the building instantly struck Lucy Dexter.

Firstly, that it resembled a modern-day fortified structure perched on top of the cliff like Colditz Castle.

Secondly, its proximity to the murder scene.

From the front of Knott's Memorial Flats, Lucy could just about make out the fish quay where, merely days ago, Bobbi Cavell's life was taken from her in such horrific fashion.

Lucy took in the exterior of the building, trying to gauge which one of the sea-facing balconies belonged to Bobbi and Leanne. She guessed it would be one of those either side of, or below, the enormous clock face which formed the centrepiece of the building's exterior.

Once inside, Lucy took the stairs to the fifth floor, gathered her breath, and rapped on the door of Bobbi and Leanne's apartment. A young woman of about Lucy's age opened it. She wore a dressing gown and had her hair in a topknot.

'Yes?'

'Leanne Soulsby?' The girl nodded. 'I'm Detective Constable Lucy Dexter, City and County CID. I wonder if I could have a word?'

'She's not here.'

'Who isn't?'

'Bobbi. That's why you're here, isn't it?'

Lucy assessed Leanne's reply. Was it genuine innocence or a well-rehearsed response?

'What makes you say that?'

'Well, she's just been in court. I've no doubt you're not happy with the verdict and want to pin something else on her. It won't work and, like I say, she's not here.'

Lucy still wasn't sure about the girl. 'May I come in?'

Leanne turned her back to the door and Lucy followed her inside.

DC Dexter looked around the apartment. From the interior design, she recognised it wouldn't come cheap. 'Actually, it's you I wanted to speak with.'

'Me? What have I done?'

Lucy resisted the temptation to suggest murder. 'When did you last see Bobbi?'

'The day of the trial. We got well and truly pissed celebrating. I spent the next day in bed. I've barely recovered yet.'

'And you've not seen her since?'

Leanne shook her head.

'You didn't think to report her missing?'

The young woman screwed her face. 'Bobbi's not missing. She's on holiday.'

Lucy disguised her surprise. 'What makes you think that?'

The girl fumbled in the pocket of her fluffy gown. 'Because she told me. Look.'

Leanne held up her phone. Lucy took it from her and read, *'I'm all booked.'*

'So, you think this means she booked a holiday. Why's that?'

'Cos we talked about it. She wanted me to go. Said she'd pay for me, but I couldn't get time off work. She'll have booked online. Have a look at her laptop if you don't believe me.'

Lucy ran her fingers through her gelled hair. The girl didn't give the appearance of someone who'd committed a heinous crime. There again, she remembered Kuldeep Thakur's words: *We have a very clever offender.*

'May I take a look in your kitchen?'

'What? Why?'

'May I?'

Leanne sighed and led Lucy through to the kitchen. Immediately, Lucy made for a cupboard beneath the sink. She opened it, took a knee, and started emptying the contents; a brown plastic bowl, a couple of tea towels, a greasy scouring pad, a bottle of Cif kitchen spray, and a cannister containing oven cleaner.

Finally, she removed two bottles of Domestos.

'What are you doing?' Leanne asked as Lucy squirted Domestos onto a tea towel.

When it didn't evaporate in a puff blue smoke, Lucy was satisfied the bottle did contain Domestos, not Chemiphase.

'Thank you. Please, we should go back in the lounge and take a seat.'

'You're frightening me now. Has something happened?'

'Just take a seat. Please.' Lucy gave a smile which wasn't reassuring.

'It has, hasn't it? Something's happened in the Caribbean. Oh hell – is Bobbi okay?'

'Last time you saw her, did she seem worried or upset? Anxious, maybe.'

'No. Not at all. She was happy. Excited, even. She was free. Look, just tell me what you're here for.'

'I'm sorry, Leanne. Bobbi Cavell has been found, dead. Murdered, I'm afraid.'

Leanne's mouth formed a perfect circle before it was hidden behind a trembling hand. 'No,' she gasped. 'Not

Bobbi. She can't be. She's on hol...' She couldn't finish the sentence before the tears came in torrents.

Lucy waited until the girl's cries subsided, uncomfortable in the company of Leanne Soulsby's grief.

'I know you were best friends. I know this must be so hard for you. But we really need your help to catch whoever did this. Is there another crowd Bobbi hangs out with?'

Leanne's head shook vigorously. 'Bobbi went away by herself. It must be someone she met over there. Perhaps someone on her flight. Get onto her laptop. Find which airline she flew with. Who sat next to her. Please, it must be somebody who was on the same plane.'

Lucy took Leanne's hand. 'I'm sorry, Leanne. Bobbi wasn't on holiday. We found her here.'

'She was still in the UK?'

'Leanne, she was still in North Shields. We found her in a unit in the fish quay.'

'What the fuck?'

'I'm afraid so.'

The tears came again. Relentless waves convulsed Leanne Soulsby into a wailing wreck. Her hair came undone on one side and hung in front of her face. When the tears eventually stopped, she tucked the errant strand back in place, sniffed noisily, and rubbed her eyes with the heel of her hand.

'Right. What do you want to know from me, Detective?'

'Did Bobbi have a boyfriend?'

'No. She dated, but not for a while. Too preoccupied with the court case.'

'I'll need names and addresses of anyone she saw. Can you get them for me?'

'We never really talked much about each other's blokes. As I say, she hasn't seen anyone for a couple of years or so.'

Lucy noticed Leanne fiddled with her phone in the pocket of her gown.

'Bobbi didn't have her mobile on her when she was found. Is it here?'

'Not sure.'

'If it is here, we'll need it so we can check her contacts.'

Leanne nodded. 'Okay.'

'Did Bobbi have any enemies?'

'Ha,' Leanne spat. 'You either loved Bobbi or hated her. So, no enemies as such, but plenty won't have a good word to say about her.'

Lucy breathed out through her nose. 'Family?'

'Yep, they'd be on the list.'

'I meant did she have any?'

'Just her parents. They didn't get on. Her dad founded the Jackdaw Building Society. He's worth a fortune. I guess you know that already.' Lucy nodded. 'Her folks thought she was a lazy cow, sponging of them and such like, so they cut off the allowance they were paying her.'

Interesting, Lucy thought. *I'll let the DCI know in case the family kept that little nugget to themselves.* 'When was this, Leanne?'

Leanne shrugged. 'Dunno. Two years ago. Maybe less. Around the time Bobbi started getting into trouble.'

'If she had no money, how did she pay for all this,' Lucy gestured around the apartment, 'And how could she afford to take you on holiday?'

Leanne didn't want to say it. Couldn't bring herself to implicate her BFF. But, she had to – it was the only way.

'Bobbi could afford it because she *did* it. She told me as much. Bobbi scammed that Paddock woman.'

Her eyes widened.

'Oh my God. Paddock's son: he threatened Bobbi. It's him. It must be!'

123

CHAPTER SEVENTEEN

Lyall Parker and Ryan Jarrod stared up at the large Victorian house in the affluent Gosforth suburb.

'Nice,' Ryan commented.

'Wouldnae expect anything less. If Bobbi Cavell could scam Mrs Paddock out of two-hundred grand, she's obviously nae living on her uppers. Come on, let's see what they've to say for themselves. Especially that son of theirs.'

They walked down an illuminated path, through a front garden framed by mature trees. There was no doorbell, only a brass gargoyle knocker. Lyall rapped it loudly.

Eunice Paddock recognised them instantly. 'Detective Inspector Parker,' she said. 'How good of you to check on us. Please, come in. You, too, Detective Sergeant...'

'Jarrod,' Ryan prompted.

'Of course.'

Eunice's husband looked up from his newspaper as they entered the lounge. 'The Detectives have come to check on us, Alan. Good of them isn't it?'

Alan Paddock folded away The Mercury. The headline stared up at them. *'Hunt for killer of local woman underway.'*

'Indeed it is, dear.' Alan looked up at Lyall and Ryan as he said, 'But we're fine. It's only money. I just wish they'd found the little madam guilty, spoilt brat that she is.'

Lyall sympathised with them. 'Aye. Sorry we didnae do enough.'

'On the contrary, Detective Inspector. You did everything you could. Not your fault the judicial system failed us.'

'Good of you to say so,' Lyall smiled. 'Is your son around? We'd like to check he's okay, too.'

The living room door opened. Tyler Paddock marched in, his dark hair raised by the Alice band around his head. 'I'm here.'

'Tyler, the Detectives have called in to check on us,' Eunice explained.

Tyler harrumphed.

Lyall Parker's tone changed. 'Actually, we'd like to ask you about court last week.'

'What about it?'

'About your altercation with Roberta Cavell,' Ryan said.

'That's all it was: an altercation. Thanks to you.'

'And if I hadn't intervened, would it have become summat more than an altercation?'

Tyler shrugged.

'What would you have done if I hadn't stepped in?'

The man shrugged again, avoiding eye contact.

Alan Paddock frowned. 'Where's this going, Detective Sergeant?'

Lyall and Ryan remained silent, waiting for Tyler to speak first. A game of verbal chess.

'Alright. I said something to that stupid bitch who scammed my mother out of her savings but that's all it was; just words.'

'Your mother's savings – or your inheritance?'

'Really,' Alan bristled, 'There's no call for this.'

Lyall ignored him. 'What exactly did you say, Tyler?'

Tyler Paddock threw up his hands in exasperation. 'I can't remember. Something about getting my own back, or words to that effect.'

'What did you mean by that?'

Eunice and Alan Paddock exchanged confused glances.

'Nothing, really. Look, I was upset.'

'Angry?' Ryan asked.

'What do you think? Of course I was angry. After what she did, I think it's my right to be angry.'

It was Lyall and Ryan's turn to look at one-another. 'Your right. You said it was *'your right'*. What do those words mean to you?'

Tyler looked perplexed. Wiped sweat from his upper lip. 'I don't understand. Has something happened?' Genuine concern ate at his face.

Lyall sat back. Folded his arms. 'Roberta Cavell has been murdered.'

The Paddock family let out a collective, 'What?'

'Yes. Murdered. Your father's just been reading about it,' Lyall motioned towards the newspaper with his head.

'Oh sweet Jesus. You don't think it was me, surely?'

Lyall played the younger Paddock like a cat with a mouse. 'Hmm. Let me think for a moment. Roberta Cavell robbed you of your inheritance. DS Jarrod and ma'sel – not to mention dozens of others – heard you threaten Miss Cavell. And, you've said you thought it was your right to threaten her.'

Tyler Paddock was floundering now, thrashing about like a landed trout. 'Proves nothing. It can't prove anything because I didn't do it.' He looked towards his mother and father huddled together on the sofa. 'Honestly. I didn't. I couldn't kill someone.'

'Tyler, Roberta Cavell's body was desecrated. She had words carved into her corpse.'

'So?'

'The words were, *'My right.'* Those were the words you've just used to justify your threats against her.'

**

Jarrod and Parker sat in silence in the DI's car outside the City and County CID's Forth Street HQ.

Eventually, Ryan spoke.

'Fucking hell. I thought we had him, man.'

'Me too, laddie. Me too.'

'It all added up. Means, motive, opportunity: we had him hook, line, and sinker.'

'Aye, we did. Until we told him the time of death. Then, he magicked up an alibi which stands up.'

'It seems to, aye, but does he really look like the kind of person who'd do voluntary work, Lyall?'

Parker sighed. 'Disnae matter what I think. We've checked it out and the charity confirms he was on duty with them.'

'At that time of the morning? Howay, man – we get paid but I wouldn't want to work at that hour if I could get away with it.' Lyall said nothing so Ryan continued. 'Could he have snuck away? I mean, how long would it take?'

Lyall shook his head. 'You're clutching at straws. The records show he called the charity from a phone in Widdrington to report his arrival, and again when he left. Tyler Paddock was in Northumberland. There's no way he could get from Widdrington to Shields and back in time to commit Cavell's murder.'

'Jesus. So, we're no further forward?'

'Disnae look like it. We'll head up to the bullpen. See what the others have come up with.'

'They won't have anything, Lyall. I'm sure of it. If it's not Cavell, it isn't any of the other suspects I listed. I'd lay good money on it.'

**

Up in the bullpen, Lyall and Jarrod felt deflated. Superintendent Maynard, on the other hand, was angry; angrier than Ryan had ever seen her.

'Fan-fucking-tastic,' she scowled. 'Three quarters of my team on the case, and we've got sod all.'

'Ma'am, I still think there's some mileage to be had with Tyler Paddock. I know he's provided an alibi…'

'Which is watertight, DS Jarrod. Of all the suspects on here,' Maynard waved a hand in the direction of the board, 'I agree he's the most likely. But an alibi is an alibi. Sorry, Ryan, even my dream team – you and Lyall – can't win this one.' The angry red in Maynard's cheeks faded and her tone

127

mellowed as she turned to Lucy. 'Anything else you can give me on the flatmate?'

'Sorry, ma'am. I've told you all I know. No-one can back up her story because she was home alone, but I'm sure her reaction to my questions were genuine. And she showed me the message Cavell sent her confirming she'd booked a holiday.'

'Have we found Cavell's mobile?'

'Yes, ma'am. It was in the apartment.'

'The apartment she shared with Leanne Soulsby. Which means Soulsby could have sent the message from our victim's phone to her own. Come on, Lucy; you can do better than that.'

Lucy reddened. 'I've checked the time of the message. Roberta Cavell was still alive when it was sent, ma'am.'

'Soulsby could have had it all planned. She could have sent the message at a time which would clear her.'

Ravi Sangar, computer forensic lead, spoke up. 'I've checked the phone records and in my view the message was sent by Cavell, not Soulsby.'

'And you're reasoning is?'

'Four years ago, before the victim and Soulsby were closely affiliated, Cavell sent a similar message to her parents, using the exact same string of emojis she attached to the message she sent Soulsby. I think it's highly unlikely Leanne Soulsby would replicate those precisely.'

Sam Maynard rubbed her forehead. 'Thoughts, Stephen?'

'I hate to say it, but I agree with Ravi. And I'm convinced it's not Cavell's parents. So, from what Lyall and Jarrod say it can't be Paddock, which leaves us with Timothy Rice – and it's not him because he isn't capable of writing on the poor lass's belly.'

'Jesus Christ,' Maynard kicked the crime board in frustration. 'What about Rice's aunt?'

Ryan shook his head. 'Sorry, ma'am. She's too frail.'

Sam Maynard tilted her head towards the ceiling, puffed out her cheeks, then looked at each of the team in turn. 'That's it, then. After the best part of a week, we're no further forward.'

The squad hung their heads to avoid the Super's piercing eyes. They remained in silence for seconds which felt like minutes. At length, Ryan spoke.

'I know the DCI prefers to deal in facts rather than speculation, but can I suggest something?'

'Go on.'

'If we assume this is a revenge crime, or something relating to the trial, our culprit has to have been in the courtroom.'

'What's your line of thought leading to?'

'Well, Judge Hogarth accepted a majority verdict, ten/two. What if one of the two dissenters took things into their own hands? Felt it was their right to dispense justice of their own?'

'They'd have to be a sick fucker to think she deserved that, though,' Todd Robson objected.

'Being a 'sick fucker' isn't on the list of reasonable grounds to avoid jury duty, much as I'd like it to be,' Danskin said. 'You could be onto something, Jarrod.'

Sam Maynard's eyes regained their sparkle. 'I agree. I'll sort the paperwork out. Ryan, you're still working with Lucy in the main, aren't you? I want the pair of you down at the lawcourts. Pronto.'

She stared at the images of Roberta Cavell's body affixed to the crime board.

'I want to know who the hell sat on that jury.'

CHAPTER EIGHTEEN

Victoria Tunnel
Ouseburn

The man awoke with difficulty. He felt nauseous, had a splitting headache, aching shoulders, and wet feet.

When he opened his eyes, things got worse.

'What the hell…'

Once his eyes adjusted to the pitch blackness, he realised he was inside a tunnel. The narrow confines of the brick-built walls closed in on him, its roof arcing inches above his head. His toes trailed in ice-cold, thick water.

'Fucking hell.' He struggled to make sense of it all, but the more he tried the less sense it made. His gut churned as gastric juices rose from his digestive tract and lodged in his throat.

His whole body ached with cold. He looked down. He wore no clothes.

'Oh fuck.'

He looked up, and panic engulfed him. He was chained to metal runners either side of the tunnel's roof.

'Oh fuck. Oh fuck! OH FUCK!!'

He felt a shoulder dislocate as he struggled against the chains. The man screamed in pain. The scream echoed again and again down the long, dank passage.

'Awake at last, I see.' A stranger's voice came from behind him. He tried to twist his head but was unable to do so.

'Where the fuck is this? What's going on?'

'This is a magnificent feat of construction. It's the Victoria Tunnel. It runs all the way from the Town Moor down to the

Ouseburn and the Tyne. We are near the Ouseburn entrance, if it's important to you.'

'No. It isn't fucking important. What the hell are you doing, you madman?'

The stranger's laugh resonated against the tunnel walls. 'That is just so ironic coming from you, William Vickers.'

'What? How do you know my name?' William thrashed against his restraints until something wet and furry brushed against his leg. 'Uuurgh. Rats. Oh no, man. Get it away from me. Jesus, please get it away from me.' William cried unashamedly.

'Rats aren't a problem,' the voice said, inching closer. 'I may be, though.'

'I know people who'll sort you out. Do you hear me? They'll come for you once I'm out.'

'Do you really think you're getting out of here?'

A figure slowly appeared in front of William. It wore waterproof clothing, gloves, wellington boots – and a gas mask.

'Oh sweet Jesus,' Vickers whispered.

'No. I'm not Jesus,' the voice came again. For the first time, it dawned on Vickers that the voice was male. Until then, it hadn't seemed important. Now, somehow, it did.

'What do you want?'

The man pushed his masked face against Vickers. 'I want what is right.' The voice came through the gasmask's filter as a serpentine hiss.

'Oh, fucking hell, man. What do you mean?'

'Exactly what I say, William Vickers. I want what is right. It's my right to have it, too.'

Vickers took the man in. 'I don't understand any of this.'

'I want what is right for Carmen.'

All remaining colour drained from Vickers' face.

'Who's Carmen?' he stuttered.

The man took a couple of steps back. Looked Vickers up and down. 'You know who Carmen is.'

'She led me on. It was all her fault. She consented. It was all her idea. She's a whoring bitch.'

The voice spoke slowly, as icy as the water beneath William Vickers' toes. 'She was sixteen. And you knew how old she was, but you didn't care. You destroyed her.'

Vickers tried to squirm away from the man. 'My childhood was fucked up, too. I got over it. So will she.'

'You didn't get over it. You proved you didn't the moment you stuck your cock up Carmen Best's arse.'

'I didn't.'

'Yes, you did. You've just told me you did. You said it was all her fault.'

Another rat reared up on its hind legs and sniffed at Vickers toes. He didn't care about rats anymore.

'Please. It wasn't how it seems.'

'Yes, William - it was EXACTLY how it seems. And now, I'm going to give you a little taster of how it seemed to Carmen Best.'

Vickers yanked at his chains, squirmed like a worm, kicked his feet until filthy water caked his legs. 'You're a bastard,' he yelled.

'No. I'm right.'

**

Half a mile along the Newcastle Quayside, Ryan and Lucy made it into the Law Courts building moments before it closed.

A cleaner already sat astride a buggy steering it in a series of figure of eight movements across the lobby floor. Bristled mops, like circular toilet brush heads, spun on either side of the buggy.

Ryan sprinted across in front of the machine while Lucy waited for the driver to pass by her. The cleaner swore as Lucy's shoes left dirty footprints across the patch of floor he'd just cleaned.

By the time Lucy caught up with Ryan, he was already knocking on the Court Clerk's perspex screen. 'Hello? Anyone still there?'

'Court's finished for the day,' a woman's voice said from behind the half-open door of a back office.

'Police,' Ryan said, firmly.

The sound of a wheeled chair trundling across the floor was followed by the face of a woman in the door's maw. 'Evening, officers. You're late, aren't you? We should be all locked up by now.'

'We're investigating a murder. They don't run to a timetable.'

'A murder, eh? We don't get many of them in here. Murder*ERS*, yes. Murders, no,' the woman said as she sauntered towards the front desk.

'I need the list of jurors for a recent trial.'

'Detective, I know you have authority to access the names of jurors, but you know that I know you need a warrant first.'

'Will this do?' Ryan held up his phone to show a scanned image of the paperwork Superintendent Maynard had sent through to him.

'I need the hard copy,' the woman said.

Ryan congratulated himself on not shouting *'Jobsworth'* out loud. 'Trust me, if we had time, I'd have brought it with me. This really can't wait until tomorrow.'

'I'd like to help, but...'

'We need to find out who may have committed this crime, man, and we need to know this instant. Like, now. If you'd just accept this image in lieu of the paperwork, I promise I'll get the actual warrant to you in the morning.'

The woman looked between Ryan and Lucy. Finally, she made a decision. 'This way,' she said.

'Cheers. I really appreciate it. Thank you.'

The woman led them into a back office. When prompted, Ryan gave the woman the case reference number. She typed out the details and swivelled her monitor so the screen wasn't visible to Ryan or Lucy.

'Do you want the full list?'

'Unless you have some way of knowing which way each jury member voted, then aye - we do.'

The woman looked up from her monitor with disdain. 'Detective, no-one but those present in the jury room know the answer to that one. No, I meant do you need the stand-by jurors, too?'

Ryan thought for a moment. 'No. Just the twelve sitting members.'

The woman's finger hovered over her keyboard. 'You shred this in front of me once you've got what you need from it, okay?'

Ryan gave an exasperated sigh. 'Aye, I will. DC Dexter will note down anything we need. Now, the list. Please.'

The woman hit print.

The paper seemed to take an eon to emerge from the printer.

The woman made to hand Ryan the sheet, snatched it away from him for a last-minute check, before finally passing it over.

'It's in alphabetical order. Take what you need, then shred it.' The woman glanced at her watch. 'I was due off duty nearly quarter of an hour ago. You've five minutes.'

It took Ryan much less than five minutes to find all he needed. As Lucy peered over his shoulder and began jotting down names, Ryan was already at the bottom of the list.

'God, no. Shit. No, it can't be. Please tell me it's not. Oh, fuck.' His voice choked with emotion.

'Not what, Ryan?' Lucy asked, perplexed.

'It's a set up. I think this whole thing is a set up to get me out in the open. Hell, Lucy; I've gone and broken cover, haven't I? None of this has anything to do with Roberta Cavell. None of it. It's all about me, and I don't know what to do. I really don't know what to do.'

Ryan handed the sheet to Lucy before he dropped himself onto a chair, shoulders drooped, head in hands.

While the Court Clerk shrugged herself into a thick coat and plugged in the shredder, the paper in Lucy's fingers began to shake and tremble.

Lucy Dexter had reached the twelfth juror.

The name leapt out and constricted her throat.

Juror number twelve was listed as a Lei Zhan Yu.

CHAPTER NINETEEN

Ryan sat in Maynard's office, head bowed, eyes red-rimmed; his left hand clasped in Lucy Dexter's right. She gently stroked the old scar on his palm with her thumb.

For the last hour, Sam Maynard and Stephen Danskin had taken it in turns to watch over him while the other kept the squad ticking over. Now, finally, both Super and DCI were in the office together.

Ryan was mumbling. 'I thought I was getting over it. I was just pulling my life back together again. It'll never end, though. Not as long as Yu's out there. This is me for the rest of my life, however long that's going to be.'

'Ryan, listen to me.' Maynard's tone was gentle yet reassuring. 'Yu is not an uncommon name in China. We have nothing to connect Benny Yu to this Lei Zhan Yu. Nothing whatsoever. I've got Rick Kinnear's crew working with Ravi Sangar on the collection of background info on Lei Zhan as we speak. And I've been on to my Met colleagues. They've confirmed they've received no intelligence which indicates Benny Yu is back in the country. This is most likely nothing more than a co-incidence.'

The thunder of a train leaving the Central Station echoed Ryan's heartbeat. Whilst he waited for the noise to subside, he considered Maynard's words. 'You're playing roulette with my life, ma'am. We don't know it's a coincidence. The manner of the killing, the torture, the pain inflicted; they're all the hallmarks of Benny Yu.'

Lucy Dexter stood, still clasping Ryan's hand, and kissed the crown of his head. Ryan leant into her. 'Ma'am, why are you so certain Benny Yu isn't involved?' Dexter asked.

'I can't be certain, I've got to be honest, but let's think about it for a moment. The Met intelligence is normally dependable. They say Benny Yu isn't in the country. Second, if we think Lei Zhan is related to Benny Yu, how could he have ensured Lei Zhan was on jury duty?'

'Why don't you bring him in? You'll find out that way.'

'Ryan, listen to me. What grounds do we have to question Lei Zhan? All he's done is perform his public duty. For all we know, he could have been one of the ten who found Cavell guilty. Statistically, he probably did.'

'Ma'am, if Benny Yu managed to get him on jury duty, it doesn't matter which way he judged her. Lei Zhan's there for only one thing: to hunt me out.'

'There's no way Yu could fix it for Lei Zhan to be on that jury.'

Danskin spoke quietly. 'With respect, ma'am, we don't know how far Yu's influences run.'

Maynard's eyes ordered Danskin to shut up. 'Most of all, the reason I think this has nothing to do with Lei Zhan,' she continued, 'Is that a killing of this nature isn't something a novice could plan and act out. Lei Zhan doesn't have previous or he wouldn't be called to jury…'

'That's not strictly true,' Danskin corrected her before her eyes froze him again.

The Super expanded on her reasoning. 'Alright, then, he could have minor cautions or a suspended sentence somewhere in the dim and distant – Ravi's checks will tell us if he has – but he won't have any majors to his name.'

Ryan vibrated his cheeks. Slowly nodded his head. 'Makes sense, I suppose. I'm still not happy, like.'

'Nor would I expect you to be. And nor would I assume my thinking is automatically correct. So, Stephen and I will look after you until we know for sure.'

Ryan tisked. 'How do you propose to do that?'

Stephen Danskin answered. 'You're off the front-line investigation, for starters.' He expected a rebuff from Ryan, but none came. 'We'll keep you involved in the case, but in the background. Here, at the station.'

'Will you re-instate my security?' Jarrod asked.

'No need,' Maynard said. She held up a hand to repel Ryan's protest. 'There's no need because Stephen says you can stay with him for as long as it takes.'

Lucy Dexter intervened. 'Won't that take your mind of the investigation, sir? Ryan can stay with me.'

'Out of the question, Dexter,' Danskin said, looking at her hand cocooning Ryan's. 'I don't see you as the sort of bodyguard Jarrod requires.'

Maynard agreed. 'Stephen's correct, but it was good of you to offer, Lucy.'

Dexter failed to hide her disappointment.

'Ma'am; sir – that's all well and good for me,' Ryan commented, 'But what about me family? My Dad and brother, and my gran. They're sitting ducks, man.'

'Only if I'm wrong. But, even if I am, Stephen and I haven't been sitting on our hands this past hour. We've things in place.'

'Oh aye. What things?'

'Well, from tomorrow we'll have a uniform presence from the Whickham station inside your Gran's care home. We've already got a marked car sitting outside the home as we speak. She'll be fine. As for your father and ...'

The office door opened. DCI Rick Kinnear poked his head into the office. 'Visitors to see you,' he said, smiling.

'You aal reet, son?'

'Dad!' Ryan rushed into his father's arms. Held him tightly. 'I'm sorry about this. It's all my fault.'

'Hadawayandshite, lad. Course it's not.'

Another voice came from the doorway. 'It is your fault, like; but we'll let you off.'

'Hiya, James. How you doing, kid?'

Ryan's younger brother shrugged. Unrecognizable from the carrot-haired young man of six months ago, James' hair was dyed jet black, bordered by a shaggy ash-white fringe. His eyes looked like Alice Cooper had applied the make-up.

James wore a long black coat, and his feet were encased in heavy boots fastened by chains and clasps which jangled as he walked.

'Christ, you'll be okay,' Ryan said. 'I wouldn't recognise you, never mind Benny Yu.' For the first time since returning to Forth Street, Ryan managed a chuckle.

A thought struck him. 'What about Spud?'

'Don't fret. He's okay. Morag Jacobs from round the corner owed me a favour for fixing her fence after the gales. He's with her. Mind, I'm not sure her cat's ower chuffed about it.'

Ryan laughed again.

Lucy stood next to him. 'We haven't been introduced. I'm Lucy.' She held out a hand towards Ryan's father.

'And?' Norman Jarrod said.

'I'm Ryan's partner.'

Norman raised an eyebrow.

'Work partner,' Ryan qualified.

'Are you sure about that?' Danskin muttered to himself.

Norman ignored her. 'The guy who brought us in – what's his name?'

'DCI Kinnear.'

'Aye, him. He brought us up to speed. He said we'll be aal reet 'til it all blows over.'

Ryan sighed loudly. 'Wish I could be so sure.' He turned to Superintendent Maynard. 'How are you going to look after them and their house?'

'We're not. At least, not the house. But your father and brother will be in the safest place possible.'

Ryan lowered an eyebrow. 'Which is where?'

Maynard smiled. 'In one of our cells.'

'Come again?' Norman Jarrod said.

'Where could be safer?' Maynard proposed. 'You'll be well fed and watered – none of the slop the others get – and I'm arranging for some camp beds to be installed for you. You won't be prisoners, obviously.'

'Brilliant idea!' Ryan exclaimed.

James spoke up. 'You're locking us up, right?'

'In a manner of speaking we are, I suppose,' Maynard agreed

James' face broke into a smile. 'Cool!'

Ryan shook his head before turning his attention to Stephen Danskin. 'In that case, sir, I won't be accepting your offer of accommodation.' Lucy Dexter took Ryan's hand again, misunderstanding his intentions. 'I'll be staying reet here with my family. I'll be staying in the cells an' aal.'

Maynard looked towards Danskin. 'Stephen?'

'Fine by me. Jarrod will be safe and, more importantly, he'll be on call twenty-four hours a day,' the DCI joked.

Lucy felt disappointment, but still clutched Ryan's hand.

'That's settled, then. There's just one loose end to tie up,' Sam Maynard said.

'Which is?' Ryan asked.

'If you're confined to barracks, I'm an officer down. We need to catch whoever did this before the press cotton on to who the victim is. If they link the killing to Jackdaw Building Society, the story will run and run. So, I've got us a replacement lined up for you, Ryan.'

Maynard brushed past him and opened her office door. 'Come in.'

Lucy Dexter released her grip on Ryan's hand as Jarrod's replacement stepped through the door.

'Evening all,' Detective Sergeant Hannah Graves announced.

**

The cells in the Forth Street basement barely had space to accommodate two people let alone three, so Danskin allocated Ryan the cell next to Norman and James. The doors were unlocked, of course, yet something about the surroundings compelled them to stay in their appointed accommodation.

Ryan spent the first part of the night standing on his camp bed speaking to Norman and James through the grill in the cell wall. 'Tell me about this Muzzle lass,' Ryan asked his brother.

'Not much to tell. She lives in Lemington near the river, hangs out around the Eldon Square green on a Saturday afternoon, likes her gaming. That's about it.'

Although the holding cells were relatively modern, their voices still echoed around the four walls.

'What's her name?'

'Muzzle.'

'No, man. Her real name.'

'No idea.'

'You must know what she's called.'

'It's not important. I'm Jam Jar to her and, to me, she's Muzzle.'

'Where'd she get that name from?'

James gave a shrug invisible to Ryan.

'James? Why's she called that?'

'I divvent know. Is it important?'

Ryan asked the first of two questions he'd been leading up to. 'Tell me one thing: is she Oriental?'

'What? Of course she's not but would it matter if she was?'

'It would, actually. What about drug use?'

'Bloody hell, Ry. You're off your trolley, man.'

'It wouldn't be the first time her type had been involved with drugs.'

James couldn't believe what he was hearing. 'By her type, you do realise you're saying my type, don't you? I'm not into drugs, and never would after all that Benny Yu shit. Don't judge a book by its cover, Ryan. I thought you were above this type of prejudice.'

Norman Jarrod joined the conversation. 'It's not prejudice, son. It's cos he's worried she might be involved in all this, somehow.'

James barked a laugh. 'You don't know her, Ryan.'

'Ah, but do YOU? Honestly, do you?'

After a few seconds earnest consideration, James' reply came back firm and confident. 'I reckon so, aye.'

Ryan stood on tip toe until he could just about make out the top of James' dyed head in the adjacent cell. 'Go on, then. Tell me something about her.'

'She went to college. Studied physical education.'

'What did she do after college?'

'Nothing.'

'So, you mean she's a drop-out.'

'No. She had a breakdown, if you must know.'

'Shit. Sorry,' Ryan apologised. He genuinely was sorry. 'Hobbies?'

'Bikes,' came the monosyllabic reply.

'That figures, with her sports studies background.'

'No, man. Motorcycles. Yamahas, in particular.'

Norman Jarrod laughed.

'What's funny about any of this, Dad?' Ryan objected.

'Have you seen yersels? Listened to what the pair of you are saying? Tonight's straight out of The Great Escape. Remember Ives and Hilts in the cooler? When Hilts asked Ives if he rode – meaning a motorbike - and Ives replied *'Yes, I'm a jockey'*?' That's where this conversation's going.'

They did remember. The film was a family favourite. Ryan and James got the reference. Their laughter broke the coldness of the exchange.

James' voice lost its defensive tension as he said, 'Ry, I need some kip now, yeah? We'll catch up tomorrow but take it from me - Muzzle's all reet.'

'Okay kidda. Sorry 'bout that but I had to ask. We'll chat in the morning. Mind, you'll have to be up sharp. I'm on duty at seven.'

'Seven?! Pfftt. Bollocks to that.'

The Jarrod family laughed together once more, and Ryan settled down for the night content that he and his family were safe. For now.

CHAPTER TWENTY

At six fifty-five, Ryan pulled open the unlocked cell door, surprised at how well he'd slept.

He'd found the camp bed comfortable and the duvet snug. The portable heater Maynard had installed helped, too, but, most of all, the sound of his father and brother snoring peacefully next door brought him the comfort of a mother's heartbeat to an unborn child.

Now, though, it was time for work.

The narrow corridor outside the cells turned at a ninety-degree angle and, as Ryan took the blind corner, he walked straight into someone heading in the opposite direction.

'Well good morning,' Hannah said, rubbing her breast were Ryan's elbow had caught it.

'Oh hi. Sorry 'bout that,' Ryan said, feeling awkward. 'What're you doing, anyway? Has the DCI sent you to make sure I'm fit for duty?'

'Not exactly, no. I've been working with Ravi on the night shift. Gathering intel on t'other Yu.'

'And?'

'Could be something, probably nothing. Stephen's bringing the squad up to speed once everybody's in. I'll let him tell you with them. I'm bushed, Ry. I need me pit.'

Ryan caught her elbow. 'You're staying down here as well?'

She looked at him. 'Aye. I am. Remember I'm in Benny Yu's sights almost as much as you are so, until we know whether this has owt to do with him...' She left the sentence hanging.

'Which *room*,' he made air quotes, 'Are you in?'

'Yours. We're sharing.'

Ryan's jaw dropped open. 'With my Dad and brother next door? Howay, man. That's just not right.'

Hannah looked at his hand on her arm. 'Don't get ahead of yourself. We'll be ships passing in the night. Super's got me and Ravi on permanent nights 'til this is all over. She still doesn't want us working together.'

Ryan checked his watch. 'I'd better get up to the bullpen. See you sometime, then.'

'Okay.'

They walked off in opposite directions. 'Hannah – it's good to have you back,' Ryan said.

She turned and offered him a smile. 'I'm pleased to be back. And it's good to be see you again. Really.'

'And you.'

Hannah turned her back on him so he couldn't see her smile as she added, 'Judging by the look she gave me, I don't think Lucy Dexter feels the same.'

**

Nigel Trebilcock doled out bacon stotties and mugs of coffee to the squad gathered for Danskin's briefing.

The DCI stood in front of the crime board, Lyall Parker to one side, Ravi Sangar the other. Looking on were Todd Robson, Lucy Dexter, and three of Rick Kinnear's team temporarily brought in as support. Lucy slalomed through the crowd until she was next to Ryan.

'Morning, Ryan.' She took a sip from her coffee mug and licked her lips. 'Pleasant dreams?'

Christ, you're so obvious, Ryan thought. 'I didn't dream.' Looking up, he addressed DCI Danskin. 'Sir, I'd like to know what Hannah and Ravi found about Lei Zhan. It kinda' matters to me, y'know?'

'I do know, Jarrod. And the sooner we rule out any connection with Benny Yu, the quicker we can get on with finding Roberta Cavell's murderer.'

'Assuming it's not Lei Zhan, that is.'

'Patience, Jarrod. We'll find out soon enough. Where's O'Hara got to? We can start as soon as…'

The bullpen doors swung open. 'Sorry I'm late, sir,' a breathless Gavin O'Hara said. 'Lift's playing up. Took the stairs,' he explained, also taking a sarnie from Trebilcock's stainless steel platter.

'Reet. Sangar, take the stage, please. Let us know what you and Graves have on Lei Zhan, then you can get off to bed and we'll get on with the case.'

Ravi Sangar pinned a photograph to the board.

'Lei Zhan Yu was a member of the jury sitting on the Roberta Cavell fraud case.' He tapped a marker pen against the image of Roberta's body. 'This is what happened to her. For the benefit of DCI Kinnear's lads, we need to rule out Lei Zhan being her killer.'

'Apart from being on the jury, why do you think Lei Zhan may be involved?' one of the newcomers asked.

Ravi considered his words carefully. 'Because of potential links, no matter how tenuous, to a Benny Yu. The latter Yu was investigated as part of Operations Tower and Sage and has gone off-map since the investigation collapsed; but not before he made threats to the life of DS Jarrod. So, you see, that's why Superintendent Maynard has bumped him up the suspect list. We must rule out any connection between the two Yu's, PDQ.'

Ryan cleared his throat. 'And have you?'

Ravi sighed. 'Yes and no.'

Ryan rolled his eyes. 'What's that supposed to mean?'

'We have a file on Lei Zhan Yu. Only, it's not our Lei Zhan Yu. Yu Senior – our man's father - has numerous minor drug offences against his name. Possession, not dealing, before anyone jumps to conclusion he's part of the YuTube drugs line.'

'Have uniform spoken to Zhan senior?' DC Trebilcock asked.

'No, Treblecock,' Sangar replied, addressing the DC by his nickname, 'We haven't. Before you ask, it's because he died three years ago.'

'Cause of death?' Parker enquired.

'Stroke. Nothing suspicious was raised at the post-mortem.'

'Okay,' Ryan said, 'Let's get this right. We've now got two Lei Zhan Yu's; the dead man and our jury member. For the sake of me heed, do either have any connection with Benny Yu?'

'Not as far as we know.'

'Not good enough, Ravi. I need to know.'

Danskin intervened. 'I understand your concerns, Jarrod; I really do. But give Sangar a break. He's worked through the night on this, and we all know we've virtually nothing on Benny Yu's background. So, it's as Sangar says: Not as far as we know.' He held up a hand to quash Ryan's protest. 'But we'll have him watched for a couple of days. See if he raises any suspicions.'

'Sir, can't we just bring him in?'

'Nothing's changed, Jarrod. We still haven't got any grounds.'

Ravi Sangar spoke again. 'We know where he lives and where he works. We can have him watched while I do some more digital forensic work on him.'

Ryan let out a breath. 'It's a start, I suppose. Where does he live?'

'He's got a place on Blackfriars Court, backing onto the old City Walls just off Chinatown.'

'And he works?'

'Grainger Market. He runs a street food stall.'

Ryan checked his watch. 'He'll be setting up soon. I might just have a wander ower and check him out.'

'You most certainly will not!' Danskin thundered. 'You're confined to barracks, if you haven't forgotten,' – he had –

'And you and Lyall were in court. We can't risk him recognising you.'

Danskin glanced around the assembled squad.

'But I do agree the Grainger Market is the least obvious place to observe him. Todd, you and me will check him out. Market will open in less than an hour. Don't take another sarnie because we're having a Chinese as soon as we get there.'

'I prefer Indian, sir.'

'Doh – with a name like Lei Zhan Yu, he's not likely to rustle you up a Biryani, is he?'

Todd shrugged. 'Fair point.'

'Right. Me and Robson will check him out. Sangar, get a few hours kip. The rest of you I want flat-out discovering which other sickos have a motive for killing Roberta Cavell.'

**

The John Dobson-designed Grainger Market, busy, vibrant, and bustling, is still one of Newcastle's secret gems two-hundred years since it first opened its doors.

Todd Robson sniffed the air. 'Man, this takes us back. I used to love coming here as a kid.'

'You surprise me, Robson. I didn't have you down as the shopping type.'

'Came here with me mam aal the time. There were cobblers, greengrocers, a place you used to get saveloy dips. You could get owt you wanted.' Todd looked up in awe at the arced glass roof and metal-railed terraces which could have been lifted from Bourbon Street. 'Fan-bloody-tastic,' he said.

'Is that a tear in your eye, Robson?' Stephen Danskin said with amusement.

'Nah but it's bloody great, isn't it? It's like summat you'd see in a period drama. I remember there was a set of jockey scales you could sit on. As soon as I'd been weighed, I'd get a load of ket from the old-fashioned sweet shop while me mother went round aal the butchers looking for a chicken for Sunday dinner.'

'Don't tell me – you had Hovis and reel butta' for tea, I bet. Bloody hell. Where's Todd Robson gone? Hello - has anyone seen Robson?' Danskin twirled around, asking strangers.

'Shut up, man. Let's find this Yu bloke.'

They explored a couple of avenues before finding Lei Zhan Yu's establishment. They walked casually by, no sign of Yu, and took refuge in a coffee bar which overlooked Yu's stall.

Outside, six black metal stools faced the counter of the understated, open-fronted stall. It was situated on the apex of two aisles. On the blind-side of the service counter, four circular tables cluttered the aisle, each surrounded by cold metal chairs.

Fifteen minutes went by. No-one approached carrying a violin case, a brick of cocaine, or anything seen in Kill Bill.

Finally, a guy wandered up to the counter. He picked up a laminated menu, beckoned his Asian girlfriend over, and Lei Zhan appeared from a tiny back kitchen as if the customer had rubbed Aladdin's lamp.

'There's our man,' Danskin said.

Yu was a short bloke of wiry build. He wore a red shirt beneath a red apron. He had black hair cut in the style of Kim Jong-Un, most of which was hidden beneath a white cap. Yu appeared innocuous enough. He noted the couple's order and slunk back into the kitchen while they occupied one of the tables.

Todd rubbed his nose and drained his coffee. 'So, what's the plan? We stay here all day, or what?'

Danskin lowered himself from the coffee shop stool. 'Fancy something to eat?' he said, leaving Robson with no choice as he exited the café.

The air in the aisle was already thick with the smell of food ebbing from patisseries, pizza stalls, a jerk chicken place, and Lie Zhan's tiny restaurant.

'Would yous like a menu?' Zhan's accent was less Guangzhou, more Gateshead High Street.

'Anything you'd recommend?'

'It's a bit nippy being so close to the exit. How aboot a bowl of noodle soup?'

Danskin wrinkled his nose as he scanned the single-sheet menu. 'I'll have a couple of dumplings: pork and cabbage and chicken and mushroom.'

'Canny choice, there. And you?' Lei Zhan asked Robson.

'Don't suppose you've got a Biryani, have you?' Danskin stamped on Todd's foot. 'Ouch! I guess that's a no.'

Todd's eyes roamed the menu. 'I'll have a Char Siu stuffed bun.' He chose it purely because he didn't have a clue what a Char Siu stuffed bun was, and it couldn't be less appetising than anything else on the menu.

When Yu disappeared into the back, Robson asked what their tactics were.

'We eat,' Danskin replied. 'Then, we go with our gut.'

'From the smell back there, I reckon wor guts will take us straight to the bog.'

**

Their food arrived in ten minutes. They perched on the counter stools and Yu went backstage to give them space.

Danskin was impressed with his dish. 'If he really is a fucked-up killer, he's a bloody good cook.'

Todd wrinkled his brow. 'You sure? It looks minging to me.'

Danskin pushed his plate towards Robson. 'Try it.'

'No ta. I'll stick to this.' He took his first bite. Raised his eyebrows in surprise. 'Hey, it's canny, man.' He brushed a piece of meat into his mouth. 'It's just like barbecued pork.'

'That's 'cos that's what Char Siu is.'

'Oh. You could have told me. I'd have ordered two if I'd known.'

'Right. Let's see what his reaction to this is.' Danskin rapped his knuckles on the counter.

Lei Zhan Yu appeared from the back. 'Enjoy it, lads?'

Danskin told him they had. He opened his wallet in front of the restauranteur and whipped out a twenty-pound note.

Yu's expression became serious as he handed Danskin his change. 'Cheers,' the DCI said as he dropped a couple of pound coins into an open-topped porcelain cat at the side of the counter.

'Thank you.' Yu's reply was curt.

Danskin slipped off his stool and made for the exit to Grainger Street. Robson followed. 'That was the grand plan, sir, was it? Get some scran and leg it?'

'Not exactly, no.'

Out on the street, swallowed up by traffic noise and shoppers, Robson raised his arms in the air. 'So what do we do now?'

Danskin turned to face him. 'You really aren't very observant, Robson.'

'Waddya mean?'

Danskin looked him in the eye. 'I deliberately opened my wallet in front of him. Did you not notice his attitude change as soon as he saw my ID and realised who we were? Now, I don't think he's our killer, but summat about his reaction stinks as much as the wet fish stall in there.'

Danskin pointed to an entrance to the market further down Grainger Street. 'You go back in via that entrance and wait for my call. I'll take the Grey Street entrance and we'll meet at Yu's.'

The DCI squinted towards Grey's Monument, standing erect between the splayed legs of Grainger and Grey Streets. 'Let's see how our man reacts when he sees us coming again. If he makes a run for it, he's up to something and we bring him in.'

**

'You ready?' Danskin spoke into his mobile.

'Yeah, good to go, sir.'

'Okay. You stay out of sight until I get there. I'll call you when I'm ready.'

Hands in pockets, Robson sauntered by Coleman's Deli, hung around outside Falafel Al Hana, and avoided Marsh Fishmonger's so the smell wouldn't alert Yu to his approach.

Danskin's journey was more eclectic. He strode by a wig store, a barber shop, and a vintage clothing establishment. He pulled his mobile from a pocket and called Robson.

'You ready?'

'Aye. What do we do?'

'Just casually walk towards him, make sure he sees us, and watch how he reacts.'

'Easy money,' Robson said, ending the call.

It seemed like easy money until Yu saw them coming.

The Chinaman vaulted his counter, veered sharp right, and was out onto Grainger Street before either could react.

'Follow him!' Danskin yelled.

Robson raced out into the sunlight. Glanced up the length of Grainger Street, then back down again. A white-capped figure weaved through the crowds.

'Got him! He's ower the road,' Robson yelled, barrelling through a group of teenagers.

Danskin emerged into daylight and joined the chase.

Yu skipped between shoppers, almost collided with a bus stop, and was approaching the Mushroom Bar before he realised Robson was closing on him. Yu ripped off his hat, lifted his arms out of his apron and, at the last minute, sprinted into the road.

'He's heading for Nun Street,' Danskin shouted. 'I think he's gonna lose us back in the market.' He gasped for breath. 'It'll be easier for him to disappear in the narrow alleys.'

'Don't worry. I'm nearly on him.' Robson swerved onto the street. 'I'm gonna get to him before he hits the market.'

Yu made a sprint for Nun Street. The market entrance was less than fifty yards away. He looked over his shoulder, legs pumping, arms flaying. He turned back just as a City scooter emerged onto Grainger Street from Nun Street.

Its rider collided with Yu. Scooter, rider, and Yu spiralled over the tarmac. Yu struggled to his feet. Yelled 'Fuck you,' at the man lying on the road and, still half-crouched and dragging a leg behind him, dashed onto Nun Street.

Straight into the path of the number seventy-one to Throckley.

'Ah Jesus, man,' Todd moaned, drawing to a stop. 'What the hell did you have to do that for?'

Danskin raced past him. Skidded to the ground alongside Yu.

Dazed passengers stepped from the bus, then at once clambered back on board, mobiles glued to their ears. Shoppers screamed at the sight of the stricken man, his body bent and broken.

Danskin felt for a pulse. 'Call an ambulance,' he shouted at the crowd.

Lei Zhan Yu raised his head from the road surface. Blood oozed from the back of his skull like yolk from a cracked egg.

Yu opened his mouth to say something. His eyes flickered, glazed over, and his head sank back onto the road.

Danskin knelt alongside him. Clenched a fist. Unclenched it. Lowered his head.

'Fucking great,' he cursed through gritted teeth. 'Just fucking great.'

CHAPTER TWENTY-ONE

Sam Maynard silently closed her office door. Two men sat with their backs to her. Two of HER men. Two officers involved in the death of a man.

'That's the Independent Office for Police Conduct informed. Now, before I hear from them again, I want to hear it from you. What the hell happened?'

Robson was more than happy to let his DCI do the talking. Danskin explained their approach to Yu, his reaction at the sight of Danskin's ID, and his dash for freedom – or death.

'You were under orders not to identify yourselves.'

'We didn't. Not formally. Not my fault if he chose to freerun all over the Toon.'

'I hope you'll choose your words with more care when the IOPC contact you.'

Danskin shrugged. 'Sorry, ma'am. Anyway, we know the IOPC enquiry's just a tick-the-box exercise. Once they know what he did to Cavell…'

'Stephen – he did nothing to Roberta Cavell.'

'No? Then why the hell scarper the way he did? It's the whole YuTube operation back in business.'

'I agree the IOPC are unlikely to pursue the matter, but Lei Zhan Yu didn't kill Roberta Cavell.'

'How do you know? Come on, an innocent man wouldn't react the way he did.'

Sam Maynard answered softly. So softly, Danskin knew it was her way of delivering a bollocking.

'I didn't say he was an innocent man. But he is innocent of the murder of Cavell.'

'How come?'

Sam Maynard rested both palms on her desk. She leant forward, and her ice-blue eyes pierced Danskin like a lightsabre.

'Because Ravi's been looking into him while you two were cocking-up.'

'I ordered Sangar to get some sleep.'

'Good job he's an insomniac, or we wouldn't know that Lei Zhan Yu is a member of an illegal gambling club. They've a den above a Chinese supermarket in Stowell Street. That's where he was at the time of Cavell's death.'

'Shit.'

'Thanks to Ravi, though, we've discovered Lei Zhan is up to his eyes in debt. Rumour has it, he's been laundering money through the accounts of a Chinatown restaurant to pay them off.'

'And he thought we were onto him. That's why he ran for it. He had nowt to do with Roberta Cavell or Benny Yu, did he?'

'Correct.'

'Ah shit and bollocks, man.'

A silence haunted the room. Todd Robson held his breath, not wanting to break it. He hoped Maynard wouldn't notice he was in the office with them. The tactic didn't work.

'Anything to add, Todd?'

'No, ma'am.'

'Right, listen to me, you two. When the IOPC gets in touch, we tell them we had our suspicions about Lei Zhan's scam all along. That's why you were at the market. You had good reason to talk to him, and you were there to interview him under caution. Is that understood?'

'Ma'am,' Danskin and Robson spoke in unison.

Maynard lowered her voice still further. 'I don't need to tell you how much this goes against everything we stand for. That said, I know how IOPC operate. They'll buy it. There'll be no further repercussions. Now, listen to me. I never want to be in this position again. Am I making myself clear?'

Both men nodded.

'Good. Now, get out there and catch me a killer.'

Neither Danskin nor Robson had left the office before Lyall Parker dashed in, face taut with stress.

'Sorry, ma'am, but you need to know. I think we've got oorselves another victim. A man, this time.'

**

Maynard refused to let Danskin and Robson anywhere near the scene. They needed time to digest and reflect on events in the Grainger Market. Instead, Lyall Parker led the operation.

Maynard suggested he take Lucy Dexter with her to provide continuity. After a deal of thought, the Super agreed with Ryan that he should also attend. With all links to Benny Yu written off, Jarrod had no reason to remain under wraps.

DC Dexter was delighted when Lyall Parker ducked into the rear seat of the car, leaving to sneak in alongside her. 'Bonnie and Clyde, back together again,' she said with a glint in her eye.

'They were bad guys, pet. Make it Starsky and Hutch.'

'Who?'

'Never mind.'

They journeyed the short distance along City Road in silence. Lucy pulled up next to a marked car, blue lights flickering brightly.

'I'm DI Parker. Where's the victim?' Lyall asked the vehicle's incumbent.

'Doon there, sir.' The PC showed the direction with a tilt of his head.

The trio passed into the inner police cordon and ducked into a tent erected around the Victoria Tunnel entrance, just up from the quayside and a stone's throw from the Hotel Du Vin.

Two uniformed officers stood guard inside the tent, with another sat on a campstool next to a man in a high-viz vest. The man wore walking boots, jeans and a checked shirt, and bore an armband with the words TOUR GUIDE emblazoned around it.

Ryan had seen the look on the man's face before. It was the same look worn by Timothy Rice at North Shields fish quay.

'Do you mind if I start the chat, sir?'

'Be my guest, laddie,' Parker said.

Ryan slowly approached the man. 'I'm DS Jarrod, and these are DI Parker and DC Dexter. You can call us Ryan, Lyall, and Lucy.'

The man nodded briefly.

'What can I call you?' Ryan asked.

'Jack. Jack Wilson.'

'Okay, Jack. I know you'll have spoken to the constables here already, but I'd like to ask you a few more questions if that's alright. Jack, is that okay?'

'Aye. I suppose.'

Ryan crouched next to Wilson. 'I see you're a Tour Guide. Is that why you were here?'

A nod.

'Doing what, exactly?'

'Checking stuff out. Getting ready for the first tour. It looked like the tunnel door was broken. It was.'

Ryan waited for the man to continue. When he didn't, Ryan gently probed for more. 'What happened next?'

'I went in.' Jack remained silent for a long time. 'I heard shrieking. Scared the shit out of me, it did.'

'He was still alive when you got here?' Ryan asked, hopeful the victim had managed to say something about the attack.

'It wasn't him.'

Balls, Ryan thought. Another idea came to mind. 'Someone else was there?'

Jack Wilson shook his head.

'So, who screamed?'

'I said shriek, not scream.'

Ryan shifted position slightly. 'Okay. Who shrieked, then? Was it a man or woman's voice?'

'Neither.'

Ryan sighed. 'I know this is difficult, Jack, but you're not making sense. Who shrieked?'

'I didn't find him,' Wilson said, eyes brimming with tears. 'The rats did. They were the ones doing the shrieking.'

Jack Wilson's spew splattered over the tent's groundsheet.

**

They stood just inside the tunnel's entrance, its red-painted door ajar.

'You know, I must have walked passed this dozens of times and never even noticed it,' Ryan mused.

'What the hell is it?' Parker thought aloud.

'Nee idea.'

Lucy Dexter did. 'It's an old wagonway. Nineteenth century, I believe. It used to take coal direct from a mine up Spital Tongues way straight down to ships docked on the Ouseburn and Tyne.'

'Really?'

'Yes, really. It even runs under the City Walls and part of Hadrian's Wall, to boot. During the war, it was reopened as a bomb shelter.'

'How do you know all this?' Ryan asked, impressed.

Lucy reminded Ryan of something he'd once said to her. 'Ah well, I've got a sense of belonging after all, haven't I?' She winked at Ryan. 'Actually, I know because I've done the tour. Jack was my guide, I think.'

Ryan snickered. 'Clever shite. Right, let's steel ourselves for this. I reckon it'll be pretty rank.'

They pulled on protective coveralls and picked up a flashlight each. Lucy volunteered to lead the way, relying on muscle memory from her earlier visit.

The threesome walked in single file. The tunnel was barely head high. Lucy and Lyall stood upright, but Ryan's shoulders soon ached from stooping.

Less than a hundred yards from the entrance, the air became stale. Pools of stagnant water dappled the tunnel floor, several of them ankle deep. A rat scuttled by as it was caught in the beam of a flashlight.

'Sweet Jesus, I've seen wee dogs smaller than that,' Lyall swore.

'Bet it bites like one as well,' Ryan added.

They heard activity around the corner as they approached a bend in the tunnel.

'You do realise we're like a Star Trek landing party, don't you? One of us isn't getting oot of here alive,' Ryan joked.

No-one laughed. They didn't laugh because Lucy's flashlight had illuminated the naked man suspended from the ceiling. The activity they'd heard was the scurry and squabble of a dozen rats inspecting the corpse.

'Oh for Christ's sake,' Lyall wheezed.

Ryan let out a lungful of air. The man seemed to dance in front of his eyes until he realised it was an optical illusion. It was the beam of the flashlight in Lucy's trembling hands which leapt and jumped.

Lucy attempted a scream which came out as a hoarse whisper.

'Fucking hell,' she swallowed. 'This is a fucking nightmare.'

Her flashlight fell from her hands and, this time, Lucy did scream.

It echoed down the tunnel like an approaching train. 'His testicles!' she yelled. 'They're moving!!'

'What?' Ryan trained his flashlight on the man's lower body. 'Jesus, Lucy. Switch your light off, Lyall.' Ryan doused his at the same time.

'Why?' In the darkness, Lyall's quiet question sounded as loud as a Muezzin's call to prayer.

'Because Lucy doesn't need see this.'

'See what?' She retrieved her torch, flicked on the light, and saw what she needn't see.

The man's testicles weren't moving. They weren't moving because he had no testicles.

What moved was the lower half of a rat with its head buried inside the man's body cavity where his scrotum once hung.

**

DI Parker ordered Lucy back to base. He told her to engage a baton crew straight away. When asked why, he replied, 'To keep the little furry bastards away from oor victim or there'll be nae body left for Aaron Elliot.'

Once Dexter had been sent packing, Lyall undertook a recce of the body. He walked around the scrawny remains, keeping as close to the tunnel walls as he could to ensure there was no cross-contamination of evidence.

DI Parker noted blood trails down the back of the man's legs. Lyall focussed the flashlight.

'For the love of God,' he exclaimed.

'What you got, Lyall?' Ryan asked.

'We've got a real sicko, that's what we've got.'

Ryan didn't want to know, but he had to ask. 'What's happened?'

'The poor guy's had a Coke bottle rammed up his arse.'

Ryan winced.

'A glass one,' Parker added. 'And by the glass on the deck, I reckon it's shattered inside him.'

Ryan screwed his eyes tight. 'Ah, man.'

Parker circled the body once more. 'That's no' the half of it. The rats didn't get his balls. He's been castrated, I'm pretty sure.'

'We've got a trophy hunter?'

'Some bloody trophy. No, I don't think the killer took them. I think the rats had his discarded Rocky Mountain Oysters for breakfast.'

Ryan swallowed down bile. 'This is seriously fucked up.'

'Och, you're getting nae argument from me.'

Ryan trained his torch on the man's abdomen. The words MY RIGHT, etched above and below the corpse's navel, screamed back at him.

He asked a rhetorical question. 'Apart from *My Right* and the chains, what's this poor bugger got in common with Roberta Cavell? How are they linked?'

'I can't see this wee guy hanging around wi' Cavell. She wouldn't be short of better offers than this fella.'

'True. We need Elliot or Thakur here urgently. See what light they can shed on this one. There might be something in the forensics. At the very least, they should provide summat to help us ID the victim.'

'Good points, Ryan. If you're okay staying here, I'll head back oot and chase their arses. We'll no' get phone signal in the tunnel.'

Ryan wasn't alright, not really. But he agreed to stay.

He agreed because he wanted time to think what could possibly link Bobbi Cavell to the pathetic specimen hanging from the roof bars of the Victoria Tunnel.

There had to be a common denominator.

Finding it was the key to both cases.

CHAPTER TWENTY-TWO

Sam Maynard led the urgent briefing in front of the Roberta Cavell crime board. DCI Rick Kinnear and his team joined Danskin's, while Stephen himself skulked at the back of the crowd, looking contrite.

'We now have two murders with distinct similarities. Joining Roberta Cavell on our board, is this poor sod.'

Maynard fixed the second crime scene photographs to the board. The squad, experienced officers one and all, gasped in horror.

'So, two bodies; one male, one female. One found in North Shields fish market, the other in the Victoria Tunnel near the quayside.' She drew a red marker pen across the two locations on a map. 'A distance of eight point six miles.'

Once again, Danskin was impressed by Maynard's diligence.

'Both bodies were mutilated,' Maynard continued. 'Cavell was scalped, had her face removed, and her fingers amputated. Our unknown male…well, we can see what happened to him.'

The men at the briefing winced. Todd reflexively crossed his hands in front of his genitals, so, too, Nigel Trebilcock.

'Both victims were alive when the mutilations began. Both victims had the words 'My Right' carved onto their abdomen. Thoughts, people, please.'

'Same killer,' Trebilcock said.

'Almost certainly. The details of Cavell's murder haven't been released. Either it's the same culprit, or it's someone who was present at the scene of Cavell's murder. Apart from us and uniform, that leaves one person.' She indicated

Timothy Rice's photograph. 'We'll speak to him again, but we have good reason to believe it isn't him.'

'Do we have an ID for the second victim, ma'am?' Gavin O'Hara asked.

'Negative. Neither his clothing nor any possessions were at the scene. We hope to know more when Dr Elliot has completed the post-mortem.'

Maynard held a silence, encouraging others to take part.

'What does the inscription mean, this *My Right* thing?' one of Kinnear's men asked.

'Good question. Short answer is, we haven't a scooby.'

'Ma'am, if it's not a copycat – and from what you say it can't be – we've a serial killer out there,' Lucy Dexter said.

'Possibly, but not necessarily. Two deaths doth not a serial killer make, though it's a strong possibility. That means we need to catch him – or her – urgently. We all know the press will feed like sharks if they get a sniff of this. Any ideas on the next steps?'

Stephen Danskin knew the answer, he just didn't want to say it. There again, he believed he'd already blown any outside chance he had with Sam Maynard over the Lei Zhan Yu fiasco.

He might as well say it.

'Ma'am, three things strike me. We need to understand what the hell this *My Right* business is all about, we need to stop this maniac from striking again, and to do that we need to get inside his or her head.'

'If it is the same killer,' Maynard reminded everyone. 'You of all people should know not to see what you expect to see, Stephen.'

Danskin ignored the jibe and the laughter of his colleagues. 'With respect, ma'am, I think we all know it's the same perpetrator.'

Sam Maynard's eyes sparkled with curiosity. 'So, what do you suggest?'

'I think we need the input of a forensic psychologist.' Danskin met Maynard's gaze.

'Ma'am, I think we need Fola Fasanya back on the case.'

**

Sam Maynard instructed Lyall Parker to fully brief Fasanya on the latest and also asked him to set up a Zoom conference. Lyall took ownership of the briefing but delegated the Zoom-thing to Ravi Sangar, not having an inkling how to do it himself.

Meanwhile, Maynard invited Danskin into her office.

'Here we go again,' he thought. *'Another bollocking awaits.'*

'I want to thank you, Stephen. I know you don't see eye-to-eye with Fola so it was good of you to suggest we welcome him back.'

Danskin shrugged. 'Seemed the right thing to do, that's all.'

Maynard sighed. 'Listen, Stephen; sit down a moment.'

He did so, fixing his eyes on the desktop.

'I'm more astute than you give me credit for. I know what this thing between you and Fola is about, and it's nothing to do with your previous experience of criminal psychologists; your experience with Imogen Markham.'

Danskin inspected his fingernails whilst reserving his right to remain silent.

'It doesn't need a psychologist to work out you have feelings for me.'

The DCI swallowed his embarrassment.

'You're a good Detective, Stephen. One of the best I've worked with. Your team has your respect, you're good with them, and they'd back you with their lives, I'm sure. What's more, I like you. I really do.'

Stephen raised his head.

'But, you know there's no future in it. None whatsoever. Firstly, you've seen my take on Ryan and Hannah. That's why I had to split them up, at least 'til things cooled down between them. Secondly, it's against the Code of Ethics. You know that as well as I do.'

Stephen lowered his head. He didn't know what to say. What he did say, he wished he hadn't. 'But it's different for you and Fasanya; that's okay, is it?'

'Stephen, look at me. Fola isn't one of my officers.'

Danskin harrumphed.

'More importantly, although it's none of your business, there's nothing between Fola and me.'

Another harrumph.

'There never will be. He's as good as you, Stephen.'

'Whoa, I never said he wasn't. I hope you're not suggesting there's a racial element to this? That's out of order.'

Maynard laughed.

'Sorry, ma'am, I don't think it's funny.'

The Superintendent smiled. 'I'm sorry, I didn't mean it in that sense. I meant he's as good as you.'

Danskin threw up his arms, perplexed.

'Stephen – Fola Fasanya is as good as you. G.A.Y. He's gay.'

Danskin groaned, closed his eyes, and tilted his head back. 'You know when you wish that hole would open up?'

Maynard laughed. 'Forget it. We never had this conversation, and I know this won't distract you from the job. Now, let's see if this conference is set up.'

'Ma'am.'

'Oh, Stephen. Just one more thing.'

She beckoned him towards her.

With an impish smile, she leant forward and kissed him on the cheek.

**

Ravi had the feed ready to go. He'd gone for video conference rather than Zoom with all its inherent 'You're on mute' distractions.

They crowded around an oblong desk with a spider-phone in the centre, mics spiralling across the table so everyone could contribute their thoughts. Fola Fasanya appeared in close-up Ultra HD, with Maynard's team showing in miniature in the top right-hand corner of the screen. Fasanya saw the scene reversed: the Forth Street crew centre-stage of his monitor, Fola on the periphery.

Maynard made the introductions, and Fasanya dived straight in.

'We must begin somewhere, so let's start with DC Dexter's serial killer theory.'

Parker had clearly briefed the psychologist well.

'A serial killer gets motivation from any one of several sources. It could be a vision. A message from above. A religious zealot of some description. In this instance, and at this moment, I suspect none of these refer to our suspect. Other serial killers believe they have a mission to rid the world of bad people. Revenge, if you like; real or imagined. Without getting ahead of ourselves, they think they have a right to do these things.'

All eyes flicked to the images of the corpses, and the words incised on their torsos. Maynard hushed their gathering murmurs. 'Carry on, Fola.'

'Next, we have those who kill for hedonistic reasons. For kicks. Sexual ones, usually. They need to dominate and exert power over their victims.'

Again, that seemed to fit the profile. 'If it was sexual, wouldn't they restrict the victims to one gender?' Ryan asked. 'We have one male and one female here.'

'Indeed we do, but the human psyche knows no boundaries. Peter Sutcliffe and Fred West focused on females, yet Brady and Hindley chose whoever crossed their path.'

Maynard's team considered Fasanya's words. Stephen Danskin broke the silence. 'They were all psychopaths. Is that what we're dealing with here?'

'Possibly. Or a sociopath.'

'There's a difference?'

'As many differences as there are similarities.'

'Let's focus on the differences for now,' Danskin asked.

On screen, Fasanya's nostrils flared as he took in air and considered how best to explain it in layman's terms.

'Sociopaths tend to be less stable, emotionally. They're impulsive. If something or someone gets their goat, they react; quickly. Generally, they lack patience and rarely work to a plan.'

Lyall Parker left the table and began jotting down random key words on post-it notes.

Psychopath/Sociopath
Vision
Kicks
Revenge
Domination
Ripper/West/Moors

Ryan joined him with another pad of yellow notes. He wrote *Impulsive* and *Planned,* then began ordering the notes into columns on the board.

Maynard smiled to herself. This was going well. She noted even Stephen Danskin watched with rapt attention. She could tell he was impressed as he continued to question the psychologist.

'Sounds like our killer is a psychopath, then. He – or she – plans everything to the minutest detail. Ticks the box, for me.'

Fasanya beamed down at them. 'That's not for me to determine. I'm just sharing my knowledge. You guys use what I give you to reach an informed decision.'

'All good stuff, Fasanya,' Danskin conceded. 'Anything else?'

'Just one closing thought for now. While psychopaths are plan-obsessives, they also take calculated risks. Part of their psyche is to prove their superiority. Sometimes, they take pleasure in outfoxing an opponent. You see, they sometimes leave clues in order to challenge their hunters.'

'*My Right.*'

'Correct, Stephen. It's quite possible our perpetrator wants us to see their reasoning; that the killings aren't random acts of violence. The culprit wants us to work out what their motive is. And, by scarring the victims with My Right, they're leaving us a clue to that motive.'

Lucy Dexter leant towards the mic closest to her. 'Was he born like this? Screwed up in the head, I mean.'

'Ah, thereby lies another conundrum. Some are, while others become seriously fucked up by lifetime events. Child abuse, often, but certainly not exclusively.'

'Your gut instinct?'

'It's not my call. However, seeing as you ask,' Fasanya looked towards the ceiling in a room somewhere in Basildon. 'I'd say something happened to make him like this.'

**

'Exciting news! I've been searching forever for this one, but I think I've found her!'

He'd awoken the old woman from her afternoon nap. Her neck, twisted to one side and locked in position, meant she couldn't raise her head from her pillow. A sliver of drool clung to her lips. Her left eyelid, glued tight with sleep, refused to open whilst she looked at the man in the doorway with her other eye.

He pulled up a chair and took the woman's hand, ignoring the stench of urine from the catheter bag which had overflowed in his absence. 'I thought I'd lost my touch when I couldn't find her, but it's all fine. You see, she doesn't have an address of her own – that's why I couldn't trace her.'

The woman's eye stared blankly at the ceiling as he continued his excited gabble.

'Not only did I not have an address, but she's changed her name, too. All I had was her first name. Jane. I knew her as Jane Arthur but she's Jane Moss, now. Aren't I clever tracking her down? I should be a policeman.'

He laughed uproariously as more piss dribbled from the woman's bag.

'This is her, look.' He held a photograph in front of the woman's unblinking eye.

'And this,' he reached for a second photograph, 'Is what she did.'

The photograph showed a second woman. Her face, pitted and scarred, oozed red from acid burns. One eye was opaque, the ear on the same side of her face dissolved to little more than a fleshy ridge. The young woman's cranium was encased in a gauze bandage. There was no hair beneath. Just red-raw flesh and, in places, exposed bone.

A tear rolled down the cheek of the old woman.

'Awful, isn't it? I'm sorry, but I needed to show you what this terrible Jane woman had done.'

He crumpled Jane Moss's photograph in his balled fist.

'Don't worry. I'll put it right. I promise I'll put it right.'

CHAPTER TWENTY-THREE

Ryan Jarrod poked his head around the Super's door. 'You wanted to see me, ma'am?'

'Yes, Ryan. Take a seat.' She set down her pen and closed a file on her desk.

Ryan sat sideways on to avoid squinting into the laser-like silver sun.

'We need to reconsider your security situation now we've ruled out Lei Zhan Yu from the enquiry. He can't get at you now for obvious reasons, and we've still nothing whatsoever to link him to Benny Yu.'

'Yes, ma'am.'

'Hear me out. There's more. I can't afford to keep your family cooped up, either. We need the cell, amongst other things. Your father and brother will be released back home this afternoon. If you're concerned, you'll have to fund alternative accommodation yourself.'

Ryan nodded his understanding.

'That said, I'm not prepared to put you at risk – no matter how small that risk may be. I'll reinstate watch on your house but that's as far as I can go.'

'Thanks, ma'am,' Ryan said, closing an eye in thought.

'I'll close the blinds if the sun's in your eyes.'

'No, it's not that.' He paused. 'Can I suggest something?'

'Try me.'

'Rather than give me an officer, can you switch his attention to my folks?'

'I'm not putting you at risk, I've already said.'

Ryan raised a finger. 'What if I didn't go home? What if I kipped in the office, just for a couple of days? Hannah's on nights here anyway and it'll mean I'll be on hand to help her if she comes across anything significant. I want this bastard caught, ma'am.'

Sam Maynard considered his words. Studied the profile of her impressive DS. Finally, she spoke. 'Compromise. I'll despatch an officer to keep watch on your family. As for you, I'm not having you sleeping on the bullpen floor. I'm sure I can free up one cell for you, under the circumstances. You can sleep downstairs after your shift – just for a night or two, mind.'

Ryan smiled. 'You got yourself deal.'

'Good. Oh, and before you go, I don't think there's a need for you to be office-bound now Yu's out the way.'

'I'm back on full duties?'

'I think that's one risk I am prepared to take. Yes, Ryan; you're back on full duties. Chaperoned, but full duties.'

'Permission to cheer, ma'am.'

Maynard laughed. 'Permission granted.'

'Yayyy! Woo-hoo!!'

Maynard's door opened mid-whoop. Stephen Danskin looked from Maynard to Ryan and back again, mystified by the events in the room.

'I'll leave you to it,' Ryan said. He left the office clicking his heels as if performing Chim Chim Cheree.

'What was that all about?' Danskin asked.

'Nothing. Really, it was nothing. Now, I've got a budget report to file, a press release to prepare, and a meeting with the Commissioner in half an hour. What can I do for you?'

Danskin squinted into the sun.

'Well?'

The DCI rubbed a hand over his mouth. 'I hear you've asked O'Hara to look over the jury list again.'

'Yes, I have. Until we know more about the second victim, we must continue with the Cavell enquiry. The jury angle is the best line we have.'

'I don't have a problem with that, ma'am. You've also asked Robson to review footage of the incident in the Court's foyer. Is that so?'

'Stephen. I'm busy. I haven't time, so stop pussyfooting around and tell me what you do have a problem with.'

Danskin shielded his eyes from the glare and sighed deeply. 'This has nothing to do with…before, you know? Right?'

'Uh-huh.'

'Ma'am, I've never worked with a Superintendent as dynamic as you in my career. You're a breath of fresh air and, generally, I appreciate you're hands-on approach.'

'I sense a but, am I right?'

'But you told me earlier, you recognise the rapport I have with my team, the dynamic we have between us.'

She looked at him intently. 'I do.'

'Then don't jeopardise it. You put Graves and Sangar together on nights, you've doled out duties to Robson and O'Hara, and you've just had a one-to-one with Jarrod.'

Maynard rocked back and forth in her chair. 'And?'

'I'm their DCI. It's my role to allocate duties to my team, not yours. Ma'am, to be honest, I feel you're undermining me and putting the team dynamics you admire in jeopardy. There, I've said it.'

'You most certainly have said it,' she agreed. 'What's more, you're right. I'll take a step back. I can't promise I won't contribute; in fact, I know I won't be able to stop myself – but you're the lead. Now, like I said, I've a shitload of work to do. I'll get on with it, and you do yours. All by yourself, like a big boy.'

She smiled.

'Go catch me that son-of-a-bitch, Stephen.'

**

Danskin, Parker, Lucy Dexter, and Ryan gathered around the crime board. The DCI lifted the photographs of the two victims from the board and laid them side by side on a desk.

They stared at the photographs, waiting for the horror to recede before they took an objective view.

Lucy shook her head. 'It doesn't make sense. I really don't get it.'

'Yet…' Danskin observed. 'It doesn't make sense YET.'

Ryan provided his input. 'The only thing they have in common is she had her hair and face removed, and he his nuts. We're sure he's not a trophy collector?'

'I spoke to Fola about the very same thing after our teleconference. He says not, because he left the bloke's balls and her hair and fingers behind.'

'Unless he was interrupted,' Ryan said.

Danskin considered the possibility. 'Perhaps, but I think it's unlikely he'd be interrupted twice, both times immediately after the murder but before collecting his trophies.'

Lucy's mouth curled in distaste. 'There really are such things as trophy hunters? I mean, apart from in the movies.'

'Oh yes.'

Ryan blew out air. 'When I collected things as a kid, they were programmes from the match, not eyeballs or dicks or faces, or whatever.'

'Why did you keep the programmes, Jarrod?'

'Because they reminded me of good times, I suppose.'

'Right in one. According to Fola, that's exactly the same as trophy collectors. The killer wants to relive the moment time and time again. Fasanya quoted Jeffrey Dahmer who kept the heads of his victims in his freezer. Whenever he wanted a kick, he'd just open his freezer door the way you or I would switch on a recording of Match of the Day or summat.'

The audience struggled to comprehend what made a person do such a thing.

'Fasanya's sure that's not the case wi' oor culprit, aye?' Parker asked.

'Not ruled out, but 'highly unlikely' were Fola's words.'

The detectives stared at the images, then at the crime board with its maps and post-it notes and spaghetti strands of coloured string.

'We need to work out how our killer selects his victims. Is it random?' Ryan asked rhetorically. 'Doesn't seem that way to me. I think there's a method and a plan behind it all; a mission, if you like.'

'That's what Fola said in the conference,' Lucy observed.

Ryan fingered the two photographs. 'What have you in common? What drove someone to do this to you?'

'That,' said Danskin, 'Is the million-dollar question.'

'We could phone a friend,' Ryan suggested.

'Such as?'

'Aaron Elliot. If he can put a name to the bloke, I'm sure we'll work oot the connection.'

Danskin glanced at the wall-clock. 'Elliot won't hang around. He'll let us know as soon as he has something. I just hope it's before he strikes again.'

'Is that likely?'

'You heard Fola. If wor killer's a psychopath, it's not likely – it's a certainty.'

Ryan closed his eyes. 'Just fucking brilliant.'

'In the meantime, we go with what he have.'

'Which is?'

Danskin pointed at the crime board several times. 'This lot. Rice, Soulsby, the Paddocks – the son in particular – and Cavell's parents.'

'Sir, we've ruled most of them out,' Dexter said.

'Then rule them oot again, Dexter. They are all we've got 'til Elliot gets his finger out his backside.'

Ryan raised a hand like a schoolkid waiting to be excused. 'Not quite, sir.'

'You've got a better suggestion?'

'Lucy's jury list.'

Danskin tutted. 'Once the second victim turned up, that theory went up the spout. Having said that, the Super's got O'Hara looking at it again.'

'I still think it's worth…'

'Bollocks, Jarrod: it's not. Like I say, we're short-handed and the Super's already got us doubling-up on that angle. I'll get uniform talking to this lot again,' he wafted a hand towards the pictures of the initial suspects, 'While the rest of us go over CCTV of the murder locations.'

'Again? Ravi's crew and Hannah have been over it half a dozen times already, sir. They've found nowt.'

Danskin stared at Ryan with a *'What else do you suggest?'* look.

Ryan sighed. 'Okay, you go over the footage. I'll chase up Aaron Elliot.'

CHAPTER TWENTY-FOUR

Elliot was in his lab when Ryan called him. 'Yes, he's working on a post-mortem,' his secretary confirmed. 'No, I don't know who it is.' 'No, I can't disturb him,' but, 'Yes, I'll make sure I give him your message.'

'Thanks a bunch,' Ryan muttered at the disconnected handset.

He wandered to the coffee machine. Ryan fumbled in his pocket for a handful of loose change, fed the machine, and selected an unsugared flat white. While it poured, he popped coins into the adjacent snack machine and waited for the Kit-Kat to drop into the depository.

Biscuit in one hand, coffee in the other, he returned to his desk.

'You should've said,' a voice behind him said. 'I think it was my round.'

'Hannah.' He checked his watch. 'Bloody hell, is that the time? You're back on duty already.'

'Aye. No sleep for the wicked. I'll sleep tonight, though. I'm back in Jesmond. Released on good behaviour,' she smiled, the dimple in her cheek winking at Ryan.

'What's your work agenda tonight?'

Hannah flicked her head towards the tech room. 'Same as that lot, by the looks of it. CCTV review. Again.' She rolled her eyes.

'They'd have found summat by now if there was owt to find.'

'I know. Still, orders or orders, I suppose. As it happens, Ravi's said he's actually going to get some sleep tonight, so I'll be on my lonesome. Means I can do anything I like.'

Ryan thought for a moment. 'Will you do me a favour, if you get a chance?'

'Such as?'

'Look, it's probably a waste of time as well, but if I give you a list of jury members from the Cavell trial, can you run some background checks for me? It'll be quieter overnight and you might spot summat the others miss.' He saw her face. Held up his hands. 'I know, I know – you won't find anything, but it'll be a break from the CCTV.'

Hannah put her hands together as if in prayer. 'We will get him, Ryan. Or her. Whoever it is, we'll find them. It mightn't seem like it right now, but we will.'

'I hope you're right. So, waste of time or not, you'll do it for me?'

She shrugged. 'In for a penny, in for a pound. Where's the list?'

Ryan pulled open a drawer. Closed it again. 'Tell you what; Lucy's got a photo of the original doc on her phone. Ask her to send you it when you join her in the tec lab.'

Hannah glanced towards the room. The door's porthole window framed Lucy Dexter's face. She glared at Hannah.

'Don't think she's very happy you and me are here together.' She made a grab for Ryan's hand. Pulled him towards her. Kissed him on the lips. 'There. That'll get her thinking.' Hannah's eyes held a mischievous glint.

'Howay, man. You've got to work with the lass. We both have. Me more than you, actually. She's still my partner. Divvent wind her up.'

'A bit late for that, I think. Look at her face.'

Ryan looked towards the tec room window, but Lucy was no longer there.

'Another fine mess you've gotten me into, Stanley,' he moaned.

'Catch ya' later,' Hannah said, almost skipping her way to Ravi Sangar's digital forensics lab.

Ryan shook his head at Hannah's capriciousness. Just when he'd come to terms with the fact they'd never be together, she filled him with hope. He smiled sadly in the knowledge she'd soon dash those hopes once more.

The ringing of his desk phone brought him out of his melancholy. He scurried to it. 'DS Jarrod.'

'I'm sorry,' a familiar voice said, 'I think I've called the wrong number. I was looking for Sherlock.'

'Aaron! Thanks for getting back to me. Any chance you could bump our man up your list?'

Ryan heard Elliot make a sucking noise like a garage mechanic inspecting a damaged engine. 'I don't think I can.'

'Bugger. Do what you can, mate, will you?'

'It's not possible. Sorry.'

Ryan exhaled loudly.

'It's not possible because I've just finished with him. Still got his smell all over me.'

Ryan smiled and winced at the same time. 'You're a reet tit sometimes, do you know that?'

'You wouldn't have it any other way. Now, do you want what I've got for you, or not?'

'Too bloody right I do.' Ryan picked up a pen, then set it down again and opened Notepad on his PC. 'Fire away.'

Elliot began with a load of medical jargon and terminology which left Ryan staring at a blank screen.

'Aaron, man. Give us something I can understand, will you?'

Elliot laughed, and Ryan pictured him tucking a strand of lanky hair into his lab cap.

'Whoever the killer is, this death confirms he wants to inflict considerable amounts of pain on his victim. I'm quite sure – in fact, a hundred per cent sure – this is the same killer.'

'How come?'

'Well, he wants to be absolutely sure his victims are dead when you find them, but only after they've experienced unimaginable agonies.'

'You say *'he'*. Our killer's definitely male, is he?'

'There's no forensic evidence as yet so, as far as any trial goes, at this moment in time I'd have to say 'no, we can't be sure.' But, off the record, I'm confident it is.'

Ryan changed font colour as he typed in the off-record note. 'How'd he die?'

'Our murderer cut the carotid artery – same as his last victim – but there wasn't the blood splatter because, this time, the victim had died of his other injuries first.'

Ryan thought for a moment. 'How did we not spot that cut straight away?'

'Rats, dear boy. The body had numerous scratches and bites. It wasn't immediately obvious. You shouldn't cut yourself up about it.' Elliot laughed at his choice of words. Ryan didn't.

'What was the cause of death?'

'Internal haemorrhaging. You wanted it in layman's terms, so I'd say there were bucketfuls of it.'

'Caused by?'

Elliot whistled down the phone. 'A broken bottle up the anus won't have helped. Horrific lacerations. The lower four inches of his rectum looked as if it'd been through a shredder.

Ryan screwed his eyes tight.

'Of course, the necrosis to his scrotum will have contributed, too.'

'Necrosis?'

'Yes. From what little tissue remained after the rats' banquet, I found significant blood pooling around the genital region. If I was a betting man, I'd say our victim had a cable tie knotted around his scrotum. Probably two or three, just to be sure.'

'Fuck's sake.' Ryan squirmed in his seat.

'Well put, Sherlock. I believe this was the first thing our killer did to the victim before performing his other rituals.'

Ryan was conscious his fingers hit the keyboard ever-harder. 'These cable ties – they made his balls just drop off, did they?'

'I wish it were so. No, there was very little tissue left to inspect, but scarring indicates he was eventually castrated by a knife. Sadly for our victim, it wasn't a sharp one.'

'A blunt knife? Seriously?' Ryan felt his own testicles seek refuge inside his body cavity. 'Shit.'

Ryan thumped away on his keyboard. He used as many of Elliot's own words as possible, typing them in bold italics.

'Anything else?'

'Would you like anything else, Sherlock?'

Ryan spoke between gritted teeth. 'Look, man, this isn't the time to play wor usual games. Just give me what you got.'

'Would a name help?'

'You've got a name? You know our victim?'

Ryan detected a triumphant note in Aaron Eliot's voice. 'Not personally, no. But I do know who he is.'

'How?'

'Remember we spoke about the medical genetic testing database? Well, our man is on it. Turns out his mother was one of the seven thousand with Huntington's Disease. Huntington's is an inherited…'

'I know what Huntington's is. One of the Toon's new owners has it.'

'Indeed so. There's a fifty: fifty chance the condition is inherited by the offspring of someone with the condition, which is why our victim was tested for it. Turns out he was unlucky.'

'He had it?'

'On the contrary. He was clear, which was unfortunate for him. If he had inherited it, it's possible he may not have lived a long enough life to go through what our culprit inflicted on him.'

Ryan typed up his final question before asking it. He looked at the screen. Waited. Took in its significance to the investigation.

'Who's victim number two, Aaron?'

CHAPTER TWENTY-FIVE

He watched her from the pub doorway whilst pretending to wait for his spectacles to demist. He continued looking at her as he shook the raindrops from his jacket.

The tapered, coffin-shaped establishment sat on a plot of land between the busy approaches to the High Level and Tyne Bridges, at the lowest reaches of Gateshead. The place was quiet, probably no more than twelve customers, but its unusual design made it appear busy.

She sat alone, perched on a barstool with an empty shot glass in front of her and a part-drained schooner of ale nursed in her hands.

'You look like you could do with a top-up,' the man side, sliding into the stool next to her.

The woman stared at the patterns of foam etched on the side of her glass, the remnants of a once creamy head. She didn't acknowledge him.

'Suit yourself,' he shrugged, 'But I know I could.' He raised a finger towards the barman and ordered a half from the nearest hand-pull. He didn't care what it was. He wasn't here for the beer.

'I'll have one of them, as well,' the woman said. 'But make mine a double.'

The barman reached for a pint glass. 'I think you should make this one your last, yeah?'

'Whatever.'

The room endured a non-stop bombardment of traffic noise which at least filled the silence until the barman moved away. Once he had, the man said, 'Penny for them.'

The woman sniffed, one nostril flaring. 'See this,' she said, holding up the almost-empty schooner. 'Looks like fairy wings on the side, don't you think?' The glass trembled in her hands. 'Tell me. What do you see?'

'Looks like dried bubbles to me.'

'Then like my dreams, they fade and die,' she sang, flatly. She pointed a grubby fingernail at her new companion. 'Seriously – what do you see?' she asked again.

The man looked at her. 'I see someone who could do with a friend. Someone who seems troubled.'

She kept her head down as she half-turned to look at him. Dark circles, almost indigo in colour, lay beneath red-rimmed eyes. 'Trouble shared, and all that shite? Nah, you don't want to know, luv.'

'Try me,' he said.

She half-sneered at him, half-smiled. She hadn't washed her hair for days and it hung in thick strands before her eyes.

'Why would you care? Huh? What's my troubles got to do with you?' Her voice was slurred, and she swayed unsteadily on the stool.

'I've been where you are, that's why.'

The woman sniffed noisily. Held out a hand. 'I'm Jane.'

'John,' he said, taking it in a loose hold.

'Pleased to meet you, John. You should have something to go with your beer. I will, if you're still paying. Mine's a Slippery Nipple.' She raised him the shot glass and ran her tongue around her lips like a lizard.

The man calling himself John felt a shiver of revulsion, but ordered the sambuca and Bailey's cocktail, all the same.

'So, Mr Know-it-all John, what's my situation?'

'You're alone in a man's bar, looking miserable, and getting pissed. That's your situation.'

She snickered. 'If only that was all.'

181

'Seriously, Jane. I've been you – only with an extra appendage, as it were – sitting in a bar, drinking myself to oblivion. It might seem like a good idea, but I promise you it isn't.'

The Central Bar door opened and the sound of vehicles hissing on the wet road flooded the room.

'Why were you drinking yourself into oblivion, Mr John?'

He caught a glimpse of nicotine-stained teeth. The last twelve months had taken a savage toll on her. He hardly recognised her, yet he knew the woman had once been attractive enough before the heroin and crack and alcohol hooked her like a squirming eel.

'The usual thing,' he said. 'Women. Always has been. Always will.'

'Don't give me the *'They're all the same'* bollocks.'

John shrugged. 'Don't know. Mine was, though.' He looked into Jane's eyes and the moment he said, 'She left me for another bloke,' he knew he had her.

The thrill made him shiver as he saw her eyes take in a distant memory and her jaw tighten. He took a sip from his glass and set it down quickly. This time, it was his hand which trembled.

'Well, Mr John. Looks like we have something in common after all. My fella left me, too.'

'I'm sorry.'

'We were perfect, yet he didn't see it. He fucked up the moment he fucked up, if you know what I mean.'

'I do.'

She sniffed and wiped her nose with the back of her hand. 'She doesn't deserve him,' she spat.

'You need to win him back.'

'It's a bit too late for that.'

He lay a hand on her bony shoulder. She jumped. Shrugged his hand away. 'I'm serious,' John said, 'It's never too late.'

'It is. Really, it is. He'll never come back. Not after… not now.'

He regarded her for a moment. 'Do you fancy going somewhere else? At the very least, it'll give us a bit of fresh air – and time to talk without him listening,' he nodded in the direction of the barman deep in conversation with a couple of blokes in flat caps.

He could tell she was about to turn him down. But John held all the cards. He leant towards her. 'I've got something that'll take the edge off,' he whispered.

She knew what he meant.

'Let's go,' she said.

**

'Hi Dad. Just checking in to make sure everything's okay.'

'No need, Ryan. We're fine.'

'I spoke to Superintendent Maynard and she said she'd have a patrol watch over you, just in case. Is anyone there yet?'

Ryan heard the window blinds crinkle as Norman Jarrod peered out.

'More than one, actually. There's a car outside with two blokes in. Bruce Willis and Jason Statham, probably.'

Ryan snickered before adding, 'It is a marked car, isn't it?'

'Now you mention it, it's not.'

'Just a minute, Dad. I need to check something. Stay on the line.'

Ryan swivelled his chair to face the monitor screen. He searched the district police station database, called up the Whickham branch, and searched the duty roster. There it was, PCs Grimes and Nicholson on Special Patrol duties.

'Are they in uniform?'

'Hard to tell, son. It's pissing down and the car window's steamed up.'

'Okay. Let me know once you can see, yeah? If they come to the door and they're not in uniform, don't answer it. Y'hear?'

Norman Jarrod sighed down the line. 'You really need to let go of this Benny Yu business, y'knaa.'

'I'm getting there. How's James?'

'I'd say he's probably managing better than you are at the mo. His time in clink's giving him a new lease of life. I've just popped up to his room with a beer for him and he's still playing that bloody stupid computer game but there's a chat window open as well and he's filling Muzzle in on his time inside. He's buzzing about it.' Norman laughed; Ryan didn't.

'I wish he'd be a bit more guarded about what he tells folk.'

'Ry, man. What've I just said aboot giving it a rest? I'm fine and James is fine. You should be, too.'

Ryan cradled the phone between shoulder and ear while he yawned and stretched his arms. 'I'll be too busy to worry tonight.'

'You need some kip, man.'

'Not gonna get it. Got a name for the second victim. I reckon me and Hannah's going to be up all night checking his background.' He heard the blinds rustle again. 'Everything okay?'

'Aye. Heard a car door, that's all. Bruce Willis has just stepped out for some fresh air. Divvent worry, he's in uniform. Guess that's me date with Shania Twain shafted again.'

Ryan laughed. 'Okay Dad. I'd best be off.'

'Aye, nee bother, son. Ta-ra.'

Norman Jarrod kept the blinds peeled apart as he watched the cop he'd named Bruce Willis saunter towards The Glebe.

Bruce Willis wore plain clothes. So, too, Jason Statham.

**

If anything, the rain had increased in intensity. Jane Moss took John's arm as they stepped outside the Central Bar.

Thunder rolled deep within a charcoal sky. Gleaming spears of rain shimmered in the beams of car headlights, and the few folk out and about scuttled about their business beneath hoods and umbrellas.

'Do you know,' John said as they waited for the traffic lights to change at the head of Hills Street, 'Gateshead's the second most dangerous town in the north-east?'

'Yeah,' Jane said, the disinterest obvious in her voice.

'Weapon possession, violent assaults, sexual crimes – Gateshead's up there with the worst of 'em.'

The lights changed and John almost dragged the woman through pools of standing water.

'You a cop, or something?' Jane said, shrugging herself from him.

'Hell, no,' John laughed. 'Got no time for cops.'

'Me neither,' the woman said. She took hold of his arm again as they made across High Street onto the quiet solitude of Church Street.

'It's reckoned folk are frightened to go out after dark in some parts of town.' How sad is that?'

'I'll go out when I want to.'

'And me, too. That's what brought us together. It must be fate,' the man smiled.

'Where are we going?' she said as they passed an Indian Brasserie and Bar.

'Somewhere quiet. You want a kick, don't you?'

'You bet.'

He pushed open the metal gates to the grounds of the St Mary's Heritage Centre. The gate's hinges squealed in protest.

'This way,' he said. 'We'll find some shelter and then...' he winked at her. Her yellow teeth glowed black in the light of a single light illuminating a fraction of the footpath which wended its way towards the Heritage Centre.

He led her around the side of the building. The Heritage Centre had once been St Mary's Church, and its graveyard stood dark and threatening, sheltered from the tranquillity of St Mary's Square.

'No-one will see us here,' he said. 'Look, we'll sit under the portico. After that, we won't care where we are.'

'Let's get on with it. I need to score. I'm gagging for it.'

He looked at the bedraggled harridan who, only months ago, had been a handsome, if not beautiful, woman. 'I bet you are,' he said with no hint of humour.

John pulled a glass pipe from his pocket. Jane watched, transfixed and fuelled by expectation, as he stuffed a small handful of white crystals into the pipe's bowl.

'Ladies first,' he said, passing her the pipe. He took a lighter from his pocket and watched as the crystals turned to brown filth.

John watched her place her lips around the end of the pipe. She shut her eyes and sucked deeply; four, five times.

He gently removed the pipe from her lips. 'Feeling better already?'

Jane blinked. Sat still. Blinked again. 'I don't feel right.' Her sight blurred at the periphery. 'I think your gear's dodgy.'

John's tone changed. 'I think you're the dodgy one.'

Jane looked up at him, confusion in her eyes. Confusion, and something else. Fear.

'I need to go,' she said.

She stood, only for her legs to buckle beneath her. She collapsed onto the sodden turf of the old graveyard. Rain anointed her face until her flesh ran slick.

The last thing she saw before she blacked out was John's malevolent leer staring down at her.

CHAPTER TWENTY-SIX

The bullpen at night was a haunting place, Ryan decided.

With its motion-sensor lighting, only the strip above the desk Ryan and Hannah sat at, and another near the exit occupied by one of Kinnear's men, were lit. The rest of the vast space was occupied by a darkness which swallowed Ryan and Hannah's elongated shadows.

Ryan shuddered. Despite the bullpen's familiarity and Hannah by his side, he felt vulnerable. A train rumbled outside. Ryan jumped as its brakes shrieked. Hannah remained unmoved, as if only he could hear it, like Hamlet's ghost.

He pulled at the flesh beneath his eyes, exposing the redness of his lower lids. 'Get a grip,' he said out loud.

'You what?'

'Nothing. Look, I'm gonna see if owt leaps out and hits me on the crime-board. You keep up the background checks on our second victim.'

She saluted sarcastically. 'Yessir.'

Ryan called up a series of images thumbnail images from his PCs library and hit the print button three times.

Hannah, meanwhile, typed *William Vickers* into her internet search bar and began trawling through the second page of hits. She found three men of that name living locally, only one of which had an associated image. It wasn't their man.

She rattled off an e-mail to Ravi Sangar instructing him to check the social media and telephone records of the remaining two names and delved further into the realms of the web.

Ryan walked to the printer, retrieved the images, and proceeded to the crime board. He noticed his heart rate drop as his movement triggered more lighting. The room no longer felt a sinister death-trap.

He flipped over the crime board to expose its uncluttered reverse side. On the left-hand side, he pinned before and after pictures of Roberta Cavell. To the upper right, he affixed the 'after' image of the emasculated William Vickers. He wouldn't get his 'before' image until Hannah's searches produced one.

Ryan took a step back and took a dispassionate view of the photographs. 'What have you in common?', he said aloud. Sure, both had been tortured and mutilated. Both had been chained. Both had 'My Right' carved into their abdomen. Yet, the mutilations were different. Why? 'What connects you?' he said again.

He began noting the injuries beneath each victim's photograph when, behind his back, he heard Hannah release a low whistle. Heard her chair wheel back from the desk. The clatter of fingers on keyboard quietened.

'Ry, come here a mo, will you? I think I've got something.'
Ryan hurried over. 'What is it?'
'Something I should have picked up on an hour ago.'
She angled her screen so he could see it.
It was his turn to whistle. 'Will you look at that,' he said. 'Get the fuck in. We might just have our breakthrough!'

On Hannah's screen was a newspaper headline featuring William Vickers. The article went on to describe how he'd been found not guilty of rape and sexual assault.

'Shit, Ryan – as soon as I had the name, I should have checked if he had a record.'

He looked at her. 'Yes, you should. But I didn't either. Anyone can make a mistake. The important thing is, you've corrected it. Pull up the court records, can you?'

It took Hannah a view minutes to track down the court transcript factual summary. Once she had, Ryan wheeled his chair alongside her, and they read it together.

The summary described how Vickers allegedly anally penetrated his sixteen-year-old victim, Carmen Best, in her bedroom while her parents were absent from the house. The prosecution claimed he broke into the house armed with a knife, ordered the girl to strip naked, then assaulted her.

Vickers had admitted doing so, but claimed the act was consensual and, in fact, Carmen Best instigated the activity. The defence painted a picture of Best as a precocious and promiscuous teenager, one who had posed willingly for explicit nude photographs for one of her 'many' ex-partners, and who was comfortable in the knowledge of those photographs being shared widely amongst schoolfriends and others.

The transcript outlined how Carmen Best had denied posing for any photographs and, when the images were shown to the jury, she broke down and admitted she had lied on oath.

The final line of the report read, '*Surprisingly, the jury found Mr William Vickers Not Guilty of all offences. Presiding Judge Goode-Parriett released Mr Vickers without further conditions.*'

'Now we're getting somewhere,' Ryan exclaimed. 'High five, Hannah.' He raised a palm aloft. She left him hanging.

'Dirty get,' she said. 'Even if she did lead him on, he's a filthy, disgusting bastard. Sixteen, she was. Barely more than a child.'

Ryan lowered his hand. 'Aye. Even the official recorder must have thought so.'

'How come?'

'Well, the Statement of Facts should be just that: facts. The Recorder's put her own opinion on it. '*Surprisingly*, found Not Guilty,' the record states. I'm amazed it wasn't redacted from the transcript.'

'Aye, but it doesn't alter the fact he's a dirty bastard.'

'A dirty INNOCENT bastard, Hannah.'

She looked at him. 'Just like Roberta Cavell.'

It took a moment for the implication to register. 'Bloody hell!' He grabbed a couple of marker pens and dashed to the crime board. Hannah followed in his wake.

Beneath the photographs of Cavell and Vickers, Jarrod wrote 'Verdict: Not Guilty.'

He picked up a red marker and wrote 'Presiding Judge: Eton Hogarth' beneath Cavell's image. He skimmed the document and, again in red, he wrote 'Presiding Judge: Warren Goode-Parriett.'

Again using red to show a difference, he put 'Fraud' in the Cavell column, 'Sexual Assault' beneath the Vickers details.

Hannah knew better than to interrupt him, so she stood back and let Ryan scribble more details on the board. He'd grabbed a dirty cloth and wiped out the injury details he'd put on the board earlier and started again.

Under the Bobbi Cavell column, in red ink he listed:

Fingers

Hair

Face.

In black, he wrote:

Carotid artery

'My Right'.

He repeated the last two entries in black ink beneath William Vickers, before switching to the red pen to write:

Castration

Rectal haemorrhage.

He tapped the tip of the pen against his teeth, staining his teeth crimson. *What am I missing? Think, man. Think.*

'Hannah, call up everything we have on Bobbi Cavell for me, will you? Her personal stuff, not the case records.'

She returned to her desk. Ryan followed. Ten minutes later, he thumped his fist against the desk. 'Yes, you beauty. That's it!'

Hannah watched him scurry to the board and, with a green pen, he arced an arrow from the alleged offences to the injuries each victim sustained.

'Ring Danskin,' he said.

'Ryan, it's four in the morning.'

He stared at her, eyes alive. 'I don't give a monkey's chuff. Get the DCI here. He needs to see this. Now.'

**

'This had better be worth it, Jarrod.' Stephen Danskin strode into the bullpen with a serious case of bed-hair. 'If I had a wife, I'd have me knackers in a sling for getting up at this hour.'

He instantly regretted his choice of words as he passed the crime board images and saw the neutered male. Danskin raised his eyebrows. 'You've had a busy night, I see.'

'A productive one, too, sir.'

'Howay, then. Hit me with it.'

Ryan inhaled a lungful of air. 'Victim number two is a William Vickers, recently declared innocent of serious sexual offences. The court record shows the verdict was an unexpected one. Just as much a surprise,' he said, pointing a finger towards Roberta Cavell, 'As her verdict was to Lyall and me.'

Danskin rubbed sleep from his eyes. 'Jarrod, it's barely five o'clock. I've raced here from me pit to find you – who should be sleeping, by the way – pointing out the bleedin' obvious. Is that it? Both victims were found not guilty?'

Ryan's eyelids slid shut. 'It's more than a co-incidence, sir. Both were found not guilty under dubious circumstances. Both were killed in a similar manner. Both have the same inscription carved into them. Most importantly, the manner of their deaths, although different, have a very important connection.'

Danskin continued to probe and poke at his eye. 'Which is?'

191

Hannah Graves picked up the theory. 'Sir, Ryan thinks the mode of both killings are connected to the allegations against them.'

'More details, please.'

'William Vickers was accused of sexual offences. In return, he had his genitals mutilated and his arse ripped out.'

'Nicely put, Hannah,' Danskin observed.

'Sorry, sir, but that's the way it is. Now, as well as knowing Roberta Cavell wore hair extensions and false nails, we've also discovered she'd had lip fillers and buccal lipectomy…'

'What the hell's that when it's at home?'

'Fat pads in your cheeks are surgically removed to thin them. It gives greater facial definition and angles the cheekbone.'

Danskin ran a hand over his bristled jaw. 'I know I'm tired, but this isn't making any sense to me, like.'

Ryan tried to clarify his thoughts. 'Bobbi Cavell had cosmetic surgery performed on her. The killer checked her breasts for implants. He didn't find any, so they remained on the corpse. Everything else, he removed from her.'

Danskin screwed up his face, trying to understand the significance.

'To put it bluntly, much of Bobbi Cavell was false.' His finger followed the path of the green arrow on the board linking her injuries to the crime. 'I suggest our killer viewed Cavell as a fraud.'

Danskin was getting there. 'And our murderer removed Vickers' undercarriage as a nod to the offence he was accused of.'

Ryan and Hannah nodded to each other.

'Sir, I'm no Fola Fasanya, but I reckon we've a vigilante killer out there.'

CHAPTER TWENTY-SEVEN

Danskin called Sam Maynard, who dashed to the station. He called the rest of his team. They, too, headed for Forth Street without a moment's hesitation. Even Todd Robson.

By six-forty-five, they were assembled around a desk below the station's plasma screen. The blue screen flashed into life and the squad were greeted by Fola Fasanya's benign smile, and his red-veined bleary eyes.

'Good morning at this ungodly hour,' he said, 'Now I know how Naga Munchetty feels every day.'

Lyall Parker and Nigel Trebilcock chuckled. The others were in no mood for levity.

True to her word, Sam Maynard stayed at the fringe of the group and let Danskin lead. 'Fola, I explained briefly what this was aboot when I asked you to join this conference. DS Jarrod and DS Graves believe, for the reasons I made clear to you earlier, we may have be looking at a vigilante killer.'

Fasanya nodded, opened his mouth to speak, then realised Danskin was continuing. 'Tell us what you understand about vigilantes, and whether it fits our killer's profile.'

'A vigilante rationalises their behaviour by believing that legal forms of criminal punishment, or justice as a whole, is either insufficient or flawed. Essentially, they mete out the punishment they believe the crime deserves.'

Danskin, Jarrod, and Graves nodded in agreement.

'For the benefit of others,' the DCI explained, 'We now believe the mutilations on our victims reflect the offences they were charged with.' He went on to explain their thinking to the rest of the squad. Most nodded, Trebilcock sat with jaw clamped tight, and Robson muttered 'Bugger me sideways.'

'So, Fola. Does that meet our profile of a psychopath?'

'In itself, no. A vigilante killing isn't necessarily a psychopathic killing. However, taking in the manner of the murders, the depravity of the mutilations, and the planning behind them, I'd say there's a good chance our killer is a psychopathic vigilante.'

His face moved closer to the camera until it filled the screen. 'It explains why he believes it is his 'Right' to do such thinks. I'm afraid, my friends, a vigilante psychopath is not a good mix.'

'Tell us aboot it,' Todd said. 'Where do we go from here?'

Fola's face moved away from the camera. 'I'm sorry,' he said, 'But that's not my field. That call is Sam's.'

'Actually,' the Super said, 'It's not. Stephen – next steps, please?'

Danskin smiled warmly. 'Thank you, ma'am. My opinion, backed by Jarrod and Graves who've done most the forensic detail here,' he noticed Lucy Dexter scowl in the background at his words, 'Is that we need an urgent warrant.'

'For?' Maynard asked.

'Ma'am, we need details of everyone who was in the courtroom for both trials. None of the details of either murder has been released. Only one person could know the links between them and mete out their own justice in the way they have.'

He looked his squad in the eye, one-by-one. 'Our killer must have attended both trials. We need names, and we need them the moment the court opens.'

'Your warrant will be ready for the court opening; you have my word. Jarrod, Graves – tremendous work! Bloody tremendous. You make a great team.'

'I appreciate it, ma'am. Thank you,' Ryan said, winking at Hannah.

Lucy Dexter's eyes hardened and became little more than slits, brows knitted together. Both nostrils flared above thin lips.

Todd nudged Lyall Parker. 'Somebody's not a happy bunny-boiler,' he whispered.

**

Norman Jarrod was awake though still in bed when the rap on the door came. Seven-fifty. Too early for the postman.

While Spud snarled and yelped and generally pretended he was a Rottweiler, Norman whistled to himself on the way downstairs.

The second knock brought a 'Had on, man. I'm comin', and more craziness from the pug.

'Shut up you daft mutt,' Norman shouted as he reached for the doorhandle. Ryan's warning dribbled into his consciousness.

'Who is it?'

'Police, Mr Jarrod. My name's Andy Nicholson. PC Andy Nicholson.'

'Okay. Do you mind taking a few steps up the path, so I can see you, like?'

'Of course not, sir.'

Norman cautiously spread open the blinds. A man in police uniform stood half-way up the path, hands tucked into the straps of his stab vest. On the road outside stood a car daubed in blue and yellow checks, a second officer at the wheel.

Norman peered up Newfield Walk, to Larkspur Road and beyond. Apart from an electric Co-operative Dairies buggy, nothing else stirred. Norman Jarrod opened the front door a couple of inches and spoke through the gap. 'Aye?'

'Morning, sir. Just checking everything is A-okay.'

'Aye, we're fine, ta.'

'And to apologise for last night.'

'Why? What've you done?'

Andy Nicholson chuckled. 'Made a bit of a mess of things, I'm afraid. Grimesy,' he indicated his colleague in the car, 'And me got our wires crossed. We spent aal neet outside your kid's house. The message about him staying at the station didn't reach us 'til this morning. Still, I can safely say Ryan's house is still standing.'

Norman Jarrod looked up and down the street again. 'You were there all night?'

'Yep. Don't tell the brass,' Nicholson laughed.

'Were any of your colleagues here last night?'

'Don't think so, sir; no.'

'Not Willis and Statham?'

'I'm not following, sir.'

Norman Jarrod crinkled his brow. 'I thought there was a car here last night, that's all.'

'Nah, not us.'

'Okay.' He hesitated. 'Will you be here most the day?'

'Aye. All of it. Either me and Grimesy or one of our colleagues will, anyway. There'll be a marked car outside at all times.'

'Okay. Cheers, mate.'

Norman Jarrod closed the door and leant against it. *No point telling Ryan,* he thought. *He'll only stress about it, and we're safe now.*

He stuck two slices of bread in the toaster and put last night's mysterious car down as 'one of those things.'

**

Stephen Danskin sent Hannah home to bed with instructions not to return until six pm. He told Ryan to get his head down in his temporary lodgings in the basement. Ryan protested, objected, and point-blank refused until Sam Maynard stepped in with a compromise.

'You've been up all night. I need you functioning. Four hours, then you're back on duty. You'll be teamed up with Lucy again.'

'But…'

'No buts, Ryan. Four hours, then you'll be ready to lead DC Dexter again.

Lucy smirked. 'Thank you, ma'am. Ryan and I make a good team.'

Danskin took charge again. 'Lyall, you head down to the Law Courts with the warrant. Once we have the names, I'll have the rest of the squad on background checks.'

'You can keep Rick's lads, if necessary.'

'Thanks, ma'am. Howay, Lyall. Shift your arse, man. I need to know everybody who got within smelling distance of the Judge's backside on both cases.'

**

Ten minutes later, Parker marched through the Law Court doors. The air inside smelled of polish and pine disinfectant, rather than judge's bottoms.

The receptionist saw his approach and crossed her arms in front of her. 'Detective Inspector. What can I do for you?'

Lyall Parker held up the warrant. 'I do it properly. Paperwork and everything.'

'Good. I'm pleased to see it. What's the warrant for this time?'

'I need a list o' folk present for each day of both these trials.' He pointed out the Court reference number.

'Well...'

'And I need them now.'

The receptionist saw the urgent look on his face, but still had to break him the bad news. 'I'm not sure I can.'

'Why the hell not?'

'I'll do what I can. I can get you jury members, witnesses, lawyers – all no problem.'

'Well, go on, lassie. Get them. Now.'

She didn't move. 'I can give you the name of press and media attendees. What I can't give you, though, is the names of anyone watching proceedings from the gallery.'

'Shite. Why's that?'

'It's not like anyone's been convicted. No-one's in jail. We don't require folk to sign in and out as if they're visiting someone in prison.

'Shite,' he repeated. He looked around. 'You have CCTV here, aye?'

'We do, of course.'

'So, I mightn't have names, but I can have faces.'

'That depends.'

Lyall groaned. 'On what?'

'Whether the tapes have been erased. We don't keep them forever, you know. I think you'll probably be lucky and be able to access the footage for one trial, but I doubt we'll still have both.'

Another 'Shite.' Lyall raised his eyes to the ceiling. 'Okay. Just get me those bloody names, will ye?'

**

It was lunchtime before Parker had what he needed. Hannah was sleeping peacefully in her Jesmond apartment and Ryan was collecting a coffee on the way up from the holding cells to the bullpen, but the rest of Danskin's team were ready and waiting.

'I hae' in ma hand a sheet o' paper,' Lyall called out, Chamberlain-esque.

The crew gathered at the crime board. Parker picked up a flipchart and clipped it over the contents of the board, careful not to erase any of the data on it.

'We have seven names present at both trials.'

'Only seven? Fantastic!' Danskin cried. 'Shouldn't take us long. We'll have this cracked in no time.'

'Not necessarily.' Parker went on to explain about the missing gallery attendees and limited CCTV material.

'Trust a bloody Scotsman to put a dampener on things.' Danskin's mood became downbeat. 'Anyhoo, give us what you've got, Lyall.'

Ryan appeared at the back of the crowd, coffee in hand.

'Okay. These were present at both cases. A Frances Harrington, local hack for the Herald and Post. Basically, it's a free advertising rag.'

Danskin made a note in a pink-jacketed school pad. He put a cross next to her name, indicating she was an unlikely suspect although they'd still check her out.

'Two Ushers were on duty for both cases,' he wrote their names on the flipchart, 'And Michael Moran was the Jury Marshall at both trials,' he scribbled his name down, too. 'The Court Recorders were Hayley Swann and Jerome Hagan,' there names went on the list.

Danskin held up a hand to say Parker should stop until he'd caught up with the crosses, ticks, and question marks on his jotter.

'Interestingly, Matty McNair was on the CPS team for both cases.'

Danskin put a tick alongside McNair's name.

'Nearly there, sir. Those seven were all present in or around the courtroom itself, but also on duty were Security Guards Mandy Lewins, Ron Paige, and Jake Blair. Finally, oor lovely not-so-little receptionist.' Parker put her name at the bottom of the list.

DCI Danskin looked over the list. 'So, really, there's eleven suspects; not seven.' He thought for a moment. 'There again, four are women, which means they're at the bottom of our list, which does indeed leave seven prime candidates.'

'Plus anyone in the public gallery, sir,' Lyall reminded him.

'There you go again, man. Miserable old scroat.' The crew chuckled while Lyall smiled. He understood Danskin didn't mean it. No matter how frustrated the DCI was, Parker knew they had mutual respect.

'Okay, then. We start with…'

'Stephen,' a voice called across the bullpen; a voice laden with urgency.

'What is it, Rick?'

Rick Kinnear held a phone in the air. 'Sounds like you've got another one, Stephen.'

'What? Jesus wept.'

''Fraid so. All the hallmarks of the other two, according to initial reports from Uniform.'

Danskin looked at the list of names.

'On the bright side, if it is another one of ours, we might get to whittle this list down further.'

'Who's drawn the lucky straw to see this one?' Ryan asked.

'Me,' Danskin replied without hesitation. 'And you, Jarrod. You know what to expect.'

'Cheers, guv,' Ryan muttered.

Danskin's final words struck more fear into Jarrod than the thought of confronting another desecrated corpse.

'You too, Dexter,' the DCI added.

CHAPTER TWENTY-EIGHT

Even Lucy Dexter had grown familiar with the routine. She slipped into the protective paper suit, fixed the cap so it covered her blonde spikes, and smacked on latex gloves.

Danskin was ready to go, but Ryan lagged behind, hopping on one foot as he tried to pull on a protective overshoe.

'Here, I'll do it,' Lucy smiled.

'It's aal reet, man. I can do it,' he said, careering into the stone wall of St Mary's Heritage Centre.

Lucy came to his aid, despite the rebuff.

'When you two have quite finished arse-farting around, we'll get on, shall we?' Danskin scolded.

The inside of the Heritage Centre provided a pleasantly cool shelter from the warm spring sunshine. Ryan, Lucy, and Stephen Danskin looked around the interior.

It was clear the Centre had once been a church. A quarter of it held the normal tourist trappings of a heritage centre: information desks, hearing loops, interactive headsets linked to pre-recorded commentaries, rotating racks bedecked with attraction leaflets, and the usual crass giftshop. The bulk of the building, seventy-five percent of it, remained as it always had - reverential and churchlike.

The interior design of St Mary's was typically Gothic. Thick columns of carved stone supported a high, timber-beamed roof. The nave and chancel remained untouched. Heavy oak doors with black metal hinges hid the vestry from view. Sun streamed through stained glass set high above the pulpit and bathed it in rainbow colours.

Danskin was in no mood to take in the finer detail.

'Where's our victim? I can't see owt here. Get one of the

Uniform lads in, we should have checked with them first. Dexter, see if you can find somebody out there who can tell us what we're looking...'

'Oh my fucking God,' Lucy whispered.

Danskin followed Lucy's eyeline. She'd found the victim, naked and hiding in plain sight.

They hadn't seen her because she was nailed to a cross over a glazed stone figurine of Christ. The woman's body covered it perfectly.

Ryan gazed at the bizarre image. He was becoming inured to the horrors of the dead and looked at the scene with objectivity.

'It's not the same,' Ryan said. 'Not quite. There's no chains.'

'He doesn't need chains, man. He's used nails.'

'Exactly. That's what I'm saying: he hasn't used chains. Let's just not jump to conclusions.'

Danskin knew, better than anyone, that assumptions were the last thing they should make. Especially as the words etched across the woman's stomach were familiar, yet subtly different. Jarrod was right - they had to keep open minds.

They kept their distance and circled the victim, inspecting her body for the killer's trademark atrocities.

A trail of blood wrapped itself around the victim's forehead. 'He's used barbed wire as a crown of thorns,' Lucy observed.

'Aye, but that wouldn't kill her.' Danskin stepped closer to the victim. 'Can't see any cuts to the neck, either.'

He climbed onto the pulpit. Sniffed the air. There was something familiar in it. He pulled himself up to full height. Stood on tip-toe and looked down on the remains of the woman nailed to the cross.

'Shit the bed!'

Danskin tumbled down the stairs and cowered away from the corpse. He landed in a heap at the foot of the cross and scrambled backwards on his arse until his back lay against cold stone and he could move no further.

Ryan hurried to him. 'Sir, are you okay?'

Danskin said nothing. Just nodded. Finally, he gulped down sufficient air to get some words out.

'I know what killed her.'

Ryan let his DCI tell him in his own good time.

'The bastard drilled a hole in the woman's skull. I mean, right through. Right down to the brain.'

'He drilled into her brain?' Ryan said, appalled.

'God no,' Lucy added.

Danskin shook his head. 'No, man. That's not the half of it. I don't think he touched her brain. At least, not with the drill. There's no blood or brain matter. No, he did something else.'

He struggled to understand how anyone could do what he'd just witnessed.

'Once he'd drilled into her skull, he poured sulphuric acid straight down the hole, directly onto her brain.'

**

A shaken Stephen Danskin sat in Sam Maynard's office, for once drinking tea rather than coffee. Ryan provided Maynard with the briefing.

The Super shook her head in quiet contemplation. 'Where do we go from here?'

'Ma'am, I've been given the matter some thought. If the killer follows the same pattern, I believe we'll find, somewhere on record, the details of an acid attack. What's more, I think the trial outcome…'

'Will not have resulted in a conviction.' Maynard was ahead of him.

'Yes, ma'am. I'm sure there can't be too many such assaults in recent months. Once we've identified it and the victim, we can cross-check names from the court register against DI Parker's list. That'll reduce the numbers for us, for sure.' A thought crossed his mind. 'On the other hand, it'll increase the number of gallery observers.'

'Swings and roundabouts, Ryan, huh?'

'Yes, ma'am.'

'Now, before we go down this route, we're certain it's the same killer?'

'Aye, it's the same bastard,' Danskin said.

'I agree, ma'am. I wasn't sure at first, but I am now.'

Maynard's eyes sparkled. 'Let me have your thinking, Ryan. And Lucy – listen and learn.'

Lucy's look told the Super she was only too willing to listen anything Ryan Jarrod said.

'Ma'am, I wasn't sure at first because the killer used nails this time, not chains as in the previous cases. Then, I reckoned he was making a statement. You know, being in a church. Crucifixion and such. I reckon the statement was more important to him than the manner of restraint.'

'Yep, it figures. Anything else?'

'Aye, ma'am. The inscription on the body. The others had 'My' above the navel, and 'Right' below. This one had both words beneath the navel, lower on her stomach.'

Maynard looked out at the Tyne, rippling like silver foil as it shimmered in the sun. 'Not much of a difference. Not sufficient for us to believe it's not our man.'

'I think so, too. I believe both words were below the navel line to make room for the words he'd carved above the navel.'

'Now, that is different.'

'It is, ma'am. But, again, I put it down to the killer adapting it to the setting. You see, above '*My Right*' were the words, '*God is.*' He changed the mutilation to fit in with the scene.'

Lucy had listened well. 'No he didn't.'

All three looked at her.

'Forget about anyone in the gallery. Our killer IS one of Lyall's eleven.'

Stephen Danskin looked at her out the corner of his eye. 'What makes you so sure, Dexter?'

'The inscription: *'God is my right.'* Don't you see it?'

'I'm afraid not, Lucy,' Maynard said.

'It's obvious it's someone connected to the court. Forget juries, forget the press, forget people in the gallery. It's someone who works in the court.'

Ryan's face lit up with understanding. 'Bloody hell, Luce. I know where you're coming from. She's right. And, once we know the victim and have her trial details, we'll be onto our killer.'

'I must be thick,' Danskin said.

'No, sir, you're not. You're still in shock. You see, *'Dieu et Mon Droit'* is the Crown Court motto, taken from the Royal Coat of Arms.'

Danskin had it at last. 'Of course! Dieu et Mon Droit – God is my Right!'

The DCI punched a fist into his palm. 'Fola was spot-on – the killer's a vigilante AND a psychopath. He's left us another clue and, this time, he's made a mahoosive mistake!'

**

In a Jesmond apartment block, Hannah Graves stirred. She opened her eyes, then closed them against the bright sunlight which penetrated her thin curtains.

Something had woken her, but she didn't believe it was the light. She shrugged, lowered her head back onto the pillow, closed her eyes, and pulled the sheet over her face like a shroud.

There it was again.

She sat upright and watched her vibrating phone jump over the surface of her bedside cabinet.

'Hannah Graves.'

'Hannah, it's me. Can you take my call?'

She rubbed her eyes. 'Depends on who *me* is.'

She heard an embarrassed chuckle. 'Sorry, hen. It's me: Norman. Ryan's Dad.'

Hannah let the sheet slip from her as she sat up. 'Is summat wrong?' She knew there was by the delay in his reply. When it came, his 'I'm not sure,' wasn't reassuring.

'Norman. Tell me.'

'I don't want to worry Ryan. He's paranoid enough as it is.'

'Worry him about what? Tell me. Let me decide if he needs to know.'

He took a deep breath. 'Last night, there was a car outside the hoose…'

'Didn't Ry tell you? You've got security.'

'I know, but there was a mix up, it seems. The security went to The Drive by mistake. The cop this morning told me they'd cocked up.'

Hannah shrugged the sleep out of her head. 'What cop?'

'Nicholson, I think his name is. The one in the marked car who should have been outside here last night.'

Hannah wriggled into a pair of jeans. 'Okay. Tell me about the other car.'

'Not much to tell. It was dark outside, and the car's windows were steamed up. There were two blokes inside. Not in uniform.'

'Norman, are you sure it wasn't a taxi picking someone up or dropping them off?'

Norman Jarrod gave a humourless laugh. 'It'd be an expensive fare if they left the meter running. It was there for yonks. I mean, like a couple of hours.'

Hannah set the phone down while she yanked a T-shirt over her head. Once she was dressed, she asked, 'Is security still outside?'

'Aye. I'm upstairs in me bedroom. I can see Nicholson and the other bloke, Grimes, I think, in the car now.'

'Marked?'

'Oh aye, it's kosher okay. It's the one last neet I'm not sure about.'

Hannah allowed herself time to think. 'Be honest with me, Norman. You think it's something to do with Benny Yu, don't you?'

'Can't pretend it hasn't crossed my mind.'

'Norman, have a word with Nicholson and Grimes. Let them know your concerns but, as long as they're outside and the other car hasn't come back, I wouldn't worry too much.' She thought again. 'We've not seen or heard from Benny Yu for months. I don't think it's anything to worry Ry with.'

In the bedroom in Newfield Walk, Norman Jarrod rubbed the back of his neck. 'Aye, that's what I thought. Thanks for the advice, love.'

'No bother, Norman. Anytime, yeah?'

'Aye. For sure.'

Norman Jarrod ended the call.

From his bedroom window, the angle of the house afforded a clean line of sight over the sportsground as far as Whickham Cricket Club. Its carpark held a lone vehicle.

Norman couldn't be sure, but from this distance it looked like the guys he'd dubbed Bruce Willis and Jason Statham occupied the front seats.

CHAPTER TWENTY-NINE

The bullpen was awash with frenetic energy.

Danskin commissioned Gavin O'Hara and Todd Robson with the task of searching the background of those who were present in the courtroom for both trials. Rick Kinnear's secondees focused on doing the same with the less-likely suspects; those present in the court but outside the courtroom itself.

The DCI charged Lucy Dexter with downloading the public gallery CCTV footage into the Forth Street archive. She reported to Danskin that the only coverage they had was of the Cavell trial, but she'd discovered the same guy had responsibility for the recording and disposal of all material recorded at the Law Courts. She added the name Larry Monroe to Kinnear's suspect list.

Lyall Parker oversaw Ravi Sangar and Nigel Trebilcock's search for the record of recent acid attacks, while Danskin and Ryan re-ordered the crime board and updated it with latest developments.

Sam Maynard stood back and relayed her observations. Finally, the board portrayed a clear and unequivocal timeline of events, suspect lists, and photographs, as well as SOC photographs of the deceased and Fola Fasanya's culprit profile.

'Good work,' the Super said. 'It's looking much better.'

'It'll look even better when we can rub the whole lot off cos we've caught the bugger.'

'True, Stephen. But we're beyond the baby steps phase. We're making giant strides now.'

Baby steps morphed into giant strides, and into a sprint for the tape when the tec lab door opened and Lyall shouted, 'Ma'am, sir – I think Treblecock's found her!'

Stephen, Sam Maynard, and Ryan dashed into the room. Ravi Sangar had called up the same screen as Trebilcock and zoomed in on a press photograph. 'Is that the latest victim, sir?'

Ravi expected an instant yes or no. What he got was silence.

'What do you think, Jarrod?' Danskin asked.

'How old's the picture, Ravi?'

'Eighteen months, according to the report.'

'Sir, it could be, but she's changed a bit.'

'I agree. And for the worse, an' aal.'

Ravi sighed. 'Well, she would, wouldn't she, with a Black and Decker and a bucketload of acid through her brain?'

'She's lost a load of weight. Aged a lot,' Danskin thought out loud. 'What's her backstory?'

Nigel Trebilcock split his screen to display newspaper report, court documents, and the police chargesheet.

'Her name's Jane Archer…'

'Now known as Jane Moss, of no fixed abode.' Ravi interrupted.

'At the time of the attack, she was living in Ouston.'

'Details. Fast as you can, Treblecock.'

'Okay sir. Sorry, sir. Jane Archer – as was – faced a charge of grievous bodily harm. She attacked a Katherine Pamela Spencer – known as Kathy - in her own home…'

'Who's home? Archer's or Spencer's?'

'The victim's, sir. Spencer's.'

'Be clearer, Treblecock.'

'Sorry sir. The facts state she assaulted the woman, tied her to a chair, and poured 330 millilitres of sulphuric acid over her head.'

Danskin took in air. Looked at the photograph on Ravi's screen. 'This is our third victim, for sure.'

'What happened at the trial?' Maynard asked.

'Ma'am, the transcript reveals Kathy Spencer had been dating Archer's husband. They were already separated, but Archer was in denial. Archer blamed Spencer for the break-up.'

'Spencer lived?'

'Somehow, yes. She did.'

'Not murder, then?'

'No, ma'am. The charge was GBH. Sadly, Kathy Spencer has since died, but beyond the legal time limits for further charge.'

Danskin's mouth felt dry. He sensed they were closing in on their killer. 'If it's to fit the pattern and profile, I assume Archer somehow got off with the charge.'

Trebilcock hesitated. 'No, sir. She was found guilty.'

'Bollocks.' Danskin looked towards Ryan. 'Doesn't fit the profile. What do you think, Jarrod?'

'I dunno. Wait a minute; if she was found guilty, how come she's not in nick?'

Ravi Sangar outlined the later steps. 'At the subsequent sentencing hearing, her brief supplied probationary and psychiatric reports indicating Archer was suffering from a mental disorder at the time of the offence, and her balance of mind was disturbed. Crown agreed, albeit reluctantly, to accept a plea of diminished responsibility.'

'A fucking stitch up,' Danskin swore.

'Yes, sir. So, although guilty, sentence was reduced on diminished responsibility grounds.'

'Reduced to what?' Ryan asked.

'Given Archer's time spent in custody, she was ordered to undergo psychiatric treatment, as an outpatient and under probation, whilst also accepting a curfew and a tag.'

'In other words, she walked free?'

'In other words, sir, yes.'

A hush came over the room. Everyone sensed this was the breakthrough they needed.

'Lyall, get me the fucking court register for that trial.'
**
Norman Jarrod tapped the side-window of the patrol car.

'Jesus, man. I nearly crapped mesel,' Andy Nicholson wheezed.

'Aye, well. That'll larn yer for sleeping on the job.'

'I wasn't sleeping. I was just resting me eyes. Besides, Grimesy's here as well.

'Hmm?' PC Grimes asked, looking up from his phone for the first time.

'I rest my case,' Norman laughed.

He straightened. Took on a serious look. 'Listen, you know that car I told you about? The one I saw outside?'

'Aye, I remember.'

'It's back.'

'What? Where?' Nicholson sat bolt upright, the seat's headrest knocking his cap askew.

'It's not here in the street, man. I think it's in Whickham Cricket Club's carpark.'

'Are you sure?'

'I said, I *think* it is. The clues in the words.'

The cops exchanged glances. 'Think we should take a look, Grimesy?'

The second cop had already started the engine. 'Back soon,' Nicholson said.

It was only after they drove away Norman thought, '*Shit. There's no-one here 'til they get back.*'

He locked and bolted the door behind him.
**
Maynard despatched Lyall Parker to the Law Courts with the signed the warrant.

He skipped the queue which prompted a roll of eyes from the receptionist but a pleasant smile. 'We'll have to stop meeting like this.'

'I hope there'll be nae need after this.' He showed her the warrant details.

211

She took it from him and squinted at the refence number. 'By, that's going back a while.'

'Problem?'

'No, none at all,' she smiled.

Twenty minutes later, he was back in the bullpen, black marker pen in hand. He scored through the list of names until only five remained.

'There,' he said. 'Only five of the buggers were around at the time of Archer's trial.

The squad looked at the list.

Michael Moran. Jury Marshall.

Matty McNair. CPS.

Jerome Hagan. Court Recorder.

Ron Paige. Security.

Larry Monroe. CCTV Technician.

'Okay,' Danskin began. 'All male, which doesn't help. But, Paige and Monroe wouldn't actually be in the courtroom, so I reckon they're outside bets.'

'Sir,' Lucy said, 'Monroe could've effectively been there, watching the CCTV feed.'

Danskin nodded. 'Very true. Okay, let's add him to the main list and focus on those four first. Robson, you take the Jury Marshall. In fact, let's double-down on the lot of them. Treblecock, you're with Robson. O'Hara, you and Sangar focus on Monroe. DS Jarrod and Dexter, take Hagan.'

'Pleasure, sir,' Lucy said, looking towards Ryan.

'Lyall, I don't like the way McNair's name keeps cropping up. You take him.'

'By ma'sel? Happy to.'

Danskin looked around the squad. 'On reflection, no. I see DS Graves has just joined us. You two work together. Lyall, bring her up to speed first.' He looked at the board. 'Now, is that everyone covered?'

'Just the security guard, sir,' O'Hara pointed out. 'Why not check on him, too? Might as well take all five of 'em while we're at it.'

'Okay. Fair enough. I don't think he's an issue, but can you lads take him?'

Kinnear's men nodded.

'Great. Right, I want everything we can on this lot. Family, social media, hobbies and interests, right down to whether they've a pimple on their arse. Everything, understand?'

'Sir,' they confirmed in unison.

'Oh, and it would help if you found one of them's as mad as a box of frogs. Now, get to it. We're gonna get this bastard, and we're gonna get him soon.'

**

PC Grimes allowed a car out of Newfield Walk before he turned the patrol car into the same street.

The passenger of the other vehicle held a phone to his ear with one hand and waved an acknowledgement with the other. Andy Nicholson saluted in return.

Grimes remained in the patrol vehicle and left Nicholson to the talking, as usual. He was halfway down the path when Norman Jarrod opened the front door.

'False alarm,' Nicholson told him.

'You don't say,' Norman replied.

'No bother, though. You did right by alerting us.'

Norman Jarrod made a noise somewhere between a laugh and a snort. 'What time does your relief get here?'

Nicholson checked his watch. 'Another half an hour. Just under, to be exact.'

'Champion. When you handover, do me a favour.'

'Of course, sir.'

Norman stood aside to reveal a young man dressed in black and deep purple, hair like a skunk. 'Give this 'un a lift to Lemington. He'll show you the way.'

Nicholson saw the young man hoist a mountaineer's rucksack onto his shoulders. 'Not sure that's a good idea, sir,' the PC warned.

'Oh aye – why's that?'

'We're here to offer you protection. We can't guarantee your son's safety if he's not here.'

This time, Norman did laugh. 'Listen, fuckwit. The reason you didn't find owt at the cricket club is because the car's been here while you were chasing shadows.'

'What?'

'Aye. Exactly. In fact, you just let him oot the end of the street.'

'No way.'

Yes, way. So, if that's your idea of protection, it's best wor James is somewhere else. Now, will you take him to Lemington, or do I have to tell Superintendent Maynard what a right pair of tits you are?'

**

The passenger ended the call as the lights turned green at the foot of Whaggs Lane.

'Well?' the driver asked, turning right.

His companion smiled. 'All's good. The man's pleased.'

'What did he say?'

'I'll be honest, I didn't think it was going down well at first, not when I told him there was no trace of the Detective.'

'I heard you tell him. I think I'd have started with some good news, if I'd been in your shoes.'

'Good job you're not in my shoes, isn't it? Cos when I said the old man and the kid were still around, with only Dumb and Dumber keeping them safe, he was over the moon.'

The driver checked the rear-view mirror as they passed Whickham Police Station. No-one followed. 'He's done with us now, isn't he? He's off our back?'

'He certainly is.'

The driver exhaled. 'Thank Christ for that.' He turned down Dunston Bank.

'Relax,' the passenger said, folding his hands behind his head. 'I told you if we scratched his back, he'd scratch ours.'

They passed the leisure centre and headed towards the long-abandoned Dunston Hill school.

'When do we get paid?' The driver glanced at his passenger. 'We do get paid, don't we?'

'Of course. He even joked about it. I told you he was in a good fettle.'

They pulled to a halt at a red light outside the Health Centre. The driver looked sideways at his passenger.

'What did he say that was so funny?'

'He said we'd get our reward in Heaven.'

The car disintegrated in an explosion heard back in Norman Jarrod's garden.

CHAPTER THIRTY

Sam Maynard replaced the telephone handset. She looked out from her office and saw her team working at high-octane pace. They were a good bunch. The best-balanced squad she'd ever worked with.

It was a shame she had to interrupt them.

She walked through the bullpen and tapped Danskin on the shoulder. So engrossed was he in his work, he jumped at her touch.

'I've just come off the phone from Rick. He's been called to an incident over the river, a possible car bomb.'

'That's all we need.'

'It is. He's asked for a couple of his team to assist, which means we're going to have to release Dolan and Montague from your investigation to backfill. How critical is it if you lose them?'

'On balance, given they're looking at the rank outsider, I'd say they're most needed with Kinnear.'

Maynard smiled. It was a wrench for Danskin to look away from the sparkle in her eyes. 'Thanks, Stephen. Good team sport.'

Maynard and Danskin became aware of a burst of excitement from the bank of desks behind them.

'You got something, Treblecock?'

The Cornishman underplayed it. 'Might be something or nothing', so it might. Worth a second look, though, oi think.'

The Super and DCI were by his side in a split-second.

Todd Robson angled his screen so they could see. 'Like Treblecock says, it mightn't be owt but this Michael Moran bloke, the Jury Marshall, lodged a harassment claim against a fella called Ian Gillies. It seems this Gillies character had copped off with Gillies' partner and was rubbing salt in the wound by sending him images of them in bed together.'

Danskin scratched his head. 'I don't see the link, Robson.'

'Moran's ex-partner was a lass called Jade Wright. One of the images Gillies sent him was subtitled, '*Me with my Wright.*'

Maynard saw the possibility but remained guarded. 'We need more than that, Todd; but it's a start. Nigel, you and Todd check Moran's social media. If there's nothing on the dates in question which categorically puts him in the clear, we'll bring him in.'

'On it, ma'am,' Trebilcock said.

'It's something, I suppose.' Danskin sounded unconvinced.

'We have to start somewhere, Stephen, and it's the best we've got until one of us trumps it.'

Ryan did more than trump it. He played his joker.

He held back the excitement building inside him, but his gut told him this was it. 'Well, will you just look at this? Sir, ma'am – here!'

Jarrod had unearthed a thirteen-year-old newspaper article. He expanded the image until it filled his screen. Danskin read the first three lines, then clapped his hands.

'Listen up, everyone. I think Jarrod might have something. Link it to the big screen, Jarrod. Let's all have a good read and discuss what we think.'

The article appeared on the bullpen's plasma screen.

'**Woman Critically Injured in Road Accident**' the headline screamed.

'*The first night of the Durham Lumiere festival ended in tragedy for Tyneside woman Elspeth Hagan when the car she was travelling in was hit head-on by another vehicle.*

Mrs Hagan received injuries described as both life-threatening and life-changing by staff treating her at the University Hospital of North Durham.

Mrs Hagan was a passenger in a Nissan car driven by her son Jerome (22) when their vehicle was struck by a VW polo travelling in the opposite direction. Her son escaped with minor injuries and the driver of the other vehicle is not believed to be seriously hurt.

It is understood the couple had a reservation for dinner at the Blacksmiths Arms, Low Pittington, and were travelling to the venue when the accident occurred at the junction of Pittington and Moorsley Roads.

Although Mr Hagan is thought to be unfamiliar with the route, Emergency Services do not believe Jerome Hagan to be at fault.

Detective Inspector John Craggs, of Prince Bishop Police, issued a plea for witnesses to come forward. 'This is an extremely serious incident in which a woman received horrific injuries. We appeal to anyone who witnessed the incident…'

Danskin switched off the screen. 'What do we think, guys?'

He knew straight away by their reaction – a quiet hush like the split-second before the ball hits the back of the net at a football match – that they were all of one mind.

'Ryan,' Maynard said, 'See what you can find about the driver of the other vehicle.'

'I'm ahead of you, ma'am. The driver was a Malcolm Holmes. He lived in Horden at the time of the accident. He was charged with dangerous driving.'

'Is that all? What were the Bishops thinking of?' an exasperated Danskin exclaimed. 'I think we should talk to him. Where's he living now?'

Ryan paused. 'He's been missing for donkey's years. He was reported missing on 4th October 2018 and is still on the MissPer register to this day.'

The room fell silent. Every one of Danskin's crew suspected they knew his fate.

'What happened in court?'

'He was found guilty. It was a first offence, and the defence successfully argued the woman would have survived the impact had she been wearing a seat belt. He was given a fine and five-year driving ban.'

Danskin lowered himself into a chair.

'So, there we have the motive.'

'More than that, sir. Remember what Fola said about psychopaths? Some are born to it; others are changed by events.' Ryan was aware everyone was looking at him.

'I think this is the event which changed him.'

'We have our killer,' Danskin announced. 'Jerome John Hagan's our man.'

**

Sam Maynard reined in the kinetic energy in the bullpen.

'Listen up. Let's not get carried away. We need to get this absolutely right. I don't want anybody going off half-cocked. We need a plan, a strategy, and we need evidence. The last is in short supply.'

The others hushed at the realisation she was right.

'Hagan hasn't left a single trace of DNA or fingerprints at the scene of either of the first two murders, and when we hear back from Forensics, I bet it's the same with the Archer/Moss crime scene.'

Maynard realised she was taking over the investigation again. 'Stephen, I need you to find Hagan, and I want you to go back over the statements and find someone – anyone – who can place Hagan at the scene of the crimes. Now, it's back to you.'

Stephen knew what she'd done, and he gave her a nod of appreciation. 'Thank you, ma'am.'

He turned to face his team.

'The Super's right. As well as picking up Hagan, we need to reinterview those first at the scene of each crime. Lyall, you spoke to Jack Wilson at the Victoria Tunnel. Take Hagan's photograph and see if Wilson has any recollection of seeing him. Who found Cavell, remind me?'

'Timothy Rice, sir.'

'Aye. Dexter, you spoke to him. He's yours.'

'Do you want Ryan with me, sir? He did most of the talking.'

To Ryan's relief, Danskin said, 'No. He's with me and uniform. We're going to bring the bastard in.'

The DCI had a second thought. 'Having said that, it's worth having a word with Cavell's flatmate, the Soulsby lass, while you're doon there. Take DS Graves with you. She can speak to Soulsby.'

'But sir...,'

'We haven't time for *buts*, Dexter. Get to it. Now.'

Lucy picked up two copies of Hagan's photograph, handed one to Hannah, and stalked off with the grace of a beaten Jose Mourinho.

Hannah shrugged. 'Oh boy. This is going to be fun.' She set off in pursuit of her chauffeur.

'Jarrod – you and I will do a bit more digging into Hagan's background, work out our approach, and consult with Fola if necessary.'

'Surely that'll take too long, sir?'

'No. I want it all done in thirty minutes. Sangar, O'Hara and Robson will be on the case, an' aal.'

'And then what?'

Danskin met Ryan with a steely gaze.

'We go after him with more ammunition than Rambo could ever dream of.'

**

They found an address for him within two minutes. Within five, Maynard had a major incident van, three uniform patrol cars, and a dog-handling team at Danskin's disposal.

Two minutes later, Ravi gave them the bad news.

'The address is a former tied cottage on farmland between Wallsend and Benton. There's only one access road, in-and-out. I can't see any way we'll manage a covert approach. He'll spot us a mile off.'

'Bollocks. What do you suggest, Sangar?'

'A single vehicle mightn't arouse too much suspicion, providing it's unmarked of course. If we manage to get someone inside by those means and provide a distraction, it might be enough for the rest of the units to make their way on foot over the fields without attracting Hagan's attention.'

Sangar called Google Maps up on the big screen. 'There's a few trees and enough hedges to provide a degree of cover.'

Danskin and Maynard nodded in agreement.

'Sir,' Gavin O'Hara interjected. 'I've the duty roster for the court. Hagan's not on it for today. He should be at home. Even better, I've ascertained he wasn't working on the day of any of the murders. Circumstantial, I know, but it gives us something to work on if comes to trial.'

'WHEN it comes to trial, O'Hara; not *if*.'

Ryan checked the wall clock. They'd used up fifteen of their thirty minutes.

'I've a bit more on the mother. Seems she was in hospital for almost five months, then Hagan insisted on her coming home, despite her being severely brain damaged and bed-ridden. He's cared for her ever since.'

'Hang on. How does that work? He can't care for her twenty-four hours a day and work at the same time.'

'He's part-time, sir,' O'Hara clarified. 'Seems he lets the court know when he's free and they roster him in.'

Danskin screwed up his face. 'That's a bit accommodating of them, isn't it?'

'It'll be part of those Reasonable Adjustment bollocks employers have to make,' Todd suggested.

Ryan pointed to the clock. 'Sir, the time. We need to get a shift on.'

'Aye, we do. But remember what the Super said. We can't afford to cock-up.'

A thought struck Danskin between the eyes.

'Whoa. Let's rewind. So, Hagan works part-time. It still doesn't explain what he does with his mother. I mean, he's hardly going to wheel her bed into the court, is he? And what about when he commits the crimes? What happens to Elspeth Hagan then? Does a nurse or a carer step in? There's so much we divvent yet know.'

They remained silent while the clock ticked on.

Danskin snapped his fingers. 'Have we missed a trick? Paddock's son does voluntary work, doesn't he? Could he be involved somehow?'

'Negative, sir,' Ryan said. 'His voluntary work is with a badger watch group in Northumberland.'

'Worth the thought, though, Stephen.' The Super, too, clock watched. 'Okay; let's get the show on the road. Stephen, you and Ryan make the approach to the cottage. Keep the other units out of sight. It's your shout how we take it forward from there.'

Maynard picked up Hagan's photograph. Floppy hair, expensive, black-rimmed spectacles, a sweet smile, even.

'He looks so ordinary, doesn't he?'

'Aye,' Danskin agreed. 'Nowt about him to arouse suspicion. That's how he's got away with it. Until now, that is.'

CHAPTER THIRTY-ONE

Smalltalk between Lucy and Hannah was non-existent. They drove from Forth Street to North Shields in a silence broken only by the occasional radio message aimed at the units attending the car bomb incident.

Lucy took the quickest route, straight along the Coast Road. They were at Billy Mill roundabout before Lucy spoke.

'You don't mind, do you?'

'Mind what?'

Lucy glanced sideways. 'Me and Ryan. You don't mind about us?'

'Working together? No, we all do what the DCI or Super orders.'

'I don't mean like that. I mean, *being* together. You know, a couple and all that.'

'Come again?'

'Oh my God. He hasn't told you. I'm so sorry. I thought you knew.'

Hannah fixed her gaze on the road ahead. 'No. I didn't. And I don't believe a word of it, anyway. I know Ry. He wouldn't.'

'Really?' Lucy took one hand from the steering wheel and waved it dismissively. 'Whatever.'

Lucy smirked to herself as she drove under the Metro bridge on Tanners Bank. 'Nearly there now. I'll park in the car park looking down on the Low Light. It's always best to survey the surroundings first.'

'*Those are Ryan's words,*' Hannah thought. 'What about me?'

'You'll see Soulsby's apartment from where I park. You've got a bit of an uphill hike, mind.'

Hannah rolled her eyes and removed a plastic wallet containing Hagan's photograph from the glove apartment as Lucy reversed into a bay.

Dexter made to unhook the radio. Hannah stopped her.

'We meet back here. Half an hour, no more, then we report in.'

'Could do, I suppose, though I thought we might meet in the pub down the road. Ryan and I went there, once. Sam Fender was having a pint with his saxophonist. Ry was a bit star-struck but me; nah, I'm not a big fan.' Lucy smiled a tight-lipped sneer.

Hannah ignored the comment. 'We meet back here in thirty minutes.'

'Whatever,' Lucy said again, annoyingly.

'Oh, just one more thing, Dexter.'

'Sure.' Lucy turned to face her.

Hannah unleashed a vicious slap across Dexter's cheek.

**

Danskin turned the unmarked car left onto a country lane just after Wallsend's Sunholme Estate. He ensured the convoy followed, then radioed for one of the marked cars to prohibit entrance or exit.

Less than quarter of a mile down the lane, another narrow road ran off to the left, down to a housing estate. Danskin ordered another car to block the mouth of the road.

Sun shone across open fields to their right, so brightly Ryan held up a hand to shield his eyes. Danskin rolled the vehicle to a halt and the remaining car, incident van, and dog handlers pulled up behind.

'Okay,' Danskin said into the radio. 'Listen up. The farmhouse and cottage is down a track just around the next corner. I want a dog front and back, out of sight, and muzzled. Don't want any of the beasts howling. I want three men at the end of the drive. Keep down beneath the wall.'

He switched off the mic and wiped sweat off his brow. He unmuted the mic.

'I want the rest of you out back. There's a line of trees just to the right of the cottage, a hundred yards or so away, and bushes to the left. The hedgerow's probably less than fifty yards from the back door. I want two men in the bushes, the rest – including the dogs - in the trees. Copy?'

'Understood,' the units reported back, one-by-one.

'To get to the hedgerow, you need to skirt the field and approach the bushes from the rear. You guys set off now. We'll give you three minutes head start, then the second unit deploy to the trees. Once there, Jarrod and me will drive to the cottage. Any questions?'

Only static hissed from the radio.

'I'll take that as a yes. Okay, lads. Break a leg.'

Danskin switched off the radio. He couldn't afford any interruptions to break their cover story, that of health visitors checking on Elspeth Hagan. Two more unlikely health visitors it was hard to imagine, but it was all they had.

'Can I check on me Dad first, sir?'

'Sorry, son. No time for that. And I need you focused on this, okay? If your mind's elsewhere, tell me now.'

'No, sir. I know what we're up against.'

'Good.' Danskin reached behind his seat. 'We'll need these.'

He heaved a couple of stab vests over the headrest and tossed one into Ryan's lap.

'Put it on in the car and fasten your jacket over it. We can't be too careful.'

Ryan swallowed hard.

This had suddenly become very real.

**

Hannah strode up to the Knotts's Flats building like a woman possessed. By the time she reached it, she was breathless but had worked the anger out of her system.

She shouldn't have slapped her. She knew Dexter would report her. She'd be up on a charge and, no doubt, shunted back to the Port of Tyne for her troubles.

From her vantage point, Hannah looked down at the River Tyne, coiled like a silver serpent, and at the fishing fleet docked in the Fish Market gut where a swirling cloud of gulls hovered.

She turned her head westward, towards the lookout tower over the Port of Tyne, where a ferry lay docked outside her office window, offloading its cargo, freight, and passengers.

She'd be back there, soon; overseeing paperwork, arguing with HMRC, querying the efficiency of Border Agency staff. After what she'd just done, she could be back as soon as tomorrow.

She shouldn't have hit Lucy Dexter.

But, boy, she felt a helluva lot better for it.

**

Lucy stayed in the car until the watery haze cleared from her eyes. One side of her face burned scarlet with the imprint of Hannah's palm.

Once her vision returned, Lucy climbed out the vehicle and felt a warm sea breeze wash over her.

She squinted against a lapis lazuli sky and watched DS Graves climb the steep uphill approach to the brown-brick apartment block on the clifftop. It wasn't DS Graves fault, Lucy decided. She'd have done the same. Possibly, she'd have done even worse.

Lucy shrugged off her thin jacket and tossed it over her shoulder. Below her, the uppermost floors of the Low Light reflected white, the lower decks – including the one housing Timothy Rice – lay in dark shadow cast by the Coquet Island Seafood building.

She ignored the temptations of the Low Light Tavern and made for her destination, the photograph of Jerome Hagan in her shoulder bag.

**

Danskin parked at the head of the drive, in full view of the cottage. He and Ryan stepped out of the car into bright sunshine.

Ryan found the situation surreal. In the distance, over fields greening with Spring's rebirth, the distinctive white buildings of the Tyneview Park DWP complex shone like beacons. Across the still air, Ryan heard whistles and breathless shouts from Newcastle United's Darsley Park training complex.

It was all so everyday, so ordinary, yet yards from them lay what he felt in his bones was a House of Horrors.

It was the warmest day of the year by far, and Ryan began to remove his jacket.

'Leave it on, Jarrod. Don't show your vest.'

'Bloody hell, aye. Schoolboy error.'

They studied the cottage as they made a snail-slow approach.

The drive, rutted with dried mud, veered away from the cottage at the front and led to a home-made carport, little more than a corrugated perspex roof held up by wooden struts, at the side of the building. The car port was empty.

The cottage was a small, single-story affair; stone-built with jagged cracks running down the frontage. The white timber window frames were pitted with rot, the glass caked with dust. One of the four panes displayed a spider web pattern of shattered glass.

'Looks deserted,' Ryan said, like a ventriloquist.

'It does. Let's find out, shall we?'

Danskin knocked on the thin wooden door.

He rapped again. 'Hello? We're here to see Mrs. Hagan. She's eligible for her fourth vaccine.'

Ryan raised his eyebrows.

'Got any better suggestions, Jarrod?'

'We're from the NHS,' Ryan shouted at the door.

Ryan tried the handle. The door was locked.

Stephen Danskin cupped a hand over his eyes and peered through a grimy window into an unoccupied dining room lifted straight out of Beamish Museum.

'Let's see if this shithole has a back door.'

Danskin whistled his way around the side of the cottage, through the open-ended car port, with no attempt to disguise his presence.

They found the rear of the cottage even more shambolic than the front. Its large, unkempt garden ran to the fenced border of a rapeseed field.

'Blimey. This could do with a bit of TLC,' Ryan commented.

'Never mind the TL bit. Just some C would be better than this.'

Tall weeds protruded through a weather-beaten footpath leading to a large garden shed. As far as they could tell, the lawn hadn't received any attention for years, and a bramble bush ran amok in its borders.

'Let's see if we get anywhere here.' Danskin knocked loudly on the back door, scattering loose flakes of paint at his feet.

Still no answer.

'Sir, while you have a nose about, I'll have a gander in the shed.'

Ryan avoided weeds and nettles as he walked to the shed. Its structure appeared sound; probably the most secure thing about the entire house. The door was padlocked shut with a heavy, new-looking lock.

Ryan reached into the pocket of his jacket and brought out a paperclip. He wiggled it back and forth until it snapped in half. He bent one half into a L-shape and forced the hook end into the lock. He rotated it downwards until the tension of the lock bit.

Ryan kept the clip in place with one hand and, with his other, pushed the straight end of the paperclip beneath the pins. He shook his head to rid his brow of sweat, and gently jiggled the paperclips.

The padlock popped open.

He felt lightheaded. He stood back and took a couple of deep breaths. He felt adrenaline pump through his veins as he slid the shed door open. The sun lay behind the shed so, even with the door open, it was dark inside.

The shed bore the smell of mildew. Ryan brought out his mobile phone and flicked on its torch. He directed its ray left to right, up and down. Dust danced in the beam of light like a swarm of insects.

He hadn't known what to expect, but he knew it wasn't this.

Ryan took a step back.

And felt a firm grip take hold of his collar bone.

CHAPTER THIRTY-TWO

'Miss Soulsby?'

A furrowed ridge creased Leanne's brow. 'Uh-huh.'

'I'm DS Hannah Graves, City and County CID. I wonder if I could have a quick word?'

'Have you caught him? The bastard who killed Bobbi?'

'I'm afraid we haven't.' She saw the glimmer of hope escape from Leanne's eyes. 'But we will. And soon. That's what I'm here about, actually. To ask you if you recognise someone. Is it okay if I come in?'

Leanne led Hannah into an untidy living room, in contrast to the furniture and décor. The wrappings of a burger meal lay on the table next to an empty gin bottle.

Hannah looked into Leanne's eyes and saw in them the hollowness of the bereaved.

'How are you doing, Leanne?'

The girl lowered herself onto a sofa, her knees curled to her chest and her arms wrapped around them. She wore Ugg boots and a zebra-patterned onesie. She looked like a child.

There was no emotion in her voice as she said, 'I just want him caught.'

Hannah gave her a reassuring smile. 'And so do we.'

She produced three photographs, two of random men on the police database, and one of a smiling, charming-looking Jerome Hagan. 'Leanne, I'm going to show you some photographs. I need to know if you've ever seen any of the men before? Did Bobbi date any of them? Have you seen them hanging around, maybe outside the building, or around Newcastle? Think carefully, it's important.'

'Do you think one of these did it?'

Hannah didn't commit herself as she handed over the first photograph.

Leanne stared at it for a long moment. Finally, she blinked and shook her head.

'And what about this second one? Think carefully.'

'No. I don't think so.'

'Look again. Are you sure you haven't seen him, or just *think* you haven't?'

'I'm sure,' Leanne said, handing the photograph back.

'Okay, Leanne. You're doing well. How about this one?'

Hannah watched Leanne carefully. The girl in the onesie pursed her lips. Looked out the windows, then returned her gaze to the photograph.

'Yes! I know him. Or, at least, I've seen him. I'm trying to think where, but I'm sure I've seen him. Is it him?'

Hannah stood. 'I'm afraid I can't say, but you've been very helpful. I'll chase this up now. I have to go. Thanks for your time. We'll be in touch.'

She shook Leanne's hand and left the apartment.

In the corridor, Hannah unleashed a sigh and tucked the photographs back into a Ziplock wallet.

Leanne Soulsby had seen what she wanted to see.

She'd picked out one of the random blokes.

They still didn't have an eyewitness who could put Hagan at the scene.

**

The instant Ryan felt the hand on his shoulder, he switched onto automatic pilot.

He raised his heel from the ground, flexed his knee, and flicked his leg upwards. His heel rammed into the groin of his assailant.

The hand released its grip and Ryan heard air escape from his assailant's lungs. He sensed the man crumple.

Ryan spun, pushed the doubled-over figure to the ground, and landed his knees centre of the stricken man's chest.

'For fuck's sake, man, Jarrod; what the hell are you doing?' Danskin managed to wheeze before he burst into a fit of retching coughs.

'Sir?'

'Jesus, you've crushed me bollocks, man. Fucking hell.'

Danskin held both hands to his groin as Ryan rolled off his chest. 'Put your head between your knees, sir. It'll help.'

'It'll help, my arse. You've ruptured me.'

'Sorry, sir. I thought you were Hagan.'

'Well, I'm not, am...' Danskin broke off mid-sentence. 'What the hell's that?' he croaked, looking deep into the shed.

'Aye, funny place for a library, isn't it?' He hoisted Danskin to his feet as he said, 'And what's the folded-up Z-bed for?'

'I reckon there's only one bedroom in the cottage, by the size of it. Looks like even Hagan's not sick enough to sleep with his own mother.' Danskin stepped inside the shed. 'The shelving looks new, doesn't it? What's he reading?'

'Lots of law books,' Ryan said, moving towards a pristine-clean shelving rack.

'He's just a bloody clerk, not a barrister at the Owld Bailey. What's he want them for?'

Ryan removed a book from the shelf. Rifled through it. Picked up another.

'Some of these are court transcripts. This is Ian Huntley's; the Soham murderer.

'I know who Huntley is, Jarrod.'

Ryan picked up the next volume. 'Charles Bronson.' And the next. 'Harold Shipman.'

Danskin moved to another rack set against the side wall.

'Well I'll be buggered. He's got '*The Oxford Specialist Handbook in Surgery*' here. Look at this one: '*Essential Operative Techniques and Anatomy*.' Aaron Elliot said the killer learnt his techniques from Dr Google. Elliot was wrong. He's picked 'em up from bloody medical textbooks.'

Ryan grimaced. 'If this is what he's got in his shed, I divvent fancy finding out what he's hiding in the house.'

'Don't look like that, Jarrod. This is pretty persuasive circumstantial evidence you've uncovered. The first we've got. Well done.'

'Cheers. Sir. How's the nuts, sir?'

'How do you think? So, don't let the 'well done' think I've forgiven you.'

'No, sir,' Ryan said with a smile. He knew well-enough Danskin had forgiven him.

'Let's get inside the cottage.'

**

Lucy didn't stop at the Low Light Tavern, but nor did she stop at the Low Light itself. Instead, she walked on by.

She'd seen the tide timetable pinned on a notice board in the car park. It was due to change, which meant Timothy Rice would be in position, mop, bucket and hose in hand, ready to swill down the Fish Market. She'd speak to him at work, away from his aunt.

The heat of the sun irritated her already painful cheek. She scratched at the inflamed skin with a fingernail. When she removed her finger from her face, she saw her nail flecked red with blood.

She dabbed at her face with a tissue. The blood was barely noticeable, a faint sliver of pink. She balled the tissue and tossed it into a bin outside The Waterfront.

Dexter wound her way to the quay where skippers supervised crew members filling their boat's holds with ice. On the deck of one trawler, three men conducted urgent repair work on a net.

The door to one unit stood open. Inside, a man removed a tray from a metal cupboard. It was laden with tools of his trade. He inspected the items, one-by-one, and held up a gleaming blade to the sun.

Lucy walked over and engaged the man in conversation. She discovered the blade was a Japanese filleting knife. It struck a chord with her.

'Looks new,' she observed.

The man looked at her. 'Aye, it is. We've lost a couple lately.'

'Lost?'

'Yeah. Gone missing. Not here. That's generally what lost means.'

'And that's a replacement for one that's *gone missing*, is it?'

'Aye. Bloody expensive, an' aal.'

Lucy looked out towards the quay. 'No sign of Timothy?'

The man set down the blade. 'Who?'

'Timothy. The bloke who swills down the quay.'

The man's face flickered in recognition. 'Ah, you mean Saddo? Never knew his real name. Nah, haven't seen him since that lass got killed.'

'Really?'

'Nah, I'm just mekin' it up, like. I aalways joke about people being killed.'

Lucy's jaw tightened. 'I meant, Timothy hasn't been back.'

The man shrugged. 'Not as far as I know, anyways. Somebody telt me he lives in the Low Light if you want to see him, though.'

'I know where he lives, thank you,' Lucy said, heading off towards the former lighthouse.

She felt the seadog's eyes drilling into her back.

She didn't see his fingers tenderly caress the filleting knife.

**

Danskin reported back to Maynard at Forth Street. The cottage appeared empty.

Before she consented to her two men breaking and entering, she asked a question neither DCI nor DS had considered: 'If there's no-one there, who's looking after Mrs Hagan?'

'She's got a point,' Ryan agreed after Maynard signed off.

'She has. Perhaps he's not such a loving son after all. Howay, then, Super's given us permission. Let's get in there and find oot.'

Danskin placed an arm against a windowpane, pulled his elbow forward, and jabbed it back, hard, at the glass.

The single glazed window broke with ease. He quickly did the same with the other three panes. He tried to raise a leg to kick out the frame, found the pain in his gonads too much, so delegated the task to Ryan.

One kick and the wooden frame splintered inwards.

The first thing to hit them was the smell.

'Oh, Jesus,' Danskin exclaimed, 'I think there's some more of them in here. Bodies, like.'

With the radio left in the car, he phoned Maynard and asked her to radio the units outside the farm for backup.

Ryan opened a door. Kitchen. Old-fashioned, but adequate. And empty.

The next room on the left housed a threadbare three-piece suite, a portable TV, and an old-fashioned sideboard. No people.

Apart from the dining room, only one room remained unsearched.

Danskin flung it open and instantly retched.

He'd found the source of the smell.

A deformed and disfigured old woman lay on a hospital bed. She was entwined within a maze of plastic tubes and wiring. Transparent sacs hung from stands, each bag containing evermore suspicious looking fluids.

What's more, the woman reeked of shit and piss.

'Ah man,' Danskin said, full of pity.

The woman stared at him with huge eyes. 'Don't be frightened, ma'am. I'm DCI Danskin and this is DS Jarrod. We're here to help you.'

He turned his back on her, his eyes awash with tears. 'You know what she reminds me of?'

Ryan did. 'Florence Roadhouse.'

'Aye, bless her.'

Roadhouse had helped Danskin and Jarrod solve their very first case together, with her dying breath. Ryan was still a Special at the time. He remembered her well.

'I'll get an ambulance.'

'Backup will be here any second. They can do it. Another minute or two won't matter. We've work to do. We need to find where the hell Hagan's got himself too.'

Ryan looked around the bedroom. On one wall, a cheap portrait of a tabby cat lapping at a saucer of cream. On another, an expensively framed charter of some description, decorated with intricate calligraphy. On another wall, the paper seemed wrinkled and out of keeping with the rest of the room.

Ryan pointed it out to his DCI, who felt around it with his fingertips. 'Well, I'll be a Mackem,' Danskin said. 'Hang onto your hollyhocks, Jarrod.'

Stephen Danskin pushed at the wall and a section of it swung around one-hundred-and-eighty degrees. It revealed a concealed whiteboard.

'We've got all the evidence we need now, son.'

The board held a large map of Tyneside, Northumberland and Durham. Red crosses were scrawled across points on the map. Danskin moved closer and saw they highlighted North Shields Fish Market, the Victoria Tunnel, and St Mary's Heritage Centre.

Beneath the map, the names of Roberta Cavell, William Vickers, and Jane Archer were scored out in thick, black marker pen.

There was one other cross and one further name on the board.

The name was *Malcolm Holmes*, and the cross was scribbled over a Go-Karting track in County Durham, little more than five miles from the spot where Elspeth Hagan was reduced to her catatonic state.

'Got you hook, line, and sinker, Hagan. Now, we've just got to find where the hell you are.'

Danskin stared at the whiteboard, frantically trying to join the dots.

Ryan turned to face the framed chart, the showpiece of Elspeth Hagan's bedroom. As he did so, he caught a glimpse of something as the sun's rays caught it. Whatever it was, the flash came from beneath Elspeth Hagan's bed.

He reassured Mrs Hagan he meant her no harm as he closed in on her and knelt on the floor. His fingers scrabbled beneath the bed. Closed around something. Ryan brought it out and stared at it, thoughtfully.

Ryan's attention returned to the glass frame. He knew what he was looking for, now.

'Sir,' he said quietly, 'I'm pretty sure I know who looks after Hagan's mother when he's out doing his dirty work.'

He traced a finger down and across the chart in the frame. His sweaty fingertip left a smear across the glass.

'More importantly, I think I know where Hagan is. If I'm right, we've got a problem. A very big problem.'

CHAPTER THIRTY-THREE

It took an age for the woman to answer the door.

'I'm...' Lucy began

'I know who you are. I remember from last time.'

'Is Timothy in?'

'No. He's at the quay, swilling down.'

'I've just come from there, Mrs. Rice. I know he isn't.'

The woman bristled. 'Isn't he? Well, in that case, I don't...'

'If I could just come in, it won't take long.'

'No! No, you can't. Not without a warrant. I'm not letting you in. Please, go away.'

Lucy peered into the compact hallway.

'I asked you to go away,' the woman repeated. 'Go. Now.'

'Let her in, Auntie Mo.'

Her eyelids drooped. 'Are you sure?'

'Quite sure, Auntie Mo.'

Mo stepped aside.

'Timothy sounds much better,' Lucy said. 'I promise I won't upset him.'

She walked into the parlour and took a seat without waiting to be asked.

'Hi, Timmy,' Lucy smiled. 'You know who I am, don't you?'

The thickset man kept his head down.

'Come on, Timmy. You can talk to me. You know you can trust me. You were fine just before. All I want to do is show you a couple of photographs, and you tell me if you recognise anyone.'

Rice kept his head down. Mumbled something incoherent.

'Look, here's the first photograph. Will you look at it for me? Please?'

Tim Rice raised his eyes. Looked at her sheepishly and shook his head. His gaze returned to the carpet.

Lucy bent forward and laid the picture on the floor where his eyes couldn't miss it.

Tim brought his head up. Avoided the photograph, and avoided looking at Lucy, too. Instead, he seemed to gaze over her left shoulder.

Lucy Dexter didn't hear the bedroom door open behind her. Didn't sense the footsteps approaching. She took a hard blow to the rear of her skull.

Lucy slumped in a heap on the floor.

**

Ryan showed Danskin the item he'd retrieved from beneath Elspeth's bed.

'I've seen this before. I couldn't remember where until now.'

'Howay, we haven't time to fart about. What is it, and where's Hagan?'

'Give us a minute to work it through in my head, sir. Like the Super said, we can't afford to get this wrong.'

Ryan rubbed his brow. Looked at the chart on the wall. Finally, he nodded.

'Right. I've worked it out, and we've already made one mistake.'

'Which is?'

'We didn't do enough research into Hagan's background at the station. If we'd taken a bit of time, given it more thought, we'd have nailed this earlier.'

'Don't beat yourself up over it, Jarrod. Maynard only gave us thirty minutes, remember. Anybody can miss summat with only half an hour to work in. Whatever it is we've missed, it's not down to you. We all worked on it, and we all had the time restraints. So, forget about it and tell me your line of thought.'

Ryan sucked in air. Began talking - and talking fast.

'This on the wall tells us all we need to know. It's a genealogy chart – a family tree, if you like – going back six, seven, eight, generations. But this is what we're looking at.'

He aimed a finger at the names of a Lawrence John and Olivia Vera Treadwell.

'Now, see here? Below the Treadwells is Elspeth Hagan, their daughter.'   Ryan talked as if the old woman in the bed wasn't present. Given her state, he was probably correct.

'It says here that Elspeth is the wife of the late Owen Hagan. Owen Hagan is shown as deceased around the time of the Falklands War...'

'Jarrod, we haven't time for an episode of 'Who Do You Think You Are?' Get on with it, man.'

'I am, sir, but all this is relevant. Now,' he ran a finger in a circle around a name below the couple, 'Here's their son, our man – Jerome John Hagan.'

Danskin looked at the chart. 'We know all this. We're wasting time here.'

'No, sir, we're not. Because, if you look closely, there's another name alongside Jerome Hagan's, but it's been covered up.'

Danskin leaned in. 'Aye, I see that.'

'So, Jerome Hagan isn't an only child. He has a brother...'

'...Or sister. Or had. If he or she's blanked out, they might be deed.'

'No. It's a brother, and he's alive.'

Danskin scratched at the stubble on his chin. 'How do you know?'

'I know, because Elspeth has a sibling, too. A sister.'

He pointed to an arrow linking Elspeth's name to another. His eyes sparkled. 'Her sister's name is Monica.'

Danskin shook his head. 'I must be thick, or summat. None of this makes any sense.'

'It will do in a minute, sir.' He held up the item he'd found under the bed. 'I've seen this before. It's an earring, and it belongs to the sister.'

'What?'

'Our first victim was found by a man living with his aunt. He called her Aunt Mo. When I spoke to her, she was wearing this.'

Danskin's jaw dropped open as he looked at the family tree in a new light.

Ryan continued. 'The man who found Roberta Cavell is called Timothy Rice…'

'…and Monica Treadwell married a Bernard Rice, who passed away in 2014, it says here.'

'You're into this family tree lark now, aren't you?' Ryan smiled.

'And you're thinking Timothy Rice is Elspeth's other son.' Danskin looked towards the disfigured woman in the bed. A tear streaked her cheek.

'I'm sure of it. I'm guessing Monica took him in after Elspeth's accident. Timothy has Down's, so it'd be difficult for him to lead an independent life, especially at the age he'd be at the time of the accident. Looks like Timothy Hagan adopted his aunt's surname. He became Tim Rice'

Danskin thought for a moment. 'If Hagan thinks for one moment we're onto him, he'll know Monica and Timothy can drop him right in the shite.'

'Yes, sir. Which is why I believe that's where he is right now. Sir, I think Rice has a new mission.'

Realisation hit Danskin like a wrecking ball.

'We need back-up. I sent Dexter there.'

**

Hannah Graves leant against the vehicle, folded her arms on its roof, and listened to the sounds of the sea and the caw of circling gulls.

Her sleeves slid up her forearms and she caught sight of her watch. Twenty-five minutes had flown by since she last sat inside the car. She glanced down the footpath leading to the Low Light. There was no sign of Lucy Dexter.

Hannah ambled along the clifftop path and took a seat on the sculpted capstan, back-to-back with Ray Lonsdale's magnificent Fiddler's Green Fisherman statue. After a few moments, she stood, brushed herself down, and wandered back to the car.

She still couldn't see Dexter. *'She's playing silly buggers, I bet,'* Hannah thought.

DS Graves ran her hand through her curls. Her fingers came out slick with sweat. She wiped them on her slacks. Checked her watch again. Thirty-five minutes had elapsed since they'd gone their separate ways.

Hannah's eyes searched the length of the Fish Quay. They settled on the Ship's Cat, then the Low Light Tavern.

'She'd better not be,' she said aloud. She unclipped her radio from her belt and spoke into it.

'Kilo November, you're late. Are you all done?'

Hannah thought she heard something, but she couldn't be sure. 'Kilo November. DC Dexter. Is everything okay?'

This time, Hannah realised what she'd heard. It was her own voice.

She looked through the car's side window. A green light showed next to the steering wheel, the green light of Lucy Dexter's radio. She'd left it in the vehicle, set to 'Receive'.

Hannah tutted and made off downhill, towards the Low Light.

**

The wheels of Danskin's car threw up stones and gravel as it fishtailed up the track leading from the cottage.

'All units, back to your vehicles. We're heading to North Shields. The Fish Quay. This is urgent!' He illuminated the blue lights hidden in the front grill. 'Blues and twos all the way. Understand?'

He heard breathless shouts over the radio as the support units fought their way out of the undergrowth they'd hidden in. The patrol car at the head of the lane stepped into line behind Danskin while the driver of the incident support truck waited for men and dogs to reach him.

'Ma'am,' Danskin shouted into the mic, 'No time to explain but we need back up at the North Shields Low Light. Jarrod's pieced it all together, but I think Dexter may be in danger. She's not responding to her radio, and we think she may be with the killer.'

'Jesus Christ, Stephen, where are you?'

'We're on our way there now. ETA fifteen minutes max, probably less if I floor it.'

'Are your support units with you?'

'Following, ma'am.'

'Right. Good. Listen, I didn't get the paperwork for Armed Response prepared in time for your mission, but it's signed off now. We're good-to-go with Firearms. I'll put in a call to change the destination. It'll take a few minutes, no more, then we'll have an Armed Response Unit with you.'

Danskin zig-zagged the vehicle through traffic on Wallsend's Station Road.

'What about Kinnear's squad?'

'You've enough of your plate without worrying how Rick's doing.'

'I'm not worrying. I'm asking if he can provide support.'

'Forget it. He's busy matching up body parts to their respective owners.'

Danskin winced. 'Okay, ma'am. I'll leave this channel open. Let me know when the ARU is on its way. I'll leave Jarrod to fill you in on events at the cottage.'

The DCI blared his horn at four motorcycles spread across the slip road leading to the Coast Road. 'Get out the fucking way!'

'Calm down, Stephen.'

'I put Dexter in danger, ma'am. I don't need to be calm; I need to be there, and I need to be there now.'

Ryan jumped in. 'DS Graves was travelling with Lucy in the same car. She's only a couple of hundred yards away. She can get to the scene before any of us.'

'Shit!' Danskin swore.

'What is it?'

'They might have shared tasks. They both could have spoken to Soulsby, then both gone to talk to Rice.'

'That's not what their instructions were, sir.'

Danskin glanced sideways at Ryan. 'Like you've never bent an order, Jarrod.'

'Get out the fucking way!' Ryan yelled at the motorcyclists.

**

Hannah had made it as far as Clifford's Fort when she was alerted by her call sign announced on the radio.

'Bravo Oscar,' she replied.

'Hannah, it's Stephen.'

Danskin calling her *Hannah* and he *Stephen* was enough to pique her curiosity.

'Sir?'

'You're okay?'

'Of course. Why wouldn't I?'

'Is Dexter there with you?'

'No, she's still speaking to Rice. There again, she might be in the pub…'

'Listen,' Danskin said with urgency. 'We're pretty sure Hagan's got a connection with Timothy Rice. We think they're brothers.'

'What?'

'We also think Hagan's there now.'

Hannah fell into a stunned silence for a second before she broke into a sprint.

'I'm on my way.'

'Wait. Hannah – we're ten minutes from you, with backup. The Super's despatched Armed Response as well. Keep out of sight until we meet you there. Do NOT engage without backup. Repeat, do not engage. Understand?'

Hannah didn't reply.

'Hannah. Do you copy?'

No answer.

'DS Graves…'

Hannah switched off her radio.

She switched it off because she heard raised voices from inside the apartment; one male voice, the other female. The voices were angry. Threatening.

Was it Lucy? She couldn't be sure, but she wasn't about to take a chance.

Hannah wrapped her fingers around the door handle. Took a deep breath.

'Police! Do NOT move!'

She burst into the apartment.

CHAPTER THIRTY-FOUR

Lucy woke with a splitting headache, blurred vision, and a sense of disorientation.

Two figures faced her. They sat stock still, like tailor's dummies. Behind them, sunlight shone through a porthole sized window and zoned in like an interrogator's torch. Lucy shrunk away from it.

Slowly, she took stock of her surroundings. She was in a small, sparsely furnished room. Lucy vaguely recognised the couple sitting opposite – then everything snapped into place.

Lucy tried to move. She couldn't. Her hands were tied behind her back, her ankles to the chair legs.

Lucy heard a scraping noise behind her. Sensed something being placed alongside her. She tried turning her head but the pain was too much. She settled on a sideways glance.

Hannah Graves sat next to her; she, too, bound to a kitchen stool.

A man stepped from behind them.

'Auntie Mo, meet our friends from the police.'

Monica Rice said nothing. Next to her, Tim fixed his eyes on a spot on the carpet.

Jerome Hagan, mad-professor hair, clean-shaven and handsome eyes behind black rimmed spectacles, wore a suit, jacket and all, despite the heat. He addressed Hannah. 'We haven't had the pleasure. I'm Jerome. You are?'

'Detective Sergeant Hannah Graves, City and County CID.'

Hagan chuckled. 'I thought you were going to rattle off name, rank, and number for a moment. Welcome to my aunt's house. We're pleased to have you here, aren't we Auntie Mo?'

Monica remained passive.

'Jerome,' Lucy began before she coughed violently. She spat blood to the floor.

'That's not very pleasant. I hope you're going to clean it up, DC Dexter. That is your name, isn't it? Yes, of course it is. You surely didn't think I hadn't done my homework on you, did you?'

Lucy frowned.

'I saw you, you know,' Hagan continued. 'You and your colleague. You walked right beneath me on your way to the Low Lights.'

Lucy's mouth opened. So, too, Hannah's.

'That's right. The day that awful Cavell woman passed away, I was having a chilled pint on the Ship's Cat balcony. You passed by without a second glance. I can't tell you what a thrill it gave me to see all the activity I'd put you to. Not to mention realising how incompetent you and your colleagues are.'

Hannah's eyes narrowed. 'You've proved yourself very clever, Mr Hagan,' she said, playing to his ego, 'But you do know this has to end here, don't you?'

'My dear, it will end when I want it to end. And my mission is far from over. It won't be over until you, your colleagues, and the justice system begin to give criminals their just desserts. And I see no sign of that happening anytime soon.'

Lucy's lips were dry as stone. She licked them and attempted to speak once more. 'Your aunt and your cousin have done nothing wrong. At least set them free.'

Hagan laughed uproariously. 'My aunt and who? My cousin? You really are so far off the pace.'

'Not as far as off the pace as you think, Jerome,' Hannah said. 'We know Timothy is your brother.'

Surprise crossed Monica's face. Tim raised his eyes from the floor for the first time. Lucy managed to rotate her head to look at Hannah.

'Oh, you're good, aren't you? Is that why they made you a Sergeant? You're so much brighter than your little spiky-haired companion.'

'Jerome, I have many colleagues more on the ball than either Lucy or me. And they will be here. Soon.'

'But they aren't as bright as me. Nor will they escape me. Why should I think they'll be any more difficult to overpower than you or DC Dexter?'

Hannah opened her mouth to reply before Hagan spoke again.

'Please don't say because they are men. That would be so sexist. It would also be immaterial. My male victims were easily overcome. Your colleagues will fall into my trap.'

Hannah shook her head. 'I'm sorry, Jerome, but you're deluded. They'll come armed. Guns, stun grenades, the works. You've got nothing.'

Hagan reached into a back pocket and withdrew a razor-sharp blade.

'I've got this,' he said. 'It's served me well to date.'

'A knife? Against an Armed Response Unit? You won't get out of this alive. Your only way is to give yourself up.'

Hagan laughed long and loud. 'If I don't get out alive, neither will they.'

He loosened his jacket and let it fall open.

Around his waist he wore a thick, pouched belt. Lodged in its pockets were four silver flasks.

They were looped together with wires which disappeared beneath Hagan's shirt and re-emerged through a loosened buttonhole near the neckline. From there, they ran to his shirt pocket.

A shirt pocket which held the obvious bulk of a mobile phone.

Hannah knew what the device was.

For the first time in her career, she screamed like a girl.

**

The unmarked car driven by Danskin spun like a Red Bull as it took the hairpin bend at the head of Union Quay.

Ryan was out the passenger door before it slewed to a halt in front of the Low Light. Danskin followed, keys left in ignition and door ajar.

The first of the backup cars pulled to a halt behind them. Danskin ordered the uniformed officers to clear the area. In the distance, the sirens of the second patrol car increased in volume as it approached at speed.

The Incident Support Vehicle containing the bulk of the backup team trailed two miles behind. There was no sign of the Armed Response Unit.

Danskin and Ryan surveyed the front of the Low Light for entry and egress points. On the arrival of the second car, the DCI despatched its occupants to perform a similar task at the rear.

'Okay,' Danskin thought aloud. 'We know Dexter's in there. We know Elspeth and Tim Rice will be with her. We're pretty sure Hagan's with them; and we suspect Hannah's in there, too. That's five people. You've been in there, Jarrod. What's the layout like inside?'

Ryan cast his mind back. 'Small. Compact. Front door leads to cramped hallway. Off to the left, a living room. Not much furniture, but not much space, either. There was a bedroom to the rear. Think it was Tim's room. Beyond that, I don't know.'

Danskin exhaled. 'Not much space, then?'

'With five inside, no. If we're looking to storm the place, it'll be nigh on impossible to pick out Hagan when we get a whole squad in there.'

'Bollocks, man.' Danskin ran a hand over the crown of his head. 'Let's think this through.'

He never got time to think it through, because that's when they heard Hannah scream.

Ryan recognised it first. 'That's Hannah!'

He made a bolt for the door. Danskin grabbed him. Ryan tried to shrug him off. 'Get off me, man.'

'You're not going in there. Not without backup.'

'That was Hannah. You can't just stand there and let this play out!'

'Ryan - slow down. If it wasn't Hannah, what would you do?'

Ryan twisted and turned, squirming away from Danskin. 'But it is Hannah. That's the difference. Lucy, as well.'

Danskin held firm. 'What would you do, Jarrod?'

Ryan bit his lip as the tears began. 'I'd wait for backup,' he conceded.

'Good. That's what we do, agreed?'

Ryan nodded slowly.

Danskin released his hold on Ryan, but his eyes never left him; aware he could yet make a bolt for the door.

He didn't.

The Incident Support Van came into view as Danskin spoke into his radio.

'Ma'am, we need the ARU here NOW. Hagan's got Graves and Dexter in there with him. They're in trouble.'

Sam Maynard's voice came out muffled against a background of noise. 'Define trouble, Stephen.'

'Hagan's with them, and we've heard Graves shout for help.'

'It was a scream, ma'am, not a shout,' Ryan clarified.

'ARU have been despatched.'

'ETA?' Danskin urged.

'Two minutes.'

'You're sure about the time?'

'Yes, I am. I am because I'm with them. We're in Shields now.'

The whup-whup of helicopter rotor blades filled the air. Had the Super deployed a chopper, too? Or was it the coastguard?

Danskin looked skywards. It was neither. A private helicopter, glistening white, followed the contours of the Tyne and wound its way towards the city centre.

When Danskin looked down, Ryan Jarrod was no longer by his side.

**

'You really should learn to keep the noise down, you know. I heard you and your friends a mile off.' Jerome Hagan stood behind Hannah and Lucy's chairs. He held a sharp, gleaming blade to Hannah's throat, just beneath her right jawline.

Ryan stopped dead. Danskin was right – he hadn't thought this through.

Hagan motioned with the blade. 'Please. Take a seat.'

'No, I'll stand.'

'No, you'll sit.' Hagan exerted just enough pressure on the blade for it to penetrate Hannah's skin.

Monica Rice shuffled to one side of the sofa and indicated for Tim to do the same. Ryan sat between them.

'The gentleman didn't lock the door after him. Auntie Mo, please lock it for him. Bolt it, too, while you're there.'

Once Monica was back on the sofa, Hagan continued. 'You're Ms Dexter's friend, aren't you? I never forget a face. Nor a name, once I have it.'

'DS Jarrod.'

'My, another sergeant. I am truly honoured.'

'You won't get away with this, you know. You're surrounded by armed officers. Why don't you give yourself up, Jerome? You know it's the best way.'

Hagan snickered. 'I'm afraid you're late to the party. We've already been through this, ladies, haven't we?'

'He's armed himself up with a bomb, Ryan,' Hannah explained.

Ryan's eyes slid shut.

'That's right. If you don't believe her…' he unbuttoned his jacket. Let it fall open.

251

Ryan quickly took in the device. At least four incendiaries, hooked to a phone. *'Shit,'* he thought, hoping his face didn't betray the thought.

'Now you see why I don't need give myself up. You're my way out of here. If I go *boom*, so do you and all your colleagues. I'm sure your senior officers would not want that on their conscience – or in the newspapers, for that matter.'

Ryan subliminally took in the room. It was as he remembered. There was no easy way out.

'I really am hoping I don't need to go boom – but I will if it means taking your corrupt and inadequate cronies with me.'

Ryan stared at the man. Saw a trail of blood weep from the wound on Hannah's neck. Recognised the look of abject terror in Lucy's eyes.

'I can see you're worried for your colleagues. That's good. It means I can rely on your help. See this,' he help up the blade reddened with Hannah's blood, 'Rest assured I'll use it before I set off my bomb. Unfortunately, I can't use it on both ladies at once. You help me out. Who goes first?'

A whimper escaped Lucy's lips. Hannah swallowed so hard she feared the filleting knife may cut deeper.

Hagan revelled in Ryan's discomfort.

Ryan's eyes darted between the two girls. Ryan looked at Hannah. Saw her freckled face beneath a tumbleweed of curls with her trademark corkscrew lock teased in front of one eye. Lucy was Yin to Hannah's Yang. Young, pretty despite – or perhaps because of – her severe blonde hairstyle.

Lucy had her whole career in front of her. Her whole life. So, too, did Hannah.

'Which one is it to be, Ryan?'

Ryan's eyes settled on his subject.

'That one.'

He pointed a finger at Hannah Graves.

CHAPTER THIRTY-FIVE

Sam Maynard scurried from the ARU vehicle, fastening up her bullet-proof jacket as she did so.

'Latest, Stephen.'

'Ma'am we've six people inside. Hagan, Elspeth and Timothy Rice; Graves, Dexter and Jarrod.'

'Jarrod? Isn't he with you?'

'No. He took things into his own hands.'

'Two civilians, three of ours, and the suspect. Shit.'

Men in helmets, visors, and jackets like the one Maynard wore swarmed from the armoured vehicle. They carried rifles, wore stun grenades on their belts. Two bore enforcers – the heavy metal battering ram used to force entry. All waited for their instructions.

'Where do we enter, Stephen?'

'I don't know if we can, ma'am. Jarrod's been in the building before. He reckons there's little room to manoeuvre. If we force entry, there's no way we can guarantee we won't bring down one of the others, one of ours. In fact, the odds are stacked against us.'

Maynard vibrated her lips. 'So, what do you suggest?'

'I think all we can do, for now, is sit it out.'

Maynard tugged at her bottom lip. She moved away and spoke to the firearms lead. He sent three men round the back. To the front, he stationed one man either side of the Low Light entry door, and two men and a female officer crouched down in the car park facing the main entrance. The final two he ordered to make their way to the Low Light roof, rifles trained front and rear exit.

'Okay, Stephen, we wait and see. For now. If Hagan comes out, we take him out like a fairground duck. If we haven't heard anything from inside in twenty minutes, we go in.'

'If we go in, we…'

'That's my final word, Stephen. Twenty minutes.'

**

Lucy Dexter's eyes widened as Hagan moved from Hannah and lay the knife against Lucy's throat.

'Nice try, Detective Sergeant. I knew you'd try to bluff me. As you see, I'm no fool.'

Ryan hoped he'd disguised his relief. His double-bluff had worked. He'd read Hagan correctly and guessed Jerome would assume whichever name he gave, Hagan would choose the other.

Thing is, Ryan didn't want Hagan to take either Hannah or Lucy. He needed to buy time. He took a deep breath to settle his thoughts and tried to recall his Crisis Negotiation training.

He'd only put it into practice once, and it had ended badly. Very badly. This time, it had to be different.

'Jerome, I'm truly sorry for what you and your mother went through. I can't even begin to wonder what it must be like.'

Ryan noticed a quiver of surprise cross Hagan's face. It passed in an instant.

'What's your but, Detective? There's always a but.'

'Not this time, there isn't.'

Hagan snorted a laugh. 'Are you saying you approve of my mission? What sort of reverse psychology bullshit are you playing?'

Ryan remembered to remain calm. 'No, Jerome, I don't approve. Not at all. But that doesn't mean I don't understand your reasons. I understand you and your mother have had umpteen years of hell and the person who created it received a punishment which in no way met the crime.'

Hagan cocked his head to one side like a wary blackbird. 'He got his punishment, take my word.'

'What did you do to him, Jerome?'

'I knocked him unconscious, that's what I did.'

'That's not all, though, is it?'

A smile crossed Hagan's face. 'I waited 'til he'd regained consciousness. When he did, he found he was tied to the back of a go-kart, face down. Thirty laps later, I'm sure you can imagine what he looked like.'

Ryan saw by Hannah and Lucy's faces they imagined only too well. He hoped he'd managed to remain impassive.

'Why don't you let Auntie Mo go? Tim, too. They've shown nothing but kindness to you. Your aunt here has looked after your mother for you while you carried out your mission.'

'Yes, but she knows what I did. As soon as I discovered you'd been to the court, I knew it was only a matter of time before you worked it out. I thought if you made the link, Auntie Mo would tell you everything. I can't let that happen. I still have work to do. It is my right to serve justice.'

'Jerome, it isn't. Not any more, it's not. Now, why don't you let your aunt go?'

'No. There's more to it than that. Once my mother had her accident, SHE,' he pointed at Monica Rice, 'Split the family up.'

'No, that's not the way it was,' Monica protested.

Ryan groaned. '*Leave the talking to me, man*' he thought. He started talking before Monica could speak again.

'She wanted what was best for your brother. You were caring for your mother. You didn't have time to care for Timothy. Auntie Mo sacrificed herself to the task. She kept the family together, not split you up.'

'Do you think I'm wrong, Detective?'

'About your aunt and your brother, yes. I do.'

Ryan thought he saw Hagan give a slight nod. 'What about the others?'

'Yes, I think that was wrong, as well. But there's a difference. I can see that their sentences were unjust. I understand your anger and frustration. I really do.'

Jerome Hagan took the blade from Lucy's neck and took a step towards Ryan. Lucy unwound like a broken spring.

'Have you never wanted revenge?' Hagan asked Ryan.

Jarrod stared him straight in the eye. 'Yes.'

'Tell me.'

Ryan closed his eyes and opened his mind. 'A man kidnapped my family. Threatened to kill them. Threatened to kill me. He was a bad man, Jerome. Evil. Not like you,' he said, playing to Hagan's ego. 'This man didn't have a mission, or a cause. Only greed motivated him.'

Jerome looked at Ryan with something approaching understanding in his eyes. 'What was this man's name?'

'Benny Yu.'

'What did you do about it?'

Ryan sighed. 'Nothing.'

'Why?'

'Because I was scared.'

'A coward,' Hagan sneered.

'No. Afraid. Afraid he would split my family apart. Not like Auntie Mo who tried to bring yours together.'

Hagan cocked an eyebrow at Ryan. 'Then you didn't have the drive within you. A purpose.'

'Where the hell's the firearms crew?' Ryan thought. 'You don't have a purpose, either. You have a condition.'

'Ha! You think I'm mad?'

'No. I think you have PTSD, and every time you witness something unfair at work, it reminds you of the accident. You believe it's your right to seek revenge, or justice, or whatever you want to call it. But it's not your right.'

'My work must continue.'

'It can't.'

'It WILL.'

'What about the rest of us in the room? Why are we here? We're not part of your mission.'

Hagan's laugh brought drool to his lips. 'Of course you're part of it. You're part of the shitty system which makes me undertake my mission.'

Ryan met Hagan's stare. 'When does it end, then? When you're killed? When you're caught? You do know you're as good as caught already don't you?'

Hagan tipped his head back and laughed. 'I think it's you that's caught, Detective Sergeant. And it's not me or Auntie Mo, or either of your bitches behind me, that's going to die. That honour belongs to you.'

Jerome Hagan raised the knife and stepped towards Ryan.

**

'You've had your twenty minutes, Stephen. We're going in.'

'Ma'am, please…'

'I know your Hannah's in there. The firearms squad know, too. They're professional. The best there is. We're going in.'

Maynard nodded towards one of the squad holding an Enforcer, and pointed towards the porthole window. He moved into position, his back to the wall. A colleague joined him.

She ordered the second Enforcer to the front door. Three riflemen, sights to their eyes, barrels forward, stood behind.

'On my word…' she held up three fingers.

Curled one into her palm.

Then a second.

Finally, the third.

'Go, go, go!'

**

The window imploded inwards.

'What the…'

The flash of a stun grenade temporarily blinded those in the room. A smoke bomb followed.

The front door splintered inwards.

'ARMED POLICE!'

'POLICE!'

'STAY WHERE YOU ARE!'

'ARMED POLICE!'

'NO-ONE MOVE!'

Smoke billowed through the room, obscuring everything and everyone in it.

Vague shadows scurried and moved in the ferment.

'He's got a bomb!' Hannah's voice.

'Jesus!' bellowed another.

'Get back!' another officer yelled.

Chaos.

There was a thud. The sound of movement within the room. A cry of pain. Furniture breaking.

'Aaah, you bastard,' Ryan's squeal of pain.

More shouting.

Swearing.

'What the hell's going on in there?' Danskin screeched at the retreating firearms officers.

'He's got a bomb.'

'Oh, sweet Jesus. Hannah, Ryan, Lucy! Get out!!'

Maynard screamed into her radio. 'ARU - if Hagan comes out, shoot to kill. Repeat – shoot to kill.'

Smoke swirled out the shattered window, through the front door, everything blurred in a shroud of smoke.

Gradually, a ghostly figure formed in the fug. Became clearer. Moved towards the front door.

'Firearms – ready,' Maynard's voice now a whisper.

The entity stepped into clear air.

'Hold your fire!!' Danskin screamed. 'It's Jarrod. He's one of ours! Hold your fire!'

Ryan took a further, tentative step. Fresh air filled his lungs. He coughed. Blinked against the sunlight and the sting of smoke. He looked around, dazed and confused.

'Where's Hannah?' Danskin shouted.

Ryan took two steps forward. Stumbled, but regained his balance.

'Is Hannah okay?' Danskin implored.

'She's in there.'

Maynard noticed Ryan clutched his arm.

'Are you okay, Ryan? There's blood on…' As Ryan neared them, she saw the extent of the blood. It painted him head to toe.

'I've had worse,' he said.

'Get the medics in. He's injured.'

Ryan gave a doleful smile. 'Ma'am, I've been set on fire, shot at, drugged half to death in this job. A little nick with a knife isn't going to do me much harm.'

'Ryan, you're in shock. You're covered in bloody blood…'

Jarrod laughed at her use of words. 'It's not mine.'

'Not Hannah's, I hope,' Danskin asked.

When Ryan didn't reply, Danskin burst into a sprint; Maynard after him.

'Stephen, Hagan's still in there. He's got a bomb, remember. Get back.'

Too late. Danskin was inside the Low Light. Inside the apartment with its smoke and its broken glass and its smashed furniture.

And inside with Hannah Graves.

'You're okay?' he cried, scarcely believing it.

She nodded.

'You're bleeding.'

'It's nowt, man. Just a nick. I'd be better if you'd untie me, though.'

Danskin let out air.

'And I'm fine, too, if you're interested,' Lucy said from the floor, tied to an upended chair.

'Hagan?' Danskin asked.

Lucy indicated a position on the floor with her eyes.

Hagan lay spreadeagled on the carpet, eyes wide, staring blankly at the ceiling.

Tim Rice knelt astride him, soaked in crimson.

He held a fishing knife in his hand; the fishing knife he'd taken from Jerome Hagan and used to sever his carotid artery.

'I need to phone police,' Tim said. 'There's something not right with him. Auntie Mo says I should call 999.'

Tim looked at Stephen Danskin with tear-filled eyes.

**

Maynard, Danskin, Dexter, Hannah and Ryan huddled around the Incident Support Unit.

'What happened to the bomb? Why didn't he detonate it when we went in?'

Ryan gave an ironic laugh. 'Empty cans of Heineken, ma'am, with the branding stripped off to leave the tin showing. Pretty bloody convincing, mind.'

'I'll say,' Hannah added. 'He was a cunning sod, I'll give him that.'

'And Fola was right – he definitely wasn't mad,' Ryan said. 'Just bad.'

'Elspeth Hagan? What happens to her, now – does she stay with her sister?' Maynard asked.

'Doubt it, ma'am. Too much for her. Elspeth's been taken to a nursing home. Best place for her, while Tim's better off with his Auntie Mo,' Danskin commented.

'How is he?'

'Not good, ma'am,' Ryan said. 'He'll need a lot of help. Poor bloke's not been dealt a good hand in life.'

Sam Maynard nodded. 'It's not much consolation, but I'll put him up for an award. It's the best I can do.'

'He'll like that, ma'am.'

They stood in silence for a while. Finally, Ryan spoke.

'Ma'am, I need a shower to get rid of this bloody blood,' he smiled. 'Can I shoot off now?'

'Of course. And well done, Ryan. You've played yet another blinder.'

'Thank you, ma'am.'

'Sir,' Hannah said, 'I've got blood on me as well.' She fingered the tiny speck of blood beneath her jawline. 'I think I'll join him.'

Danskin covered his ears. 'I don't want to know.'

'What about you, Lucy? Are you okay?' Maynard asked.

Lucy looked wistful as Ryan and Hannah walked off, arm in arm. 'Aye, I suppose.'

'You work really well with DS Jarrod. Excellent work. Off you go. Get some well-earned R&R.'

Lucy looked around. Her eyes fell on the Low Lights Tavern.

'Think I'll see if I can cop off with Sam Fender.'

'And then there were two,' Maynard said, eyes on Stephen Danskin.

'I s'ppose, aye.'

Maynard scrolled through her phone. 'I meant to mention this earlier. Look.'

'What is it?'

'E-mail from IOPC.'

Danskin rolled his eyes. 'About Lei-Zhan Yu?'

'Unless there's some other cock-up you haven't told me about?'

He shook his head.

'Well, stop looking so shame faced. They're not taking the matter further. You and Todd are in the clear, and quite rightly so.'

'Ma'am.'

'So, I think we should celebrate.'

Danskin glanced at the Low Light Tavern. 'I'd love to but you know fine well I can't drink. Not with my history.'

Sam Maynard's clear blue eyes smiled at him.

'Who said anything about celebrating with a drink?'

CHAPTER THIRTY-SIX

The End
and
The Beginning

The helicopter DCI Danskin watched buzzing overhead followed the route of the Tyne and cut a sharp right towards the city centre.

The pilot made a few last-minute adjustments as the craft hovered like a sandfly. He dipped the tail slightly, the body of the copter twisted right, and straightened as the tail lifted once more.

Finally, the helicopter settled. Landing it on the angled roof of Newcastle's tallest building had been far from easy. The passenger shook hands with the pilot, slipped open the door, and ran at a crouch towards a raised manhole.

His necktie, whipped by the downdraft from the blades, wrapped itself around his throat as he approached the open cover.

He turned backwards and descended the metal staircase. Once he'd disappeared into the building, the helicopter lifted from the roof and headed into a blazing sunset.

The man counted the steps as he descended the ladder. After sixty-one, his feet settled on soft, thick shagpile carpet, not the bare concrete surface he'd expected.

He was greeted by a bearded man, swarthy-skinned, coal black eyes. 'Please – this way.'

The pair headed down another flight of stairs until they stood outside a fire-door. His escort rapped on it. Put his ear to the closed door. When he heard a mellow, 'Come,' he pushed down the metal rail and pulled the door towards him.

'Your guest has arrived, your Excellency.'

The guide disappeared into the background.

The man stared into a lavishly decorated room, stained pink and fiery red with sunset hues radiating through the floor to ceiling window.

A man dressed in robes manifested from the shimmering haze like Lawrence of Arabia.

'Welcome,' he said.

'As-salaam 'alaykum,' the man replied, giving a deferential bow.

'Wa 'alaykum as-salaam,' his Excellency Sheik Adnaan al-Ahmadi said. 'You speak Arabic, my friend. I am impressed. Mabsut 'enni softak tani.'

The man looked blank. Sheepishly, he told the robed man he'd exhausted his repertoire.

Al-Ahmadi chuckled a throaty laugh. 'No matter, I appreciate the effort you made. It means *'Good to see you again.'* Come, come – step inside, please.'

The man took in his surroundings. The room afforded a panoramic, three-hundred-and-sixty-degree view of the city and its surrounds.

'Wonderful views,' he said.

'They are, indeed. I seldom visit here but, when business demands, my apartment serves me well.'

'You own this place?'

'I do. All twenty-eight stories of it. Most believe the building holds one fewer floor. Few, if any, know my personal suite sits above this restaurant.'

'I am impressed,' the man said, taking in the view once more. He noticed three men in sharp suits with bulging pockets guarded each entry point.

'Ha,' al-Ahmadi laughed, 'I see you notice my friends. They are an unfortunate necessity but they are discrete. We can talk openly, my friend.'

The Sheik showed his guest to a window seat and ordered one of the men in suits to bring a drink.

'Thank you, your Excellency,' the man said, sipping a mint julep.

'We talk business, yes?'

'Of course. I must say, I was surprised to receive your invitation. I didn't see the Middle-East as a market for my produce.'

'Really? Then it would surprise you to learn Riyadh, for example, has a significant number of customers who would be most interested in your services.'

The man looked shocked.

'Yes, my friend. Many are prepared to risk the penalties to get their hands on what you offer.'

'I am more shocked than surprised, your Excellency.' He took another sip from the greenery-filed glass.

'No matter. I am not after business for those markets. I have many clients in this country, many rich and famous clients. They are willing to pay much for what you offer, and they afford me many opportunities to expand my global interests in return.'

'Of course. I understand.'

'Do you? That is good, because I do not understand why you ask for no payment.'

The man opposite steepled his fingers. 'I have other priorities, as I told you earlier. All I require is the use of your premises for a set purpose. That is payment enough. You shall not be brought into it, I promise.'

Al-Ahmadi smiled. 'Good, because if I am...' he motioned a slitting gesture across his throat. 'You understand, yes?'

'Perfectly.'

Al-Ahmadi narrowed his eyes. 'This man must have caused you many troubles to bring you such anger.'

'Oh yes.'

'Tell me.'

'He tried to ruin my business. I had to discover new markets. Start afresh. I swore vengeance on him. The time has come.'

'Why? Why now?'

'Business is one thing, but when he and his colleagues bring death to my family, it is time to bring death to him.'

'Ah, I understand perfectly, now.'

'Yes. It may only be a second cousin, but it is enough for me to act now.'

The man stood and stared across the Tyne, up towards a village perched on a hill overlooking the great river.

'It is time for me, Benny Yu, to rid the world of Ryan Jarrod, once and for all.'

****

COMING NEXT FROM
COLIN YOUNGMAN:

THE
TOWER

A Ryan Jarrod Novel

'One of them will die.'
Is this the end of the road for Ryan Jarrod?

Acknowledgement:

To you - for taking the time to read Low Light. Your interest and support mean the world to me.

If you enjoyed this, the sixth Ryan Jarrod novel, please tell your family, friends, and colleagues. Word of mouth is an author's best friend so the more people who know, the greater my appreciation.

I welcome reviews of your experience, either on Amazon or Goodreads. Alternatively, you can 'Rate' the book after you finish reading on most Kindle devices, if you'd prefer.

If you'd like to be among the first to hear news about the next book in the series, or to discover release dates in advance, you can follow me by:

Clicking the 'Follow' button on my Amazon book's page
https://www.amazon.co.uk/Colin-Youngman/e/B01H9CNHQK

OR

Liking/ following me on:
Facebook: @colin.youngman.author

Thanks again for your interest in my work.

Colin

About the author:

Colin had his first written work published at the age of 9 when a contribution to children's comic *Sparky* brought him the rich rewards of a 10/- Postal Order and a transistor radio.

He was smitten by the writing bug and has gone on to have his work feature in publications for young adults, sports magazines, national newspapers, and travel guides before he moved to his first love: fiction.

Colin previously worked as a senior executive in the public sector. He lives in Northumberland, north-east England, and is an avid supporter of Newcastle United (don't laugh), a keen follower of Durham County Cricket Club, and has a family interest in British Gymnastics and the City of Newcastle Gymnastics Academy.

You can read his other work (e-book and paperback) exclusive to Amazon:

Operation Sage *(Ryan Jarrod Book Five)*
High Level *(Ryan Jarrod Book Four)*
The Lighthouse Keeper *(Ryan Jarrod Book Three)*
The Girl On The Quay *(Ryan Jarrod Book Two)*
The Angel Falls *(Ryan Jarrod Book One)*

The Doom Brae Witch
Alley Rat
DEAD Heat
Twists *(An anthology of novelettes)*
****

Printed in Great Britain
by Amazon

44413777R00152